The Devil in the Wide City

By Justin Alcala

ALL RIGHTS RESERVED

Publisher's Note:

This is a work of fiction. All names, characters, places, and events are the work of the author's imagination.

Any resemblance to real persons, places, or events is coincidental.

Solstice Publishing - www.solsticepublishing.com

Prologue

Azazel was running late again. It wasn't that he had anything to do. *The Atoning Asshole* practically ran itself. It was just that Azazel didn't really enjoy schedules. They were silly. Plus, he was meeting his brother Armen and really liked pissing him off.

Azazel had been walking through the third circle of Hell, where the vagrants lined up along the building walls, pouring liquor that they could no longer taste down their gullets. He wore the lucky leather jacket that he'd permanently borrowed from Baal, along with a Tom Waits t-shirt, jeans and black boots. The night air was nippy so Azazel lit a cigarette.

He had no idea what his brother wanted, but knew it was going to be stupid. It always was. Armen, for some sick reason, felt obligated to do something with his eternal damnation. Progress never really did much in Hell. Nevertheless, since Armen still owed Azazel a favor, he'd hear out his dear old brother before asking for another loan.

Azazel arrived at the lounge, *Hung, Drawn and Quartered*, an hour late. The doorman was a wart-covered demon with dreadlocks that protruded from his beret. He had sunglasses, though there was no sun, a violet polyester suit and a hideous gold neck chain. The creature held out his hand, cutting off Azazel's path before the fallen angel could enter.

"Whoa," grunted the door-demon in a glassy voice, "I'm afraid you'll need to put that cigarette out." Azazel gave the demon a cross look. The bouncer shrugged, a pleading expression painted across his warty face. "Sorry, but they're doing it on Earth now and Lucifer likes pissing off smokers."

Azazel's jaw set as he shot a repugnant look. "Fuck off demon," he said boldly. Knowing he was untouchable, Azazel pushed his way into the lounge. The demon stood up and watched with a helpless frown as Azazel entered the building.

The lounge, one of Armen's favorite places to do business, was something out of a bad noir detective novel. The lighting was dim with small candles flickering on top of each cocktail table that surrounded the stage. The men wore suits with fedoras. The women fashioned cocktail dresses. There was even an old fashioned bartender with a white puffy shirt, sleeve garters and a vest wiping down the overcrowded bar. He looked about as excited to be there as Azazel was.

A saxophone cut through the place with a howl. On the stage was the house jazz band "Bertha's Mule," which consisted of a saxophonist, bass player and pianist. At the helm was a beautiful long legged succubus wearing a crimson colored dress that sparkled in the spotlight. She had midnight hair, long and glossy, which draped just above her heavily mascaraed eyes. On her brows were two small ivory spikes that were more nubs than horns, mostly covered by a curtain of dark bangs. The succubus straddled the nostalgic steel microphone, nearly kissing it with her ruby lips as she sang. Azazel recognized her right away as Sasha, his thickheaded pal Nedonius' former girlfriend.

Azazel took another minute to admire her, wondering what it would take to test drive the vixen before breaking out of his trance and looking for Armen. It wasn't too hard. Armen had his usual table near the kitchen entrance. Azazel made his way there and found his brother, who was a near spitting image of him, waiting impatiently. Armen had extinguished the candle at his table and was sitting just outside the reach of the stage's spotlight.

"Eww, real mysterious brother," said Azazel dryly. He shook his hands in a false tremble. Armen took a sip of his bourbon before kicking the chair across from the table out.

"Shut up," Armen growled, "and sit."

Azazel sat down and as his eyes focused, he could see that his brother's usually slicked back mane was messy and disheveled. He had bags under his eyes and was pinching his lips together with his fingers, a trademark sign that he was having a bad day. Azazel sighed and after adjusting in his duct taped chair, used his devilish ability of telepathy to read his brother's surface thoughts.

"Just ask me what's wrong," Armen's mind argued.

"Okay," Azazel tried to use sleight of hand to steal his brother's drink. Armen slapped Azazel's palm. He winced and while rubbing his knuckles asked, "So what's wrong?"

"I'm glad you asked," Armen quipped. He leaned in so that the surrounding light colored his face. His cheeks were pink with splotches of purple as if he'd just swallowed hot peppers. Armen bent down near his feet and came back up with a black leather bag. He placed it on the table and unbuckled the snaps before removing a crumpled letter from inside.

"Nice purse," Azazel criticized.

"Oh hardy-fucking-har-har," Armen grumbled. He pushed the paper at his brother. "Just read the note."

Azazel looked down. The header was stamped with the official seal of Lucifer. It read…

Dear Armen,

We have recently received word from the surface that your attempt to recover a certain Corruptor that shall not be named has proven unsuccessful. As you may know, this is unsatisfactory to our Dark Lord. As a one-time act of leniency, the Dark Lord has agreed to give a subsequent, and final, extension in order to repair your blunders. You have an additional one-hundred-and-sixty-eight hours to recover the Corruptor before certain reprimanding actions are taken.

Sincerely,

Morax

Personal Assistant of Lucifer and Manager of Marketing Operations

Visit Us Online at

www.Afutureforhellfoundation.hell/.com

Azazel tossed aside the paper, unimpressed. "You have plenty of time. What's one-hundred-and-sixty-eight hours, like a month?"

"It's a week," Armen bit back.

"So what if you get reprimanded. Who cares?"

"Who cares?" Armen repeated loudly. "This *is* a big deal. What do you think reprimanding means in Lucifer's eyes?"

Azazel leaned back in his chair. He stretched his arms back, and in the process, slyly swiped a half glass of gin from a harpy sitting next to him. He sniffed at the drink before looking over his shoulder and then having a taste. "I don't know," he said as he winced from the drink's kick. "I'm assuming they'll fire you, which, brother, that might not be a bad thing. You're crazy stressed."

"Wrong," Armen growled through his teeth, showering spit as he did. "I'll get obliterated."

"Oh," Azazel said meekly before pausing. "That's bad."

"Yes it is. And since you're the idiot that advised me to use Nedonius for the job in the first place, I'm taking you down with me."

Azazel spit out what little drink remained in his mouth. "You wouldn't!"

"You bet your ass I would. It's because of you that I'm in this predicament."

"What?" Azazel said with a grimace, "how?"

"You told me he was foolproof."

"No," Azazel protested. "I told you I could prove he

was a fool-- as in he'd be too clueless to ask questions."

Armen dismissed his brother with a wave of his hand. Azazel, who was clearly feeling betrayed, tried to read his brother's surface thoughts for insight. Unfortunately, the pair had been together for centuries, and Armen knew exactly how to stop his brother from reading his mind. He blocked out his brother with the Kenny Rogers song, "The Gambler."

"Damn it," Azazel groaned, "you know I hate that song. Come on, I just want to know what's on your mind."

"What's on my mind, little brother, is that I need to figure out a way to fix this."

"Wait," said Azazel calmly, trying to make sense of it all. "Why does Lucifer care about Gethin anyway? He's just some jerkoff."

Armen sighed before finishing his drink. He rubbed his temples a moment before slapping his hands on the table as if for Azazel to inspect. "Fine," Armen surrendered. "I give you permission to read my thoughts, as I need what's on my mind to remain a secret."

Azazel jumped into his brother's head. He could hear the subconscious voice of his brother's thoughts, which strangely sounded British.

"*Now, listen,*" Armen's subconscious voice called out, "*this is highly classified information, so stay quiet or else it's both of our heads on the chopping block.*"

"Yeah, yeah," said Azazel out loud.

"*There are very few souls who know that Gethin and Lucifer used to have a thing,*" said Armen's conscience. "*It's why Gethin received the job in Chicago in the first place.*"

"No shit?" said Azazel with surprise.

"*No shit,*" said Armen's subconscious. "*Anyway, as they started to become more serious, Lucifer began to get a bit too vocal about some of his future plans for hell, and might have told Gethin about a giant soul sucking portal that he wanted to open up over Lake Michigan. When Gethin heard this, he volunteered to oversee the project himself so long as Lucifer taught him how to open portals. Well, of course Lucifer was stupefied by his new boy toy and agreed."*

"Naturally," said Azazel, crossing his legs and nodding a few times.

"Since I hold the position I do," Armen's British subconscious voice persisted, *"Lucifer's assistant, Morax, gave me a call and informed me of their plan so that I could figure out a way to get Gethin past the red tape and into Chicago. Luckily, Nedonius' dumb ass had just burned down the entire city, so it was the perfect cover to get Gethin into the area. While things were going according to plan at first, it didn't take long for Gethin to start fooling around with some mortal and abandon the portal project. Lucifer, being the jilted lover that he is, demanded that I find Gethin or else."*

"Ah ha," said Azazel as he straightened his posture and pointed his index finger towards the ceiling.

"Hence little brother," Armen continued, *"Why I asked you to find me someone who wouldn't ask questions. You gave me Nedonius, but now he's missing too."*

Azazel studied his drink for a moment. Armen watched as Azazel tapped his fingers together, swaying his head from side to side as he mumbled in thought. Then suddenly, Azazel slapped the surface of the table, shaking everything on it.

"I got it," he announced triumphantly. "Pierce Brosnan! Your subconscious sounds just like Pierce Brosnan."

Armen dropped his head onto the table face first with a heavy thump. Azazel wore a grin between his cheeks. He waited for his brother to look back up before rubbing his hands against one another as if he were about to dig into dinner. Armen rose up lazily and sat upright once more in his chair.

"What is it?" Armen asked unenthusiastically.

"I have an idea brother."

"Yes?"

"Her," Azazel pointed to the stage. Armen took a look at the succubus on platform and shook his head with a dumbfounded expression.

"Please put on this tie," she sang, her voice dripping with venom, *"made from your guts."* The saxophone moaned low before letting her continue. *"I'm gonna' take my knife, and cut off both of your nu-*

"What on Earth are you talking about?" Armen cut in.

"Oh Armen," Azazel gasped, "if only you were half as smart as you are pissy, you'd know exactly what I was getting at."

"The anticipation is killing me brother."

"That succubus on stage is Sasha. She's Ned's ex-girlfriend."

Armen rose out of his chair in revelation. He hadn't been this hopeful in ages. Azazel, seeing his brother's interest, leaned back in his chair and presented a wide cocky smile that would make the Cheshire cat jealous. After taking a moment to gather his wits, Armen slowly gravitated back down into his chair.

"You're a genius," Armen complimented.

"Well," Azazel said, polishing his fingernails on his jacket lapel. "I do what I can."

"Once a succubus shares herself with someone, she's connected with them forever."

"Uh huh," Azazel agreed. "She dumped him because he never made anything of himself like he promised. Now, here he is, up on Earth, parading around as a corruptor."

"And they *do* still share that link. Who better than Sasha to hunt him down and exact revenge?"

"Exactly. Plus, he still owes her money. A girl with spending habits like that isn't quick to forget an ex-boyfriend's debt."

"Okay, so here's the plan then," said Armen, still forming the details as he spoke. "First, I'll get her to locate Nedonius. Once she does, I'll torture the shit out of him in order to see what he knows about Gethin. Hell, the two might even be hanging out."

"Yup," said Azazel simply.

"Then, I'll grab Gethin, bring him back to Hell, and earn the Dark Lord's eternal gratitude."

"Well," said Azazel doubtfully, "I'd be glad if he simply spared our lives."

Armen didn't seem to be listening. "So all we need to do now," said Armen in recognition, "Is convince Sasha, and then get her to Earth."

"Hell hath no fury," Azazel smiled.

Armen stood up again, gawking at Sasha as she sang about eating her lover's face off. She was Armen's potential golden ticket-- more beautiful for the part she might play in saving his skin than her elegant face and stunning breasts. Armen, now ecstatic, grabbed Azazel by his shoulders and lifted him up out of his chair before squeezing him into a hug. People stared, uncomfortable with the awkward scene.

"There, there brother, it's alright," he said, patting Armen on the back with his half pinned hand. "I'm sure you'd do the same for me."

"No, I wouldn't."

"Oh sure you would. In fact," he said daringly, "now that we're talking about favors, what are the chances that I can borrow a thousand bucks? I'm kind of hard up for cash and late on the bar's rent."

Armen pulled away, a large gracious grin pasted across his face. "No," he said bluntly through his smile, "but you're coming with me to Earth."

"I am?"

"Yes," Armen said flatly "You screwed us, and now you're going to help fix this."

"Oh."

"And one more thing," added Armen as his face went sober. "My subconscious sounds like Sir Roger Moore, not Pierce Brosnan you idiot."

The pair sat at the table until Sasha's set was over. Every song she sang was about getting revenge on her old lover. As the twins waited, they recollected where it all went wrong. No matter what angle they sliced it, blame always came back to just one fallen angel. Ned.

Chapter One

It was one Hell of a day, and that's saying a lot where I'm from. It began as cliché as one might expect when living in the nine circles of Satan's abyss. My girlfriend dumped me, my dogs ran away from home, and work gave me the pink slip. Things were looking dismal. If only I knew then that by this time tomorrow I'd be back on Earth, I might not have been so whiny.

My name is Nedonius, and I'm one of the countless fallen angels who retreated with Lucifer into the depths of Hell after losing the war for heaven. Most people just call me Ned. For the last few centuries I've been trapped here in the inferno, working in the Torment Department as a scorcher. I'm the person who tortures the wicked with blistering flame and sizzling coals. Two things about my job; first, yes it's absurdly stereotypical, and secondly, no, not all parts of Hell are fire and brimstone.

Hell for the most part is a boring place. The fringes of the nine circles are plagued with sterile suburbs, all of them crowded with carbon copy homes, manicured lawns and tiresome roads that take you nowhere. Downtown isn't much better. It's a maze of ominous black skyscrapers that tickle the tops of looming smog clouds. Each building is stuffed to the brim with cramped offices and tiny cubicles. We copied the design from the humans, who know how to nail dreary and uninspiring. In fact, now that I think about it? Nowadays we copy nearly everything from the humans.

Once upon a time Hell was just barren land and cave dwellings. We had no real history of our own besides the uprising, no Renaissance or Industrial Revolution. So we started copying mortals. Not everything, mind you, just the obnoxiously trendy. It's all part of Lucifer's campaign for improving hell's future. We watch their television, read their books, and listen to their radio. The result -- well, things aren't exactly what they seem to be on the surface, more of a cheap imitation, but the implemented distractions like daytime television, overpriced coffee houses, and pop music keep most of the damned from wanting to take their toaster into the bathtub. By the way, no one feels sorry for suicidal damned. Not even the ones who work in the business district.

You see, since the baby boom, souls have really begun to pour in, and processing them has been no easy task. The business district is completely overworked and underpaid. Most damned don't last more than a week. So, when it came time to find another job, I felt that the torment division was far more appealing than pushing papers all day. Being a scorcher is grunt work typically left for demon spawn. It's where mortals go to be punished until the end of days, and what typically comes to mind when people think about classic Biblical hell. As grueling as the pits can be, I tolerate my duties mostly because I'm good at it. Plus, it's just a rebound job until the Corruptors Department calls me back, but that's another story.

Anyhow, my last day in Hell started off pretty rocky. Now keep in mind, I didn't know it was my last day in Hell at the time, so I was a bit stressed by the entire thing. When I woke up, there was a letter from my girlfriend on the kitchen table. She was sick and tired of hearing about my aspirations of becoming a corruptor again, and felt that I'd never amount to anything. She wanted all the money back that I owed her, and wished me nothing but pain and suffering for the rest of my days. Typical *Dear John*. I wasn't happy, but it wasn't exactly unexpected. She was a high maintenance succubus with looks to kill, but an appetite for spending. It was only a matter of time before she finally cut the cord. Not only does my job pay shit, but I'm pretty uninteresting as far as being Forsaken goes. Yes, I have a big mouth, but I'm far less devious and exciting than my brethren. What came next though was far more serious.

After I'd crumbled up her letter, a loud shriek burst from the streets. My eyes immediately shot to the backyard. To my horror, the reinforced fence door I'd installed had been left open.

"No, no, no," I said, grabbing two chain leashes and hurrying outside, "not again."

While the ex-girlfriend was storming off from my flat, she must have left the back gate open for my two hellhounds, Simon and Hecubus, to run rampant through the subdivision. The beasts were massive shadow mastiffs that I'd adopted after they'd devoured their first owner. They were as vicious as they were clever, and although they had a knack for getting me into a lot of trouble, they at least pretended to be obedient to my face. *Then again, maybe they were plotting my murder.* This time around, things went really bad. By the time I'd caught the two escaped beasts, seven of my neighbors were maimed, and one sin-cat had been eaten. Not only would I be getting a nasty letter for the township's office, but also to add injury to insult, I was now late for work by two hours.

Typically, my supervisor, Ragmauth, tended to look the other way when I was running a little behind schedule because he loved having a fallen angel, or *Forsaken* as we're called, on the crew. Torturing was mostly reserved for lesser demons, so having a fully bona fide angel on staff was something he enjoyed bragging about to the other imps and fiends he worked with. Plus, I loved fire, and practically perfected the art of pyromancy. Unfortunately, as much as Ragmauth enjoyed keeping me around, he was powerless once our Director of Operations, "Bowlauf the Jerkoff," took notice of my tardiness. Bowlauf had it out for me from day one. By the time I'd made it into work, my locker had been emptied and the contents were waiting for me in cardboard boxes next to my workstation.

"Sorry Ned," said Ragmauth as he helped me carry my boxes to the car. "My hands are tied on this one. I tried defending you, but Bowlauf says that your tardiness today was the last straw. He thinks you don't take your position seriously, and that you have no respect for the rest of the team."

"That's because this job is stupid," I argued, slamming the trunk of my manly compact car. "And my coworkers *are* idiots."

Ragmauth kept his head down. "Well," he sighed, "maybe you're right, but it doesn't change anything."

"It is what it is," I tried to say coolly as I opened my car door and squeezed inside. "Catch you later I guess."

"Catch you later Ned. I hope things get better."

Brokenhearted and jobless, I decided the best thing to do was go somewhere where I could properly sulk, the pub. *The Atoning Asshole* was a favorite tavern of mine not just because of its cheap liquor, but because it was just around the corner from my house and owned by Azazel, one of my oldest pals. Azazel was a fellow Forsaken who'd been part of the legion during the War for Heaven. We'd seen it all together, and although you can never really trust anyone in hell, he was the closest thing that I had to a friend.

Azazel was watering down bottles of liquor behind his empty bar when I stepped through his doors. I shambled in like a zombie, my head down and moping as I made it towards a stool. George Thorogood was singing "I Drink Alone," through the static of the jukebox's beaten speakers. I waved feebly to Azazel's goat demon, Lazlo, who was scrubbing green vomit off of the wood paneled walls. Lazlo didn't give me so much as a nod as he scoured the avocado colored splatter. Azazel however perked up as I bee lined it towards him, unusually eager to see me. I plopped onto one of his shabby looking bar stools and sighed.

"Line 'em up Azazel," I sighed while slapping the bar's sticky surface. "Today has been a nightmare."

"Let me guess," Azazel hummed, pouring me a shot of toxic yellow alcohol, "Sasha dumped you, the hounds tried to destroy the neighborhood again, and you lost your job." *Did I mention Azazel could read minds?*

"Yeah," I said lifelessly, succumbing to my circumstances, "but don't forget that I'll probably get kicked out of my apartment soon since I don't have a job that can pay the rent any longer."

"Ah yes," he said amid a snort, "you can't forget that." I shot Azazel a frustrated glare.

"Well then you jerk, why in the Nine Circles are you so happy? Last time I checked, your friend's life is in ruins. Show a little compassion."

Azazel shook his head. "Because it's *not*," he said calmly, slipping me an envelope that was tucked near the register. The cover simply read, *Nedonius*. It was stamped by the Department of Corruptors.

"What is this?" I asked innocently.

"Just read it you moron," said Azazel through a grin. My hands greedily raced to open the envelope, slipping the parchment out from its paper pocket. It read:

Dear Nedonius,

After reviewing several of your appeals for reinstatement, management has decided to move forward and offer you a potential fulltime position within our branch. You are hereby summoned by the Department of Corruptors to report for duty, where you will be required to attend a brief new-hire orientation. This training will include an outline of your new responsibilities and territory. Failure to arrive at headquarters by tomorrow, July 10th, at nine-o'clock sharp will result in your immediate expulsion from the Corruptors program.

Sincerely,

Armen, Senior Manager of Corruptor Affairs

I could hardly believe it. The Corruptors Department had finally decided to overlook the little mishaps I'd had more than a century ago and give me a second shot. I'd be a corruptor again, my dream job since becoming Forsaken. I swiftly reread the note, my wings now fluttering with uncontrollable excitement. An assortment of black feathers began to rain down all over the pub's floor.

"Hey now, come on!" yelled Azazel. "I just swept." I hopped from my stool and grabbed him by the shoulders.

"You beautiful fool! How did you get this?"

"I told you," said Azazel, pushing me off, "my brother Armen is part of their hiring board. I put in a good word not too long ago, and he kept an eye out. It took some time and patience, but he finally found a spot for you. He'll be your account manager while you're on the surface." I was overwhelmed with joy, which was a bad thing because soon my powers of spontaneous combustion accidentally lit the entire bar aflame. Hellfire blazed over the serving table, popping bottles and shattering mugs with its intense heat. "Damn it Ned," said Azazel as he poured a nearby cleaning bucket's sudsy water onto the blaze, "you'd better not do that shit during your meeting tomorrow. Remember, the job's not yours *yet*."

"Azazel, what do I owe you?" I asked. "Just name it and it's yours." Azazel slapped the last of the hellfire out with his cleaning rag while Lazlo fanned the smoke. "Seriously, would you like my first born? They're yours. Write up the contract."

"Hold on a second," Azazel said over me. "I haven't told you the catch yet."

"Catch?" My brows climbed up my forehead, racing each other to the top. "What catch?"

"I don't know all of the details," said Azazel as he held his hands up in surrender, "but Armen admitted to me that there was an incident on the surface. It's why he says you're a perfect candidate. He'll let you know more when the two of you meet tomorrow."

I mused over Azazel's words. I mean, sure I was already trained for the job, but for the most part, being a corruptor was one of the most coveted positions in hell. Your job consisted of helping mortals condemn their souls to the grips of the dark lord. You worked freely on the surface without production goals or time constraints. Competition was fierce, and I assumed that there were at least a hundred other candidates who were just as qualified as me.

"Well," I said, raising my drink, "whatever. I'm sure it'll all make sense tomorrow. All that matters now is that it's finally going to happen." Azazel poured us a shot of his yellow colored liquor in a cracked glass before raising it and toasting with me.

"That's the spirit," he said before we took down our drinks. The burn in my throat reminded me of the time I'd accidentally bit into a battery. "Now," he slurred after wincing from the drink, "get your ass home and practice what you're going to say in the mirror. I'm sticking my neck out for you. I don't want you screwing this up."

"Ha!" I hooted…and then immediately ran home to rehearse.

For the rest of the night, I prepared for the meeting. My clothes were ironed, shoes shined, and I even managed to scrub all of the soot from my fingernails. I practiced answering any tricky questions that Armen might spring on me, including why I'd been demoted so many years ago. There was a renewed vigor in me that I hadn't felt since that dick head Lucifer talked us into his idiotic rebellion. I was going to use this newfound energy to my advantage. By the time I was finished rehearsing, there wouldn't be a question I couldn't answer or requirement that I couldn't complete. Tomorrow was the beginning of my new life. I was just hours away from becoming a corruptor again.

Chapter Two

Being Forsaken is tough on your wardrobe options. We were originally intended to be God's personal servants, conducting his most holy tasks with the utmost speed and might. That means we're a bit larger than your average human, taller with muscles to match. Add the fact that we have an enormous pair of wings sprouting from between our shoulders, stained black to remind us of our disloyalty, and it can make buying clothes a bit of a challenge. Everything needs to be custom tailored. So, once I'd torn apart my closet looking for the best outfit for the interview, it dawned on me that my choices were limited. Luckily, I had just the suit. It was an ashen ensemble that my ex-girlfriend had picked out for me before the breakup. I looked pretty damn good in it.

I'd been awake since the harpy's crow, practicing all the things I would say. It could take little more than me clearing my throat incorrectly for Armen to second guess his decision. I tried to keep my mind preoccupied until the meeting took place by taking the hellhounds with me for a little jog. By the time I returned home, most of the jitters were out. After the walk, I ate my microwavable bacon sandwich, *yes we like bacon too*, and then finally showered before getting dressed. Traffic in the fifth circle of Hell can get pretty busy in the morning, so I left early to give myself a bit of extra time.

As expected, the rows of cars trying to get into the city were uncountable. I waited in my rusty compact Toyota amongst thousands of other demons and damned, trying to get downtown. Finally, after what felt like an eternity through stop-and-go traffic, I'd arrived at

Corruptors headquarters. The drab building rose for miles and drooped at the top like a tired willow tree. I decided I needed something with teeth to keep me in fighting form, so after ordering a café' misto with extra foam from the Starsucks Coffee House in the lobby, I made my way to the security checkpoint. *Nothing says go-getter like froufrou coffee.* The Ifrit, who's under bite and long sharp teeth made him look like one of those anglerfish from Earth's oceans, guarded the main doors. After confirming my appointment, he made me a laminated visitor's badge and then with a grunt, guided me to the appropriate elevator.

After a sluggish ride up, I arrived at the instructed floor. I hurried to the correct suite as if I were already late and quickly made my way inside. The room was decorated with tanned enamel floors, twitching fluorescent lights, and a wobbly ceiling fan that squealed every time it spun full circle. There were screaming phones and a waiting area filled with impatient demons. A secretary took my name before requesting that I take a seat with the dozen or so imps and Hell spawn already waiting. Even with all of my delays, I'd made it to the office with time to spare. The agonizing wait recalled my jitters, making me shaky, but eventually the backdoor near the secretary's desk swung open, and Armen strode out.

The well-dressed Forsaken looked eerily similar to his brother Azazel, except that the long messy hair, torn jeans and Tom Waits t-shirt I was used to had been replaced with a shorter slicked back mane and tailored business suit.

"Ned?" he called out as he scanned the room. His eyes quickly locked on me, and he gave a grin that said, *you look pathetically nervous right now.* Well, I couldn't help it. I was. Everything was riding on this moment. I needed to get back to Earth.

"Hello," I shouted, jumping up anxiously from my seat. My left wing bumped a stack of *Homes and*

Gardening magazines, causing them to fall. The dozen or so subscriptions spread across the waiting room floor, causing the secretary to moan. An imp in the corner snickered through his serrated teeth. Armen ignored my clumsiness and beckoned me to follow him back into the area he'd sprouted from, where a hall of endless doors awaited.

"Fifteenth door on the left," he called out as he waved me inside the corridor. We made it to his Spartan office where only a naked desk awaited. There were hardly any other pieces of furniture or decorations within the room, which made the experience only that much more isolating. On his desk was a calfskin satchel leaning along an old computer with a spinach green monitor. There was a single leather recliner with small tears and wobbly legs sitting opposite of Armen's brand new office chair.

"Please, be seated," he said, pointing at the shabby chair prepared for guests. He unbuttoned his suit coat and slipped himself into his comfy seat. I reluctantly went to sit in the patchy recliner, and as I did, the squeal from the leather along my bottom made a distinguishing noise similar to cutting cheese. Armen raised a brow. I tried to recover by blurting out the first thing that came to mind.

"Nice computer," I barfed, "Is that an 88'?"

"It's an 86'," he said coldly, "but I didn't have you come here to talk about computers." Armen took a breath before leaning into his desk. "Ned, remind me how long you lived on Earth?" *Here come some of the tricky questions I was worried about.*

"From 1850 to 1871."

"And your territory was?"

"I worked out of Chicago sir. It's in the Americas."

"And remind me what happened again that caused you to be sent back to hell?" he asked while crossing his arms.

"Well, it all depends on who you ask, but there

might have been a malfunction with my pyromancy-"

"Ned," he said bluntly, "you were showing off for some girls and started the Great Chicago Fire."

"Sir, I wasn't trying to show off. I merely was displaying the great majesty of hellfire when-"

"Ned," Armen interrupted, "Technically, you should have been eliminated from the corruptors program altogether." I shrugged. I didn't agree, but now wasn't the time to argue. "But, the fact of the matter is that your replacement, Gethin, has gone missing, and I need you."

"Gone missing?" my voice squeaked.

"Yes. As in disappeared, no more, M.I.A. We weren't too worried at first, but it's been months now, and Chicago is a big city with a lot of desirable souls. We need production again, but not before we find out what's happened." Armen combed his hand through his greased head of hair. "Now before you ask, we did try sending up one of the basic Hell spawn to investigate, an office quasit, but he never came back. It's our fear that he's been obliterated."

"Obliterated!" I hollered.

Angels, devils, demons, we don't fear death like mortals do. That's because we can't die in the literal sense. You can run us through with a saber, burn us at the stake, and we'll just keep on ticking. But being obliterated is different. Only otherworldly beings of powerful malevolence or divinity can obliterate us, and unlike mortals, whose souls immediately get whisked away to the afterlife, when we die, we're gone for good.

"Yes obliterated," Armen confirmed. I'd hoped that I wasn't coming off as cowardly, but the O-word wasn't something I was used to.

"So what do you need me for?"

"Well obviously you're familiar with Chicago."

"No I'm not," I objected. "It's been over a hundred years. All I know now is what I see on television, hear on podcasts, and read in trashy magazines. Everything will be different."

"The city might be, but not the people. Well, not the ones that matter." Armen opened up a nearby filing cabinet, and struggled to pluck out an overstuffed manila file labeled *Chicago*. He dropped the file onto my side of the desk. I fumbled with the folder for a moment before gripping onto its surface and opening it. Stamped on top was a crushed cockroach followed by reports of every *spooky*, a nickname we dubbed for all supernatural beings that weren't divine, who lived in Chicago. I had access to the profiles of any ghoul, phantom, hag or werewolf living in the city. I'd met a lot of them within my brief time in Chicago, and the majority was mostly harmless. "Your replacement isn't dead. If he was, I'd feel his release, being his manager and all. But you can't just hide a Forsaken either. Our aura is kind of hard to miss. That is, unless you're talented enough to do so."

"So," I said intrigued, "do you think Gethin has been kidnapped by some powerful spooky who's killing anyone who gets too close to the trail?"

"One would assume. And seeing that Gethin was a demon maker before his induction into the Corruptor's Department, he could cause all kinds of havoc on the surface if he were forced to." Armen's stern voice became something more daring, and yet flattering. "That's why I need someone brave and resourceful. Seeing that you're not only a former legionnaire, but also familiar with most of the spookies in Chicago, I feel that you'll be the perfect fit." My chest puffed out uncontrollably. "Nedonius," Armen said as he planted his fingers on the desk's surface, "are you the fallen that will help find our missing corruptor and save Chicago?"

"Well, yeah," I replied, my ego stroked, but still confused. "Of course."

"Perfect," said Armen. "Now, I need-"

"Wait," I cut in, "so am I a corruptor or just some dog chasing a trail?" Armen smiled for the first time. It was an eerie smile that made me wonder if he was up to no good. After a moment, he stood up, grabbing the buckskin satchel that had been placed atop of his desk. He walked over to my side of the table and leaned on top of it.

"Both," he said affably while resting the bag in my lap. "Due to an agreement we have with the *Global Council of Supernatural Beings*, we can only allow so many of our kind on Earth. So, I need you to have the title of a corruptor in order to get you through the red tape. You'll do everything that you did before. In the meantime however, I need you to do your best in order to find our man. Hunt down Gethin, and depending on the circumstances, I might send him back to demon making, and give you your spot back permanently."

"Great!" I said loudly, too excited to contain the volume of my voice. Armen gave me a doubtful look.

"Oh and there's one other thing," he added reluctantly. "Due to new legislation between Hell and the Global Council, we only have until tomorrow before new, more stringent regulations on portals and teleporting goes into effect." Armen leaned his arm over to his side of the desk, and dug through the top drawer. After a few seconds, he removed a stick of chalk and a rusted stiletto. "So I need you to leave for Chicago immediately."

"Whoa, wait a second," I protested as Armen drew a circle around my chair. "Can I get a bit more information about Gethin before I go?" Armen was now on his knees and drawing gate symbols around my feet. He looked up at me with a frighteningly toothy grin, his dark bangs swathed over his eyes. He curled his lip, blowing breath onto his blades of hair in order to clear them from his face.

"What's there to know Ned?" he asked, dusting chalk off his hands. "Corruptor vanishes, no one knows where, so we're sending you to find him." Armen stood tall again and stared at my folded hands. "May I have your palm please?"

"Well for starters," I said, offering my left hand," I don't even know what he looks like."

"Damn it Nedonius," he moaned, "Do you want to be a corruptor again or no?"

"Well," I said thoughtfully, "yeah."

"Good, then no more questions." Armen jabbed my finger with the point of the stiletto. A flicker of flame and black blood spit from the wound. Armen dipped the knife's tip in the blood, and then used it like a pen quill to write images across the satchel resting on my lap.

"Everything you'll need is inside that satchel Ned. Just use the handbook I put in there if you're not sure about something. Now," he said through a smile, raising the blade, "let's get you to Chicago."

Armen began mumbling incantations, and all at once a sphere of flame and shadow appeared behind me. I could feel the powerful vacuum of the vortex pulling me in.

"Hold on. I need someone to take care of my hellhounds. Who's going to feed them?" Armen laughed.

"Oh those things?" His smile turned mischievous. "I thought someone put them to sleep already." I frowned at his callousness. Armen could see the disapproval in my eyes. "Oh, alright Ned. If you're that close to them, I'll have someone retrieve the beasts and send them over. Now hurry, we need you to find Gethin. Once you do, use the manual to call me." And with that, Armen lifted his leg and kicked me square in the chest. I flailed helplessly while falling backwards into the portal. My sight blurred and the room began to feel as if it were spinning.

Voip!

The portal had completely enveloped me. I was now on a one-way trip through a wormhole back to Earth. My body felt weightless as I floated through the passage, whirling aimlessly through God knows what. A flapping of wind filled my ears and a blanket of red blinded my vision. I don't know how long I remained like that, but the sensation was intense and overwhelming. Then as abruptly as I'd been consumed by the portal, gravity kicked in again, and I planted facedown onto a hard surface.

***

The cool cement tasted like stale urine. I lifted my head, and found that I was in an alleyway. The sting of gravel stabbed at my chest, and as I pushed myself up from the ground, I could hear car horns in the distance. From what I could tell, I was between two towering brick buildings, at least ten stories tall. There was a canopy of blue sky between the structures, and a sliver of sun peaking down. I'd landed between two dumpsters over brimming with garbage. A rat that had been digging through the plastic bags took notice of me and scurried down to the bottom of the waste container.

"Well," I said as I regained my balance, "looks like Chicago hasn't changed as much as I'd thought." Then suddenly…

"Hey you!" someone hollered from behind me.

It was a gruff and hostile voice. I turned around to find a pair of men hurriedly coming towards me. One, an olive skinned mortal with groomed facial hair that partially hid the sore on his lip, wore a Chicago Bulls jersey with loose-fitting pants. His fists balled tightly near his waist as he approached. His partner, a black man with bushy hair, kept his hands in his coat pockets. He was wearing a wide brimmed baseball hat and oversized shorts that drooped off of his backside.

"Oh hello," I greeted.

Without warning, the man with the wide brimmed hat drew a silver pistol from his coat pocket and held it sideways. His chest quivered, and his hands shook. I could tell he was teetering between nervousness and anger. "Give us your phone and money and we might let you live."

"Whoa, whoa, take it easy Ke-mo sah-bee," I smirked. *I love the Lone Ranger.* "Why don't you pull your pants up and we can have a real conversation like civilized people."

Bang!

The firearm shot a flare of orange from its barrel, kicking my head back as a bullet drove into my forehead. I fell rearward onto the pavement with a heavy thump. *Owie.* This was just my luck. Here I was, my first minutes back on Earth, and everything was already going to shit.

Chapter Three

The impact had not only knocked me off of my feet, but also caused my vision to spin. I could hear a loud ringing in my ears and tasted copper in my mouth. Like I said, bullets can't kill Forsaken, but they certainly have a way of stupefying you when they burrow their way through your forehead. I tried to focus, but it wasn't easy. My vision was blurry, my eyes sluggishly following my attackers as they hovered over me. The pair looked over their shoulders before hurriedly patting down my body. I could tell from the frowns on their faces that they didn't exactly find what they were looking for.

"Hey cabrón," said the man with the penciled beard, "this bitch ain't got shit." I could feel a trickle begin to run down my crown. The two hoodlums stared at my bleeding brow until one of them finally took his index finger and smeared it along my temple. He raised his hand, which was now covered in oily goo. "Damn man, it's hot. What the Hell do you think was wrong with him?"

But before his partner could answer, a pair of ferocious growls rumbled from the alley, directly behind the assailants. The men leapt up to their feet, spinning around to see what was stirring. My body was still paralyzed or else I would have joined them.

"What are they?" asked the bushy haired man as he edged his way backwards.

"Are those dogs?" asked the other mugger anxiously.

Simon and Hecubus! A heavy howl erupted. Suddenly, a blur of shadow leapt on top of the mustached man, tackling him to the ground. The gruesome sound of tearing skin came from just above my head. Warm blood splattered onto my face, which immediately broke my trance. *Forsaken are weird that way.* I lifted my neck to get a better look at things. Amid the chaos, the other assailant was retreating towards the street in a panic, his right hand holding up his pants as he tried to get away. I couldn't help but feel insulted. Without second-guessing, I held out my hands, focusing on all of my anger, and willed it towards him.

A tendril of flame leapt out from my fingers, chasing my attacker and whipping into his back like a scorpion's tail. The goon lit up in a blaze, his flesh and bones withering down to singed grains of ash before he could take another step. His now charred and blackened remains peppered the alleyway just feet away from the main avenue, unrecognizable to anyone who might stumble upon him. I stood back up and wiped the mess from my face. Simon and Hecubus had earned a well-deserved scratch behind their ears for a job well done. But as I spun around to pet them, I was taken aback by what I found.

"Oh no," I cried aloud, "It can't be."

To my dismay, my once frighteningly enormous coal colored mastiffs now paled in comparison. The portal had seen to that. It was all coming back now. The portal, as it had done to me during my first tenure as a corruptor, helped anyone traveling through it blend in with their surroundings. Last time around, I was a handsome Irish bruiser with fists like anvils and a glare that could scare away a crowd. Such was not the case for Simon and Hecubus. My once vicious killers were now ankle height with matted fur coats of black and silver. Their heads were rectangular with bushy mustaches and a pair of v-shaped folded ears. The flesh in their teeth stained their snouts and whiskers cherry, making them look more like canine clowns than ferocious demons. I'd gone from massive mastiffs to ankle biting terriers. While they still might have had the strength of Hell in them, they no longer possessed any of the majesty.

"Is this one of Armen's sick jokes?" I said as I bent down to greet the animals. "Simon, Hecubus, come here boys."

The two tiny terriers traipsed their way to me, licking at my hands. I gathered them up and stuffed them in the satchel. The dogs tried clawing at the mouth of the bag before being forcefully sucked into the depths. The weight of the bag hadn't changed, nor could I feel the hellhounds moving around inside.

"Sweet," I mumbled to myself as I clasped the buckles on the bag, "pocket dimension."

From there, I made my way towards the main road, which was marked Michigan Avenue, ready to finally get a glimpse of the twenty-first century. *Man was I in for a surprise.* The old cobblestone streets and dusty brick buildings I'd remembered about Chicago were replaced by smooth avenues and towering steel skyscrapers. Advertisement signs played videos of pretty young women posing around whatever beer they were promoting, while blinking traffic lights flashed with different colors. The smell of fried food fragranced the air, and the faint sound of music echoed from all around me. Tiny cars zoomed past massive busses that unloaded droves of humans. Across the road, a giant sculpture, bigger than most houses, planted itself in a large park. It was shaped like a bean and covered in a mirror like coating. Hundreds of people gathered around it, posing for pictures. My senses were in overload. *What in the Nine Circles had happened to this city?*

Before I could give it any more thought, someone large and heavy shoved me. He was a round man, wearing a khaki colored coat and dress pants. I turned angrily to address him, but he was already half way down the sidewalk. He didn't stop to apologize or even dignify me for that matter. No, he just kept on walking. Then another bump, this time the person was twice as plump and a bit flabbier. At first I couldn't even recognize that it was a woman, but I soon realized she was wearing a skirt and a pair of high heels that were screaming for someone to put them out of their misery. Beside her was another thick woman with red hair, and behind her, a giant man who was going bald. In fact, the more I saw of Chicago, the more I realized I was surrounded by nothing but fat people.

There were portly old women in long fancy coats shuffling into stores, hefty men in hardhats balancing themselves on ladders, and one hideously obese policeman guiding traffic with a pink donut clutched between his teeth. They wobbled, bobbled, and floundered all throughout Michigan Avenue. I could hardly believe my eyes.

"Excuse me young man," blabbered a butterball in a denim jacket as she pushed past me.

Young man? What the Hell was she talking about?

Then it hit me. I'd been so engrossed in all the changes to Chicago that I'd completely forgot that much like Simon and Hecubus, I'd been changed as well. Oh boy, what did the portal turn me into this time? Was I some young Latin stud from Spain or maybe a Herculean athlete? I rushed to the large silver bean across the street to check myself out along its reflective surface. Several cars nearly hit me on my way over, and a man in a yellow cab threw a cup of coffee at me.

I didn't care. I was focused on making it to the bulbous statue's mirrored surface. And once there, I straightened out my posture posing in order to take in my visage. To my disappointment, staring back at me from the bean's reflection was not some statuesque figure, but a young slender guy, perhaps in his early twenties, with wild jet-black hair, a narrow face and big ears. His features were sharp and pretty to the point of feminine, and his face was so smooth that it looked polished. He had light gray eyes with small dark pupils, and a pierced lip. He wore a black t-shirt with a shambling ghoul on it that said, "Zombies Just Want Hugs," blue jeans that were fastened by a spiked belt and a pair of raven colored gym shoes. Both of his scrawny arms were covered in tattoos that crept out from his shirtsleeves and stopped at his wrists.

Armen's satchel had changed too. The accessory, once ideal for an Indiana Jones movie, was now made of gray canvas and decorated with heavy metal band patches. It had decorative buttons that said, "Vote Cash," and "Have You Pooped Today?" pinned across its sides. There was a zippered pocket where a phone should go. Curiously, I opened it, but when I did, all that was inside was a single barbershop red and white mint. *Great, no phone either.*

"Son of a bitch," I shouted angrily. "This is the form I've been given? I look like an evil elf from one of those terrible fantasy movies." A heavyset young man who'd been standing next to me took in a deep breath and exhaled as he stared at his own reflection. He was about the same age as my disguise, though his rust colored hair and freckles made him look younger. He had a wide head and pointed nose that resembled a penguin's beak and an extra chin that made him look like he'd forgotten to put on his neck this morning.

"I know," he moaned, "why does God hate me so much?" I gave the ginger haired young man a second glance. He was heavy set to be sure, and a bit funny looking because of his unusually snug shirt and shorts, but he wasn't repulsive by any means. It appeared that his bruised ego was far more damaging than his actual appearance.

"I'm sure if God had anything to do with it," I replied, "I'm partially to blame." The boy gave me a curious look. 'Well not just me -- my brothers and sisters played a part in it as well." I started to think more than I should have. "Maybe you're what happens to mortals when

God needs to let out his anger, like a stress ball or something." The young man gave an uneasy half-snicker.

"Okay, you're not weird or anything," he said in good humor.

"No, I'm not weird," I said simply. "I'm Ned," I extended my hand, offering it to him with a friendly smile. "Well, Ned is short for Nedonius, which I guess is a little weird." The young man smiled and shook my hand, staring at the ink across my arms. The body art, which I hadn't really taken inventory of until now, was mostly flames and skulls with the occasional ninja and naked woman. After studying the art a bit longer, the young man paused, and then, as if coming out of some daze, shook his head and looked up at me.

"Oh man, I'm sorry. The name is Billy. Billy Shanahan. I'm a freshman at Roosevelt University. How about you?"

"How about me what?"

"What college do you go to? You're obviously an art student, right?"

"Oh," I said absentmindedly. *Ten minutes on Earth and I was already blowing my cover.* "Well duh?" Billy gave a smile. "Which school do you think I go to?" I said with a game show host's voice, trying to build my cover out of thin air.

"Well," he hummed, taking a step back to better examine me. "You don't look like one of those rich Art Institute kids, so I'm guessing Columbia."

"That's the one," I said with false enthusiasm. I'd have to remember Columbia in case anyone else asked. "But enough about school."

"Yeah, school is lame."

"You said it. School is for dummies."

A devious plan began to form in my mind. If I wanted to find Gethin, I'd need to get a hold of a local spooky, but I didn't know where any of them lived any longer. If I wanted to find one, I'd need to bring them to me. I wasn't too keen on magic, but had learned a couple tricks. If Billy could get me to a place with summoning tomes, I could call forth a local specter to help me out. I didn't think that any of the Polish gypsies that once lived in Chicago ran shops around the corner any longer. But perhaps there was one of those new age bookstores around. You know, the ones on bad T.V. sitcoms where a psychic hippy is married to a scientist. If so, there might be a chance that they had a basic summoning tome for purchase. The Boy before me was the perfect candidate for a guide.

"Hey Billy, you know what isn't lame?" I said as I combed my fingers gracefully through my hair like *The Fonze.*

"What?"

"The ladies."

Billy smiled guiltily. "Oh yeah. No arguments there. Once again though," he said, waving his hands above his tight striped shirt and bulging gut, "I'm not exactly a ladies man."

"Ha," I chortled, "Do you think I am? No way. The trick isn't always in presentation though. What you need to do is find out what girls our age like."

"That's true."

"And do you know what I discovered?"

"What?"

"They like weird shit like magic and the occult."

"You mean like Twilight?"

"Uh, sure. You see, where I'm from, the occult is something that the cool people do."

"And where are you from?"

"The South," I said quickly, trying to dodge the question. Billy looked puzzled. I was losing him.

But then, as if my luck were finally taking a turn for the better, a young blonde beauty with a thin blouse, short dress, and high boots walked beside us. She had a camera dangling from her neck, resting perfectly on her oversized breasts. She sauntered to the bean, lifting her camera and snapping a couple of photographs. Billy stiffened up like he was being electrocuted. Now was my chance to win him over. I leaned on his shoulder, trying to look smooth and uncaring, like one of those cigarette ads. The young lady studied the bean for another moment before finally noticing our stares from the corner of her eye. She turned to us, and raised a thinly plucked blonde brow.

"Um, hello," she greeted innocently.

"Sorry for gawking," I apologized, "but I can't believe what I'm staring at." The girl narrowed her eyes, clearly puzzled. "You see, we're art students, and you young lady, are confusing the Hell out of us."

The young woman gave a look of concern. "What do you mean?"

"Well," I went on, "I know for a fact that Botticelli painted *The Birth of Venus* in 1486." The girl gave a half smile, uncertain how to react. "Yet," I paused, "here you are, the model for his inspiration, standing amongst us in the modern world."

The girl snorted. "Smooth," she complimented, tucking a strand of gold behind her ear, "but I don't go out with Goth guys."

"Oh no?" I asked, giving a fake look of shock, "Well maybe you just haven't found the right one. We really know how to make things fun you know? Perhaps," I strutted a bit closer to her, "we could get together sometime, and I don't know, see if we can raise the dead."

Now, I'd definitely blown it. Surprisingly though, just as I'd thought that I'd ruined my chances with the young photographer, she paused and looked me over. I half expected her to sprint for the nearest police officer, but instead, she pulled out a pen from her camera bag and grabbed at my hand. Without saying another word, she wrote her name, *Linda*, along with her phone number across my palm.

"Call me some time," she said with a wink, "maybe the dead will walk again." She smiled before turning around, slowly parading back through the park. I watched as she did, giving her a moment to get out of earshot before looking to Billy. His jaw was hinged open. I held my hand up in the air, begging for a high-five. Billy obliged.

"That was amazing," he hooted.

"I told you man," I said as I tried to disguise my relief, "girls dig weird. I have it down to a science. And there's nothing weirder than the occult."

"Seriously?"

"Seriously," I lied. "That's why, as we speak, I'm looking to find a bookstore that caters to my need. I want to meet darker, freakier girls, ones that make old Linda there look like Shirley Temple."

"You mean like one of those Emo bookstores? The ones where they listen to sad music, wear all black, and talk about how life is just one big letdown?"

"That's the one."

Billy nodded in understanding. "I think I know a place in Lakeview, but we'll have to use the Redline."

"Wait," I said in confusion. "Are you telling me someone painted a scarlet line all the way to this bookstore? How do we go about following it?" Billy tilted his head as if looking at abstract art.

"It's a train," he said bluntly. "There's an entrance just off of Randolph Street. I have a transit card if you need me to pay for your ride?"

Currency. I'd forgotten all about it. I dug inside the satchel for money that all corruptors are supposed to have. *It's kind of hard to tempt mortals without it.* Inside was the manila file Armen had given me, a book that read *Manual*, and an array of basic spell components. There was also a wallet with a picture of a man carrying a machinegun on it. "Scarface" was stitched across the top. I opened up the money holder and found some basic paper printed cash and a few plastic credit cards. One in particular was silver with the words *Platinum* written across the face. I plucked the plastic square out and showed it to Billy.

"Will this do?"

"Whoa, looks like someone got a hold of their parents' credit cards. Heck, screw walking to the train. Why don't we just use the card and take a cab? It's way quicker."

Ah, my first potential candidate for corruption. He was fat, lazy, and ready to spend my money. That's at least "Gluttony" and "Sloth."

"Sounds good to me," I said, patting Billy on the back as we walked towards Michigan Avenue. "Hey Billy," I said with a calm voice, "you hungry?"

"Come on man, look at me. I'm always hungry."

"I'll make you a deal. Like I was saying before, I'm from the South. Big cities like this are a lot to take in. Chances are that I'm going to get lost quicker than Oceanic Airlines flight 815. Keep showing me around Chicago and I'll buy you all the meals you can handle."

"Cool, but I have to be back downtown in two hours for my last class of the day."

"Not a problem. I'll get you back in time," I said carelessly. Billy raised a nervous brow as he waved for a cab. A yellow car with a sweaty looking driver pulled up along the curb.

"Dude," Billy pleaded, "my dad will kill me if I miss school. This is a big city. You have to promise me we'll get me back in time Ned."

"I promise Billy," I said as we entered the vehicle. "You can trust me."

Chapter Four

Lakeview was around during my tenure as a corruptor, but it was by no means what it is today. The early settlers were mostly Germans and Swedish farmers who humbly tried to raise crops in the frozen soils. Now, apparently, it was the place to be. From what Billy told me, there were several different party neighborhoods inside the large community, from Boystown to Wrigleyville. It was easy to see what he meant by the amount of corner pubs, nightclubs and drunken pedestrians we passed by. *Sinner's paradise.*

We arrived at *The Prologue* just fifteen minutes after getting in the cab. The exotic bookstore made its modest home between a Greek gyro restaurant and brightly painted adult store along Belmont Avenue. Upon entering, we were welcomed by the aroma of stale paper and incense. There was a melancholy melody crying from the overhead speakers. In it a young woman wailed like a banshee over an acoustic guitar, giving the black library an even more somber feel. A few customers were scattered throughout the store casually reading worn books along the racks.

"See, I told you this place was emo," said Billy as he took a look around. "I hate places like this."

"Here Billy," I said, handing him the platinum card. "You go and get yourself a gyro next door. I'll be done shortly." Billy hesitantly removed the plastic card out of my hand. He took a reluctant step towards the exit while giving me a bug eyed stare. "Off you go," I said with a wave of my hand. Billy shrugged with an ecstatic grin before tottering out of the store. Once he'd gone, I began perusing through the aisles in search of any sort of book that would help me summon a spooky.

I'd never been much of a practitioner of magic except when it comes to pyromancy. Truth be told, it's not that I don't want to know how to manipulate mana, as much as it is that I'm lazy. Regardless, when you live in my world, you occasionally pick up a trick or two. Calling forth spookies, be they bodaks, slaads, or any other creature isn't so much about your beliefs as much as it is your methods. You need to conduct a ceremony properly, with passion and contempt. Wiccans and Catholic priests can be equally efficient at binding a spooky so long as they are methodical.

Unfortunately for me, the only book that I could find that catered to my basic skillset was an eighteenth century gypsy codex written in Polish. I'd found the book by chance, hiding between a *Wizards for Dummies* manual and vampire romance novel. I hadn't spoken the language in ages and was worried I'd be a bit rusty. With little other choice, I took the codex and went to find the register to buy it. However, before I could get out of the aisle, a light tingle sparked inside my stomach.

Forsaken have a way of sensing other supernatural beings. Think of it as another instinct, a gut feeling, with different sensations based on who the spooky is. If they're evil, it's pleasurable. If they're good, it hurts. It can feel like a light pang in your belly or a heart attack, depending on the subject. This makes meeting powerful do-gooders a pain wracking experience.

The light prickle in my belly told me that I was in the presence of a weak and wicked spooky. I looked the store over and spotted a shorter man in my aisle with a heavy wool grey trench coat and matching scarf. He was pretending to read an old book while staring fervently towards the front of the store. He reeked of cigarettes and mint gum, and had a set of white ear buds blaring music that sounded like two electric guitars having sex. His oily russet hair was highlighted purple and plastered down to the side, swathing over one of his mascara painted eyes. He had a thin goatee with pointed chin hair and a slender mustache that only further made him appear out of sorts.

"Louie?" I asked aloud, recognizing his face. The man ogled me suspiciously. "Louie Joliet, is that you?"

Louis Joliet was a French Canadian voyager who explored most of the Mississippi River in the late sixteen hundreds. Unlike his partner, Father Marquette, Joliet strayed away from God when he started getting sick. He was terrified of death and bartered a deal with my predecessor in order to grant him immortality in return for his measly soul. Although everyone publicly thought that Joliet had simply disappeared, most likely killed by Native Americans, he'd actually started a new life with one of his many mistresses in a settlement that would one day become Chicago. He was a crackpot and scumbag. Even I didn't trust him.

"Who are you?" he hissed.

"Louis, come on man, it's me Ned. Remember, I was there when you signed your special contract?" He inspected me with revulsion, scrutinizing my appearance. Then after a brief lock of his eyes and sudden pause, he jumped backwards as if frightened.

"Oh, dear," he said with a look of shock. "Nedonius? No, it can't be. What happened to you?"

"I know, it's not as inspiring as the last time you saw me, but I don't really get a choice in the matter." A few of the store customers looked up at me suspiciously. I gave a middle-aged lady with a tatty *Aerosmith* shirt a wink before returning to Louis. "Anyhow, what are you doing here? I thought you swore off magic."

"Shh!" Louis spat, putting his index finger over his lips. "I did your Excellency. Please though, not so loud."

"Well," I said quietly, "if you don't want to draw attention to yourself, it's probably best if you lose the wool coat in July." Louie looked down at his heavy jacket and frowned. "Now why are you lingering around here all creepy-like?" Louis looked back and forth between aisles, studying the customers who went back to reading their books.

"Your Grace, if I tell you why I'm here, will you please leave?"

"It all depends," I said while leaning on the bookshelf, "But if you don't tell me, I may have to talk to someone about making an addendum to your contract."

"Okay, okay, no need to get nasty," he complained. "If you must know, I'm here for her," he confessed, returning his gaze to the front of the store. I looked lackadaisically towards the cashier area. I had no real interest in finding out who Louie's latest crush was, but as my eyes tottered their way towards the register, I found a young woman like I'd never seen before reading a tattered old tome.

She had a strawberry shaped face with black silky hair that she held up in a simple bun. Her features were flawlessly mapped out like a masterfully crafted mask, striking and symmetrical. She had milky skin with a splash of freckles that colored the area between her dimples and the lower bow of her smoky raven eyes. Her ruby lips were lightly mouthing the words of her book, and as she scratched at her cherry shaped nose, I noticed that she had a small pin sized piercing glittering from her nostril. There was an array of intricate tattoos that cascaded down her thin neck and onto her elegant shoulders. She wore a tight white tank top shirt with a V-shape slit that cut near the break of her cleavage, exhibiting the tops of her voluptuous breasts, and a pair of jeans that started at her curvy hips and made their way down her rounded legs. *All and all, she was amazing.*

Louis saw me staring and slapped at my shoulder. I glowered at him for a moment, disgusted by his audacity, before opening up the flap of my satchel and giving a little whistle. A neon blue poured outward before the heads of both Simon and Hecubus peaked out. Their eyes glowed red as they started to snarl. Louis jumped back.

"My word, what are those little monsters?" he asked, tucking his hands into his chest. I pushed the beast's heads back into the bag.

"They're my hellhounds, and they'll bite your freaking head off if you ever do that again Louie."

"Well then stop staring my lord. She's the owner of this store. I've been prospecting a courtship for some time. She's mine."

"Louie," I leaned out of the aisle to have a better look, "does she even know you exist?"

"I said," he pouted before licking his lips like a snake, "*she's* mine."

I shot Louis a glare that said *back off,* before returning my attention to the bookstore owner. Louis fidgeted with his hands, fretful to my intentions.

"Come now Master," he muttered pleadingly, "I told you why I was here. Now please, go away."

I knew that ignoring Joliet's plea wasn't the right thing to do, even if I *was* Forsaken, but I couldn't let the creeper get his hands on the bookstore owner. Even if he wasn't planning on doing something disturbing, a woman like that deserved better than a soulless toad like Louis Joliet. I'm not saying that I was the best candidate, but I certainly wasn't about to pass up the opportunity to introduce myself. This woman, this dark goddess, was everything a guy like me could ask for. I'd be damned if I didn't at least say hello.

"Sorry Louie, I'm afraid I can't do that." Louie frowned, squeezing at the book in his hands. I shoved past him and made my way to the register while trying to think of a good opening line. The woman paid me no mind, continuing to flip of the pages of her leather bound tome.

"Ehem," I announced, attempting to clear my throat.

"No," she said bluntly.

"No what?"

"No, there's no such thing as *Tobin's Spirit Guide*."

"Wait," I said confused. "What do you mean?"

"I can tell from the douchebag Ghostbuster tattoo on your elbow that you were going to ask." I took a look at my arms. Sure enough, a cartoon ghost sitting inside a crossed red circle was inked on the end of my elbow. *Dr. Venkman would be so disappointed in me.*

"Oh...uh, no I wasn't going to ask that." The girl rolled her eyes. "My name is Ned."

"I don't care," she said dryly.

"Wait, come on, give me a chance here. I just wanted to ask how much this gypsy summoning codex cost?"

Her eyes finally peeled from the pages of her tome. She stared at the Polish summoning book before yanking it forcefully from my hand.

"Huh," she said, studying the blank cover. "I'm impressed. Most people don't know what that is."

"So," I said with my best smile and leaned an elbow onto the counter, nearly knocking over the donation jar dedicated to kids with disabilities, "are you impressed enough to give me your name?" She rolled her eyes again before placing the book on the counter.

"It's Chelsea," she said with a lack of interest, "and I warn you, that book isn't cheap. It's priced at three-hundred bucks."

Here was my chance. I'd have to risk big, to win big. "Okay Chelsea, so if I buy this book can I take you out sometime?" Chelsea sighed and angrily threw the book on a stack behind her.

"Ugh," she shook her head, "I knew it. For one second, you showed promise Ghostbuster boy, but you ruined it. This is a bookstore, not a dating service."

"Oh, come on," I said while combing my fingers through my hair. "Give me a shot baby. I'm not like other guys."

Chelsea's face went blank. "You know what, forget it. The book is not for sale anymore."

Damn, I'd blown it. Not only that, but I'd also just lost the recipe for summoning my spooky. *Double-damn.* I wasn't about to turn around and dignify Joliet, but I could hear him snickering in the background. Instead, I just stood there with my bruised ego, elbow still planted on the table.

"Okay, I'm sorry. You're right. I'm an idiot. Can I just have the codex please?" I took another platinum card from my wallet and waved it at her. "I'll gladly pay double." Chelsea stared at my card for a moment before picking up the codex again. She took a deep breath, than after starting at her register, grabbed the piece of plastic from my hand before swiping it through a machine.

"You're lucky I need to pay rent," she said as she handed the card back to me. I lowered my head and meekly watched as she wrapped the book up in tissue paper before placing it in an ugly plastic bag. She jabbed the shopping bag into my shoulder and added, "On that note, I'm obligated to tell you something about that book. What you have in your hands there is no trick shop Ouija Board toy. It's very rare, and very real, written only for *real* conjurers. Buyer beware." I was impressed. This girl really knew her stuff. "Now," she added with a fake smile, "have a nice day."

I took my purchase, and with my head still down, shuffled out of the store. The hot air from the streets hit me in my face. I made it to the curb, where a man and woman donned in matching Cubs jerseys were drunkenly making out. *At least someone was getting lucky.* I took out the book and examined it, ignoring the slobbery sounds of tonsil hockey next to me. It was the real deal all right. I could definitely use the book in order to call forth a spooky. Not shortly after I closed the book back up and placed it in its plastic bag did Joliet follow me out of the store.

"Too bad Nedonius," he said with a deadpan expression. "I was really rooting for you my Master. If only you would have taken my advice. Chelsea is a tough specimen."

"Drop dead Louie," I hissed.

"I *can't* Master," he said snidely, "Remember my contract?"

"Let's not test the boundaries of that contract you little shit."

Louis paused for a moment, a jeering half smile on his face. "My apologies Master. I'll be going now." He walked away while whistling down the sidewalk. I mulled over melting him into the pavement, but Billy came out from the Gyro store just in time to distract me. He was dabbing a napkin onto fresh grease stains marked across his shirt.

"So," he said with onion breath, "did you find what you were looking for?"

My mind raced back to Chelsea and the small serving of humiliation she'd served me. I never really had a mortal talk to me like that. Although it was a bit embarrassing, the more I thought about her, the more it occurred to me that *I kind of liked it.* I can't say for sure if it was because how amazingly gorgeous she was or her unfettered behavior, but I wanted more. I needed to somehow salvage the encounter. I checked the store hours painted on the main entrance and saw that the bookstore didn't close until ten. It looked like it was going to be a late night. Billy tapped his foot on the sidewalk, waiting for me to answer.

"I don't know if I was looking for it," I replied, "but it certainly did grab my attention."

Chapter Five

Billy still had some time to spare before his next class so we went to a diner across the street where I treated him to some ice cream. We made light conversation, and I was pleased to find that Billy was actually a pretty interesting guy. His mother had passed away when he was just a little boy, leaving his father to raise Billy and his two younger brothers. They lived inside a small house near Midway Airport along a blue-collar neighborhood that some would label as *dodgy* at best. His dad was a Chicago Policeman who worked extra hours to pay for Billy's school. That meant that there was a lot of pressure for Billy to do well in his studies, not only because of the cost, but because it would make him the first of his immediate family to graduate college.

Billy was studying to be an engineer of aeronautics. I had no idea what that meant until he explained it to me. Long story short, he studied flight vehicle designs so that he could someday assist in making better airplanes, space satellites, and don't forget humans' favorite past time, military weapons. When he wasn't knee-deep in textbooks, he and his roommate, Stevie, built remote control helicopters and planes out of any scrap that they could salvage. They rigged cameras to the drones in order to do all sorts of things that young horny college students shouldn't, like spying on girls outside of their windows and messing with some of the jerks on campus.

I kind of liked Billy, and couldn't see myself trying to corrupt him even if he deserved it-*which he didn't*. Truthfully, he would have been an easy mortal to manipulate due to his greed and sloth like tendencies, but I felt that he could be more useful as a pal during my investigation. I needed a local that I could rely on and Billy was just that. He was honest, humble and pleasant to speak to. Although it was evident that he had a few image issues, it was something that I thought I could perhaps coach him with so long as he kept helping me.

After ice cream, Billy wrote down his dorm address so that we could meet up later, and then headed back downtown for his next class. I lingered in the diner's booth, stationed directly across the street from *The Prologue,* so I could see the entire store. I planned on patiently waiting for Chelsea to close up shop so I could try to persuade her to give me another chance at getting to know her. In the meantime, I ordered several coffees and kept keen and focused by studying the gypsy summoning-codex. It took me some time to reacquaint myself with Polish incantations, but I eventually managed to find an appropriate summoning ritual near the back of the book that I felt would work. Finally just a few hours after dark, the lights of the bookstore turned off and Chelsea emerged. I promptly paid my check, slapping a handsome amount of cash on the counter before running out of the diner in order to catch up with her as she locked up the store.

However, I'd only made it about halfway across the busy street when a dark figure emerged from the bookstore's side path. The shadowy silhouette was taller than Chelsea, but not by much. He hurriedly strode up to Chelsea, getting intimately close before tapping her lightly on the arm. Chelsea leapt back, her fists balled up and ready to strike. But she soon seemed to recognize the figure, and after a moment, lowered her arms. Shaking her head, she returned to locking the front door of the store while the mysterious man rested along the wall next to her. He leaned into her ear and whispered before grabbing her by the hand. *Damn it Ned, how did you not figure that she already has a boyfriend?*

Chelsea and the man stared at each other for a

moment, before slowly turning around towards me. Now exposed, I rushed to a nearby car with an unrolled rear window, and dove into the backseat before Chelsea could see me. I kept my head low and climbed down to the footrest, feeling incredibly idiotic that I, a *Forsaken*, was afraid of looking like a stalker to a mortal. But before I could catch another breath, the jingle of car keys and Chelsea's drone voice alerted me that she was standing next to the car. I could hear the driver side door open, and someone slip behind the wheel. The smell of vanilla perfume let me know that it was Chelsea.

"Hold on, I'll unlock your side," she said lowly, fiddling with the lock mechanism. The stranger opened up the passenger side door and settled inside. I heard another jingle as Chelsea fiddled with her keys. A twinge of nervousness quivered in my gut, causing me to grab at my stomach. *Damn those dozen coffees.*

"Now what?" Chelsea asked in a monotone voice as her boyfriend closed the door. I could see the obscure reflection of the passenger gleaming from the backseat window. The man leaned over, reaching his arm around Chelsea's seat.

"How about your place?"

Clearly, I was in the midst of some sort of lover's rendezvous. The car started up with a quick cough from the engine and kicked into motion. I tried to keep as still as possible, ever fearful that I was just seconds away from being discovered. I was half tempted to just blow up the entire vehicle with hellfire, but that might draw unwanted attention. Plus, the last time I did anything like that, I burned down the city. Armen would be pissed.

The pair of lovers silently drove for what seemed like an eternity, hitting every bump and pothole along the way, torturing my bladder. It would be my first piss back on Earth, and as I fantasized about the encounter, I feared that I might crack the ceramic shell of the toilet if this kept up. To keep the pain in my gut from becoming overwhelming, I tried practicing Polish in my head, singing the alphabet nearly a dozen times. Finally, the couple came to a long stop, and Chelsea popped the car into park.

"So," she said with her bored voice, "I'm guessing you want to see me naked?" *Whoa, this is escalating quickly.*

"That would be nice," said her boyfriend in a wily voice. "I've waited a long time for this."

"Alright, you can do whatever you want," she said bluntly. *Wow, is this girl kinky or what?* "Just promise you won't kill me." *Wait...What?*

The passenger gave a devious laugh as he shuffled in his seat. I wasn't too sure what was happening, but I was curious enough to find out. So, with my face halfway smashed down into the carpet, and my hands squeezing at my guts, I finally made my move.

"Uh," I called out from the backseat floor, "Chelsea I don't want to freak you out or anything, but...are you okay?"

"Who said that?" hollered the man. There was a moment of near silence as the passenger's shuffling made the car lightly rock.

"Ned?" Chelsea asked with uncertainty. "Is that you?"

"Ned!" the man shouted angrily. His voice was now eerily familiar. I lifted my head and found Chelsea, stone faced with her hands tightly gripped on the steering wheel, being held at gunpoint by none other than Louis Joliet. She tried not to make any sudden movement so that the pistol, that was just inches from her face, wouldn't go off and spread her brains all over the car window. Meanwhile, Louis eyeballed me wildly. His lips trembled with a fearful frown. Before I could say another word, he reached out his free hand and pulled Chelsea by the hair, jabbing the barrel of the gun deep into her cheek. "Easy now Nedonius, I don't want any trouble."

"Damn it Louie," I bellowed, "just when I thought you couldn't get any more bizarre, you go ahead and do something like this."

"No offense my lord," he spat back, "but I'm not the one hiding in the back seat of a woman's car."

"Touché," I replied, "but you *do* have a gun to her head."

"Well I had to make a move after you came in the picture," he hissed. "She might have given you a tongue lashing at the book store, but I saw the way she was watching you when you left. You've piqued her interest, forcing me to make a power play." *All right, score one for Nedonius.*

"First," Chelsea snapped back coldly, "no one has *piqued* my interest." *Or not.* "I was making sure that the asshole didn't try to steal anything on his way out. I wasn't exactly a sweetheart at the register, and thought that he might try something stupid in retaliation. And second, what the Hell is going on here?"

"Chelsea," I said modestly, keeping an eye on Joliet, "I'm sorry. Alright, I confess," I frowned, "I was waiting at the diner across the street because I wanted to catch you on your way out of work so I could try talking to you again. I wanted to apologize for my behavior and see if you'd give me another shot. You know, acquaintances, friends, star-crossed lovers." Chelsea groaned.

"You don't even know me Ned," she argued, her head still stiff so that Joliet wouldn't accidentally pull the trigger. "I attacked you with insults at the bookstore. Why would you want another shot?"

"I get that," I said in a reasoning tone, "but where I come from, insults are a form of flattery. Trust me, compared to my last girlfriend you were being nice. Besides, I might not know you well now, but that doesn't mean we can't change things for the future. I mean yes, from first impressions, I *did* notice that you are incredibly hot, but that's not solely why I'm interested. There's more to you than meet the eye."

"Like what?" she grimaced at the gun that was squishing her cheek.

"Take your bookstore for example," I sat up fully in the backseat before patting down my hair, "it shows me that you're incredibly smart and open-minded. And when you put me in my place…that tells me that you have respect for yourself. I mean there are a hundred reasons I think you're neat from your donation jar to the fact that you are willing to admit that you verbally attacked me. That's something you can't find in this world," I paused, thinking about my words, "or any other for that matter. Trust me."

"Really?" she said with a slight pinch in her voice. "Thanks."

"*Hello!*" Joliet hollered, "Have we forgotten about the gun I have to her head?" I was seconds away from starting Louis's head on fire when the idiot added, "Plus, Ned here isn't being completely honest with you, are you *Nedonius?*" *Uh oh, Joliet was about to squeal on me. It was time to take action.*

I sprang my arm out like one of those cool Kung Fu guys and went for the gun, cupping my palm over the business end of the barrel. Joliet seemed surprised, but it didn't stop him from pulling the trigger. *Fucker.* Though my hand blocked the bullet from killing Chelsea, the kick from the pistol forced my knuckles to clobber her in the head. Chelsea slumped over onto the steering wheel, seemingly unconscious. Joliet pushed open his car door and leapt out, leaving his ugly wool scarf behind. I tried to channel my anger on him, but had a hard time focusing through the steamed glass and gun smoke. Plus, I was just relieved that Chelsea wasn't dead. It's hard to be upset when you're busy being grateful.

Regardless, I couldn't let the little purple haired

pipsqueak get away unharmed. I climbed over the seat and jumped out of the passenger side door. Standing beside the car, I could tell that Joliet wasn't much of an athlete because he ran like a T-Rex, his big head lurched over his coiled up arms as he clumsily sprinted as hard as he could. The sight of him scampering through the streets in a panic while scrutinizing the wall of buildings he ran past, searching for somewhere to turn, was pretty damn funny, making it even harder to concentrate. In spite of my laughter fit, I focused my eyes on him and mustered up what little anger I could, extending my hand and willing hellfire down the street. A tongue of weak flame reached out from my palm, chasing after Louie, and barely reaching his backside. A sudden howl followed by a pumpkin orange glow let me know that I'd hit my target. Joliet wailed in agony before turning a corner, his ass ablaze.

I thought about pursuing him, but once I looked to Chelsea and saw a raw pink mark swelling along her face, I decided against it. I kneeled back into the passenger seat and hovered my hand over her nose and mouth in order to confirm that she was still alive. Her breaths were slow but steady. She'd have one Hell of a headache tomorrow, but otherwise, she'd merely been knocked unconscious. Once I determined that she'd be okay, I found her purse next to her feet, and rifled through it for any clues that might help me figure out where she lived. After a brief search, I uncovered her driver's license, and after reading the address, gathered that her apartment was just directly outside of the parked car.

Her apartment, unit 3B, was most likely on the third floor of the building. I lifted her from the driver's seat, dragging her out through the passenger side. While doing so, the receipt from my earlier book purchase slipped out of her jeans pocket. The crumpled paper, now between the driver's seat and emergency brake, had my phony name and address circled in pen. Maybe Joliet was right. Maybe

Chelsea was interested in me in a weird, tough chick sort of way. A guy could dream.

In any case, I had a job to do, and as I carried her out of her car, along with her belongings and Joliet's scarf, I remembered how odd all of this might appear. I was a gangly looking guy in the eyes of anyone who might be watching, but I was carrying a full-grown woman with ease. For the most part, our disguises are just that, disguises. They don't inhibit us in any real way. So as I made my way to her building, Chelsea strung across my arms, I pretended that she weighed several hundred pounds.

Once I made it to the main entrance, I used the keys procured from the ignition to get past the front door, and after confirming with a collection of mailboxes that she did indeed live on the third floor, climbed a long set of stairs. After unlocking the security bolt perched above her doorknob, I lightly booted open the door in order to get inside Chelsea's flat. Her place smelled like honey and was decorated with a patchy couch, small flat screen television and a collection of old bookshelves overflowing with tattered books. Her kitchen, which was in open view, appeared to be something out of *The Brady Bunch*. It had a pea green refrigerator, ugly floral design wallpaper and an outdated stove. Simple, but charming. Then I saw it. The most important room in her house- the bathroom.

Although the pains I'd felt in the car were probably a combination of Joliet's presence blended with a bladder full of coffee, it didn't stop my belly from feeling as if it were about to explode. I hurriedly carried Chelsea to her room, flipping the light switch with my elbow. A flickering bulb under a red lampshade lit up the space. There was a crooked nightstand with unmatched socks on top, a single bed with satin sheets, and compilation of framed Betty Page paintings furbishing the walls. I gently placed her down on the bed before taking off her boots and covering her in a blanket. Afterwards, I collected one ugly stray sock decorated with Christmas trees, stuffed it in my back pocket, and shut off her light. Hopefully, if I were lucky, the hit on the head would help her forget the whole night.

Meanwhile, I had a date with destiny. I ran to the washroom, which had some type of forest theme going on, and hurriedly closed the door shut. After running the sink in order to muffle any sounds, I took the longest bathroom break ever historically recorded. *It was epic.* Once that was done, I tried to gather my thoughts.

I still had a spooky to summon, and if there was time, Joliet to murder. So, after washing my hands, I gave Chelsea one last glance over before locking and barricading her apartment door. Once it felt secured, I hurried to a slightly cracked kitchen window, and after opening it enough to slip through, leapt out. The weight of my true form smashed into the sidewalk like it was made of glass, leaving an impression of my feet along the path. After dusting myself off, I put my hand in the pocket-dimension hidden in my satchel and plucked out a sleeping Simon and Hecubus. The two hellhounds had apparently been napping for quite some time because their drowsy eyes were barely aglow. I put them down on the front lawn of the apartment, and let them wake up. The pair slowly started to come to life, the pace of their ugly little tails wagging faster as they stretched out their legs.

I didn't think that Joliet would be back. Hellfire for the most part is so hot that it incinerates its victims within seconds. Even with the weak dosage I'd delivered due to all of the distractions, it was probably a serious burn. Joliet's ass most likely looked like Freddy Krueger's headshots, and it would probably take years for him to recover. Still, you can never fully count out a madman. I'd need to take other precautions.

"Listen up you two," I removed Joliet's scarf from my satchel and offered it up to them. The little beasts sniffed at the cloth for a moment before sitting down on their hind legs. "I need you both to guard this building for the night. If any spookies show up smelling like that scarf, rip them to shreds." Simon bared his teeth while Hecubus gave a deep woof that sounded like a Great Dane over a loudspeaker. I flinched at the earsplitting bark before removing the ugly Christmas sock I'd procured from Chelsea's apartment. "This person," I said, letting them have a whiff, "is to be protected at all times. Do not hurt her. She is my friend."

Simon whimpered while Hecubus barked again, causing a nearby motion light hanging over a garage entrance to trigger. They gave me one last dutiful look before scuttling into a nearby evergreen bush, hiding in wait for Joliet, their red eyes glowing.

"Good boys," I said approvingly.

"In the meantime," I said under my breath, "I need to find somewhere private so I can finally summon my guide."

The hour was late, and my libido had gotten the best of me. If I was going to get back on track and find the missing corruptor, I needed to get busy. I'd already wasted an entire day getting acclimated with the modern world with nothing to show for it except for a new enemy in Joliet, and a young woman named Chelsea who might join his hatred for me as soon as her headache kicked in. It wasn't going to be easy to find Gethin, but I had a plan. Now the only question was, where the Hell would I go to summon a ghost in Chicago?

Chapter Six

Ghosts make great informants. They're undetectable and have nothing better to do all day than to spy on people. But summoning can be a delicate process. The stronger the spooky, the harder it is to compel them to assist with whatever task you may have for them. This is why most mediums and psychics stick with puny spirits who can barely snuff out the flame of a séance candle. However, if I were going to find a spirit who was savvy enough to find where someone was hiding a Forsaken, I'd need to go full throttle.

It was very late and I needed to go somewhere remote in case my summoning backfired. Much like Armen needed a special ritual in order to get me to Chicago, a spirit needs a way to leave the hidden realm that exists between the mortal world and that of the dead. A conjuring ritual empowers them to leave it by giving them a semi-physical form. Frighteningly enough, if I managed to botch the summoning ritual, I might have an enraged poltergeist running rampant through Chicago in physical form. If that were the case, and dozens of innocent mortals were harmed, you could bet the farm that I'd attract a lot of unwanted attention. And when you're a fallen angel hiding on Earth, all attention is unwanted. Hence why I don't toy with magic often.

Unfortunately, I was starting to learn that Chicago had grown exponentially since my last time here. There was no such thing as seclusion in the city any longer. You couldn't find a nearby cornfield or swamp where you'd be away from people. Once you were downtown, you could travel for hours in any direction and still technically be in the heavily populated Chicagoland area. Since *real* solitude was out of the picture, I opted for the next best thing-what was close and what was closed.

Navy Pier was a docking area near downtown that had been transformed into a tourist attraction some time ago. It stretched out for a city block into Lake Michigan, and was known for its massive Ferris wheel, indoor market center and boat tours. Navy Pier closed just before midnight and protruded far enough that it wouldn't risk any mortal lives if I needed to battle it out with whatever ancient spirit I'd summoned. Plus, it looked really cool in the advertisements.

By the time I'd arrived, nearly the entire place was powered down. I scouted the pier and found that there was a single weary security guard posted along the entrance of a massive barred fence. I snuck to an area of the gates farthest from the guard station and climbed over. Once I'd safely slipped passed security, I trudged across the long concrete pier until reaching the edge where cement cliff meets water. The wide-open space was muted of light and remarkably silent except for the occasional crashing wave. This place was perfect for summoning a spooky.

After removing several conjuring tools that Armen had provided me inside the satchel, I began drawing a conjuring circle along the pier cement. Next, I opened up the gypsy codex to my marked page and began reciting the incantations in order to charm my spirit. The ritual's incantations would call forth any nearby ghosts to me like fire does to a moth, challenging only the strongest to take form. I used a small needle from the satchel to prick my finger, allowing a few droplets of blood to drip into the summoning circle. Not to toot my own horn, but my blood is a potent offering in the arcane world, more precious than any black magic candle, Wiccan sage or Shinto incense that common practitioners might use. With the words spoken and contribution provided, there was nothing left to do but wait for my spooky to arrive.

I didn't have to wait long for something to happen. The spirit's appearance started as a hundred whispers all around me. Then, a cool wind blew in from the lake top, spraying a shower of sudsy water onto the cement that formed a puddle. At first the small pool stood still, but as the winds picked up again, the liquid slowly began to bubble. Suddenly, the puddle took life, drooling its way towards the conjuring circle. The puddle dribbled over my gift of blood and drank it. The acceptance of my offering caused a supernatural transformation, turning the grey lake water completely red. Afterwards, the crimson liquid spiraled upward into a mist that took shape.

The materialized form was that of a short elderly woman with a maid's bonnet and long gown. Though most of her features were blurred by mist and rippling liquid, I could make out a pair of sunken eyes, short nose and puckered lips. She raised her hands out above her head and stretched, yawning as if she'd just awoken from a long rest. The wind picked up and swirled about. The glow of a nearby lighthouse posted along the harbor twitched several times before going out altogether. It was one Hell of an entrance.

"Who is it that calls upon me?" the old woman bellowed, rising higher in the air. A sharp pressure from my supernatural senses stabbed along my side. It wasn't painful, nor pleasing, just intense. I stepped forward and cleared my throat.

"My name is Nedonius." The old crone whooshed her misty body closer towards me, dripping blood-water along the pier and chalk outline.

"Nedonius," she said curiously. "As in Nedonius the fallen angel?"

"Uh, yeah. It's great to hear that I made an impression on people the last time I was here. To be honest, I'm not sure we've ever met. How do you know my name?" The eyes of the old hag shined a poison green.

"Because it was *you* who started the great fire, but it was I that received the blame."

"Uh, oh," I said aloud.

I'd kept up with the details of my little accident after being sent back to hell, so I was quite informed about the ghost whom I was speaking with. Catherine O'Leary was an Irish immigrant living in Chicago when my pyromancy first sparked the Great Chicago Fire. She was held responsible because some dipshit from the Chicago Tribune spun a tale about her cow kicking over a lantern in her barn. Though the idiot later admitted he'd made the whole thing up, O'Leary spent the rest of her life shunned until her death nearly twenty-five years later. Clearly she'd been doing her homework since then, as she obviously knew who I was. On a side note, I'd always felt awful about it, but what could I do about it when I was cooped up in hell?

"*Uh oh,*" she wailed and dyed red lake water sprayed from her pickled mouth. "Is that all you have to say for yourself after ruining my life, uh oh?"

"Is that a rhetorical question?"

O'Leary shrieked with an anguish that made my skin crawl. Her form took on more substance, rippling along her body like waves during a great storm. Lake Michigan's watery surface, which was usually quite calm along Chicago, began to mimic her shape. Wave after wave began to grow, crashing along the pier and causing it to shake. I was a bit unnerved, as a ghost who could do that was nothing to laugh about.

"Nedonius, I have been waiting for this day for a very long time. You will pay for what you've done to me."

O'Leary pressed forward, but immediately smashed into the invisible wall created by the conjuring circle. She studied it indignantly. Clearly, no one had ever tried to summon the likes of a spirit as powerful as Catherine

O'Leary before. I didn't want to hurt the old bat's feelings, especially because I understood exactly what she was going through. I'd been persecuted from heaven for listening to Lucifer. All my friends and loved ones turned on me because the Angel of Darkness had manipulated us into thinking that the war was something virtuous when in fact it was the opposite. Nothing is worse than being an outcast, condemned from the world that you once thought you knew. With that being said, O'Leary was forgetting that I'd bound her to the location with my ritual. As long as I didn't break my concentration, she wouldn't be able to harm me.

"Now Catherine, I'm sorry for what happened to you. I really am. And yes it's true. I did accidentally start the fire, but I wasn't the jag off who blamed you. That title goes to a reporter named Michael Ahern. He accused you and your cow of starting the fire to sell papers. He's the guy you want to kill."

O'Leary shook her head as if she refused to accept my explanation. "So, you would rather blame this reporter than accept your fate?"

"Okay, two things about me Catherine. One, I *do* take responsibility for creating the fire, and am truly sorry for the grief it caused you, or anyone else for that matter." Which was true. "Two, I don't take well to threats. Even if I didn't have you bound under a summoning spell right now, you seem to be forgetting what I am. If I wanted to, I could have your haunted little soul sucked into the abyss of Hell as we speak," I bluffed. O'Leary paused. She seemed to buy it, as her once proud stance shrank and recoiled a bit. "What I *will* do for you though Catherine, should you agree to help me with something, is not only promise that I won't have your soul sucked into the abyss, but make sure that this Michael Ahern pays for what he's done to you once I get back home. That is, if he isn't already burning in the flames of Hell as we speak."

Catherine deliberated. I could see in her face that

she didn't want to accept the fact that I had the upper hand. After mumbling a bit, she finally crossed her watery arms, as if she'd suddenly become bashful, nodding her head.

"Fine," she said with a twinge of resolve in her voice. "In light of the new circumstances, we have a deal. What is it that Nedonius the Fallen requests of me?"

I needed to know about Gethin. I knew very little about my replacement. It wasn't anything personal. I just hadn't wanted to hear about his achievements once I'd lost the job. What I did know about him was that he was a herald before the rebellion and a demon maker afterwards. The two of us had very little in common both pre-and-post-war. He was an artist and I was a soldier. He created and I destroyed. The two of us never really mixed. What I also knew was that he took more of a muse role on earth, tempting men and women through vain promises and conceited assurances while I...well, I just plain sucked at the whole thing.

"Are you familiar with Gethin? He is a corruptor of ours." O'Leary nodded again, this time more poised.

"Oh yes, he is a delight. He always has such lavish parties. I once attended in secret and danced the night away with some handsome stranger. Of course, the gentleman thought that he was dancing alone, but little did he know I was by his side the entire night."

"Okay Cat, let's stick to the questions. Do you know where he is now?"

"Now that you mention it, I haven't seen him in days," she said thoughtfully. "I wonder what he's up to."

"So does the rest of hell. He went missing some time ago and no one can seem to figure out where he is." Catherine sprouted bare feet from the bottom of her bloody gown and landed on the pier. She sloshed around with her new appendages, pacing back and forth.

"Hmm, last I checked he'd been inspiring a new artist- some painter boy. Oh, what was his name?" O'Leary tapped at her liquid chin, splashing droplets onto the ground. "Oh, I remember, it was Thomas Elsberry. He's a contemporary artist who was fairly unknown until recently. Last we spoke, Gethin had been trying to corrupt the young man by helping him with his works. Gethin threw a marvelous debut party for Elsberry at the Art Institute not too long ago. It was quite the gathering, and garnered a lot of public attention."

"Perfect. Do you know where this Elsberry lives?"

"Oh, let me think," she said as her eyes rolled in the back of her watery head. "Give me a second. I rarely forget anything." I waited, watching the lake's waves absentmindedly as Catherine hummed like a refrigerator, apparently attempting to recall where Thomas called home. "Ah, yes. He owns a small apartment up in the Sauganash area. It's one of the most northern neighborhoods in Chicago. It's quite beautiful. The address is 1212 Kenosha Lane."

"Did you just use Ghost-Google?" I asked.

"What is this Ghost-Google you speak of?" she asked curiously.

"Never mind."

I could feel the bond between my summoning ritual and O'Leary's essence weakening. The window between the spirit world and my own was shrinking. If I didn't let her go soon or bind her to this plane, I'd lose the mystical anchor that she'd been fastened to, allowing the angry ghost to free herself and do as she wished.

"Alright Cat, you've been a big help. I'll release you now."

Catherine seemed upset. Her face twisted into a frown. "When will I have my vengeance then?"

"Well, first I have to find Gethin, and then I can go back to Hell and find your reporter. Go get some rest, and I'll send you a message once I'm back in hell."

"And how long will that be?"

"I don't know. Gethin seems to be hidden pretty well. Maybe weeks, months, I can't be sure."

"Wait," she insisted, "What if I helped?"

"Oh," I said innocently, "I couldn't ask you to do that. You've already helped me find Thomas's home. Hopefully that'll be enough."

"No, I can assist you. I want to."

"Are you sure?" I asked, trying to hold back a smile.

"Yes, yes. Bind me to your will, and I'll continue searching."

"Okay Catherine," I said through a surfacing half grin. "You have yourself a deal." I walked towards her circle and kicked at the outline of chalk, creating a break. "Go out and search for Gethin, and if you find any information about him, come to me immediately. The sooner I find out, the sooner I can report to Hell and get you your much deserved vengeance with that asshole Tribune reporter."

"Of course." She bowed. "Then vengeance will be mine. Oh, do I have plans for him," she said through her tightly clenched jaw. I tried not to shudder. Lifting my arms, I whirled them round and round towards O'Leary for dramatic effect.

"Catherine O'Leary, I release you into this world. So long as my blood flows, you may keep your materialized form."

My broken circle smoldered like an egg on a frying pan before dissolving. The old woman closed her eyes in relief. Then as quickly as she'd come, her form flowed into a drape of red water that splashed onto the ground. The splatter of blood looked like something from a horror movie. Catherine could now weave in and out of the physical world, and I crossed my fingers that she wouldn't use her newfound capacities to do anything nasty.

I collected the gypsy codex and placed it into my

satchel. It was day one on Earth and I was exhausted. Weary, I decided to get some rest before starting the next phase of my plan- a phase that I fully planned on initiating, *right after* I went to visit Chelsea again.

Chapter Seven

Billy was right. School was lame. Or at least his school dormitories were. I was exhausted after my first day back on Earth and needed to get some rest. So, I'd followed the address that Billy gave me and made it to his dormitory. What I didn't know was that downtown dorms aren't like the ones you see on sitcoms. There are no quads or beautiful garden campuses with kids reading on the lawn. No, in downtown Chicago, universities use skyscrapers to pack students on top of each other much like they do in hell. Everything a student needed was inside one tightly packed fifty-story building, from the library to the cafeteria.

I had to check in with a security guard on the first floor since it was afterhours. The three hundred pound man, who was transfixed on an obnoxiously colorful anime cartoon playing on his phone, didn't look like he could get up from his seat, let alone catch me if I ran past him to get to Billy. But I was too tired to be mischievous, so I complied with his rules and waited to be checked in. The fat security troll, who wouldn't be winning employee of the year anytime soon, lazily dialed up to Billy's dorm phone. Once Billy gave him permission to let me up, the guard opened an ugly leather book and had me sign in.

I wrote, *Ned Onius, 4 a.m., visiting Billy Shanahan. It isn't what you think.*

The security guard closed the book up rather impatiently, nearly catching my fingers, and slothfully pointed me to the dormitory elevators. I rode up a high tech cart that felt more like a spaceship than an elevator to Billy's floor, its shiny buttons and steel shell sending me upward at lightning speeds. Once I'd arrived, I found my way to his room and rapped ever so gently at his door.

Billy was obviously surprised to see me. Luckily, there wasn't a mean bone in the guy's body. If it were me in Billy's shoes and someone had come to visit me after midnight, the door, and person knocking on it, would be smoldering like firewood. I made up some elaborate excuse about not having power, which seemed to be enough to earn a spot on Billy's floor between his and his snoring roommate's beds. Things were dark when I'd arrived and I didn't get much time to take in the scenery. I was given an ugly Teenage Mutant Ninja Turtles sleeping bag, a couch pillow, and about twelve inches of floor space to sleep. Regardless, my body was exhausted. It took me less than a minute or so to drift off into an angel's torpor, which is mildly similar to human sleep, except a little less farty.

I opened my eyes again to find myself chained to the dorm beds I'd slept between. Louis Joliet stood above me, his boot firmly pressed across my chest. He was wearing a wide-brimmed cavalier hat, puffy clothes and a painfully flamboyant cape. In one hand he carried a blue flamed torch, and in the other arm he held Chelsea. She shook her head at me, squeezing closer to Louis.

"You burned my ass," Joliet screeched. "And now, I will burn yours."

It felt like it would never end. Joliet branded me over and over again with the blue torch. Chelsea watched and laughed. Not shortly afterwards, Billy woke up from my screaming and asked if he could have a turn. The three passed the torch amongst each other, torturing me for hours on end as they shared in cruel banter. After what seemed like an eternity, Joliet decided to try and extinguish the flame in my eyes, and with a thrust of the torch all went black.

Finally I awoke from my nightmare and hurriedly searched the room for signs of Joliet. He was nowhere to be found and the room was now bathed in sunlight. After I gathered my wits, I studied the walls, furniture and décor stuffed inside Billy's dorm. His home was what some might call a *nerd sanctuary*. There were Star Wars action figures posed along his dresser, an authentic Captain American shield hanging over his bed, and a poster with two twenty-sided dice that read, *That's How I Roll*. Scattered over his nightstand were miniature plane pieces and incomplete helicopter propellers that I could only assume were for his drones. His roommate's side wasn't much better.

There were stacks of computer programming books along his roommate's bookshelves, an array of medieval swords hanging over his bed, and an official Stark Trek Voyager chessboard resting on the corner of his cluttered computer desk. Stationed at that very desk was a gangly young man with sandy blonde hair that was prickly like a cactus, thick glasses and acne speckled across his cheeks. I assumed this was Billy's roommate. He was crowned with some type of headset that plugged into his computer, and was shouting with his nasally voice into the mouthpiece. I crawled out of my sleeping bag as he hollered instructions at the screen.

"Damn it Zendor, keep your area spells at bay. If we need to single out orcs, I'll use my holy sword."

Ouch, talk about nerds. I looked around for Billy, but he was nowhere to be found. His bed was neatly made and his backpack was missing. I scratched at my scalp, waiting for the grogginess to fade away. After a few agonizing moments I began to feel a bit better and tried making it to my feet.

"Where's Billy?" I asked without reserve. Billy's roommate went mute. There was a brief pause filled only by the clicks of a mouse. Billy's roommate kept his gaze fixed on the gold knight jumping across his computer screen.

"He has summer classes," he finally answered. His

voice was calmer than the one he'd been using to scold his fellow warriors.

I watched over his shoulder as his digital knight bravely fought off evil in a forest filled with green creatures that had glowing labels over their heads that spelled "Evil Tribal Orcs". Wouldn't that be nice in real life? *Dickhead, Dickhead, Sweet Old Lady.* Though some of the roommate's computerized companions fell to the mighty orc-chieftain, the roommate forged ahead, clicking his keypad repeatedly so that his holy crusader could survive the long and bloody passage of arms. It took a few minutes, but the digital knight vanquished countless enemies with his absurdly oversized sword until the issue was settled. Dead orcs and allies alike lay across the computer screen's battlefield. Billy's roommate cracked his fingers together before leaning back into his chair with a sigh. I had to admit, nerdy or not, it all looked kind of neat.

"Well done," I complimented. Billy's roommate picked up a green can of soda next to him labeled *Wamo!* slurping its contents. After finishing the drink, he crushed the can with his hands and slammed it next to a dozen other discarded containers that met the same fate. Beside the cans were several crumpled *Taco Hut* papers. Some rolled off of the desk like boulders on a mountain, falling to his feet and joining a collection of other random fast food wrappers.

"We could have done better," he said in a stale voice. "Our kobold thief, Meepow, failed to disarm the orc traps. Never trust a rogue." *I had no idea what he was talking about.*

"Oh, too bad. I'm Ned by the way. I'm a friend of Billy."

"Steven," he said, keeping his eyes locked on the screen. "But most people like to call me Stevie for some reason." Stevie placed both hands onto his keyboard like a pianist and began to type away. "If you want some breakfast," he offered between keyboard taps, "we have fiber-grain bars inside our pantry."

Between the two beds was a set of Tupperware shelves labeled "pantry" in sharpie marker. It was littered with cases of soda, boxes of Twinkies and a stack of brightly tinfoil wrapped bars that read *Fiber-grain Sticks*. I'd seen better slop fed to demons. If Billy had been eating bars of granola glued together with preservatives and honey since going to college then the poor guy was due for a good meal. I needed to fix this. I took out my wallet, plucking out one of the many credit cards, and placed it on Stevie's computer desk. Stevie paused.

"Stevie, tell Billy I'll be by later. Meanwhile, go and pick yourselves some real food. Don't worry about cost. I might be sleeping here for a bit since my power is out. It's the least I can do."

Stevie's pupils slipped to the corners of his eyes, though his head remained locked on his monitor. He studied the credit card before returning his gaze to his game.

"Can I order pizza?" he muttered. "I haven't had Giordano's deep dish in a long time."

"Sure. Get whatever you want."

Stevie's hand leapt from his keyboard, pouncing on the silver plastic card like a lion does prey. He hastily tucked the credit card in the breast pocket of his button shirt, and then went back to playing his game. I could see the slightest smile curl up from the corner of his mouth. Apparently, Stevie needed a change from the fiber bars as well, and I couldn't mind helping in the least. It may be true that money doesn't buy happiness, but I know all too well that it will temporarily help gain allies, especially if they've been reduced to eating Twinkies and Fiber Sticks for an entire summer.

"Well Stevie," I added over the videogame sound effects, "maybe I'll see you later tonight. Until then, take it easy."

"You too," he said with a faintly satisfied tone.

I left the room and headed to the dormitory elevator, cramming in with several other students. The mechanical doors shut tightly, shining our reflections off its shiny steel surface. Although I felt slightly out of place next to these young and promising students, my disguise fit right in. However, I was still wearing the same clothes from yesterday. As I rode down, I wondered if there was anything in the satchel that could help change my wardrobe. I hadn't seriously examined most of the knickknacks in the bag as of yet, but I did remember seeing a book titled, "Manual."

Outside, the Chicago air was muggy with a hint of thick car exhaust and fresh asphalt. I pushed my way past a line of smokers lingering near the building and lumbered towards Michigan Avenue. There I found a trendy coffee shop with a public bathroom. I ordered my favorite manly drink, a café' misto, and took a spot at one of the empty tables. After sipping the foam off of my coffee, I dug into my satchel and began examining some of the items that Armen had left me.

There was a sacrificial dagger, jarred baby tears and an array of other magical components that, at the moment, did nothing for me. Armen must have thought that I was more talented than I was. I mean, after all, I was a corruptor at one time. What he didn't know was that I'd slipped through the cracks of Corruptor Testing before they added an examination for magic. Once I'd sorted through several other knickknacks, I opened the manual.

Printed on flesh and scribed in blood, hell's standard printing method, were sections about avoiding heaven's forces, making peace with spookies, and the differences between Hell and Earth. Believe it or not, most of Hell has never actually experienced Earth first hand, and assume that it's all one big Full House episode. Demons *love* David Coulier. Finally, I came across a section dedicated to basic, but useful spells for corruptors. As I'd said before, I was an expert pyromancer, but I didn't have the patience for some of the more practical magic. It involved years of scientific knowledge, an in depth understanding of the arcane art, and most problematic-- a calm disposition. Don't get me wrong; pyromancy has its own technical methods, but it's mostly blind fury that makes it work.

Inside the pages were techniques for creating spirit wards, controlling human emotions, and transforming one's clothes. I looked over the last spell's description. According to the manual, all it took was a spool of thread, which was provided in the satchel, some incantations, and the caster's complete concentration. If done right, the spell would instantly tailor the user's clothing, transforming their garments into any fashion the caster wished. So, I removed the spool of thread from the satchel and headed to the coffee house's bathroom.

After waiting my turn in line, I went into the closet size lavatory and locked the door behind me. Grabbing at my t-shirt, I said the provided words and concentrated on the transformation, thinking of clothes that a noir college kid would wear. At first nothing happened except for the toilet flushing from its motion sensor. But as my mind went still and my thoughts sharpened, slowly my clothes began to change shape and color. Soon I was adorned in a plain grey t-shirt that simply read, "I may be crazy, but at least I have each other", black jeans and charcoal gym shoes. The smell of the material had changed too, and was now scented with fresh fabric softener and a splash of cheap cologne.

"Sweet," I said aloud as I looked my clothes over.

I left the washroom only to be met by the next person in line. A paunchy man in a pink polo and dress pants challenged my speedy makeover with a hoisted eyebrow, looking me over as if I were trying to fool him.

"There's fast, faster, and then there's me," I said with a smirk. The man shrugged in confusion and then hurried past me and into the lavatory.

I left the cafe in my sharp new digs, ready for round two with Chelsea. I hailed a cab in order to get to her bookstore without delay. Unfortunately, what should have been a ten-minute ride turned into a thirty-five minute snail crawl due to Lake Shore Drive traffic. By the time I'd arrived it was high noon and the sun was blistering. Hell hosts a dry heat, a cozy kind of pain wracking warmth, but it had nothing on Chicago. Lake Michigan, combined with the Midwest's natural climate, created an excruciating humidity. Everything I wore was sticky and wet, as if it had been dipped in syrup.

The bells along The Prologue entrance chimed as I stepped inside. A waft of cold air from the electronic chiller cooled my skin, giving me goose bumps along my arms. I could hear the laboring melody of a dejected woman on the ceiling speakers once I entered the shop's main area. I wasn't sure how Chelsea was going to react to me after last night, but I was terrified to find out. I peeked into the storeroom where the register was stationed, ready for a book or coffee mug to be thrown at me. But nothing could prepare me for what I'd found.

Simon and Hecubus, the hellhounds who had earned their ill-famed reputation after slaying the mayor's barghest howler, were being coddled in Chelsea's arms like babies. Chelsea, who wore a Dr. Who Band-Aid over the stinger she'd received last night, rocked the little pups, which now had skull print bows on their heads, like little girls. The two hellhounds rested along her incredible breasts, licking at her fingers. *Lucky little shits.*

"Oh hello," I said as sweetly as I could. The trio simultaneously turned their heads to me. Luckily, Chelsea wasn't looking down, as a red flash glimmered in Simon's eyes.

"You!" Chelsea hissed. Her expression shifted from caring to fuming as she put the dogs down onto the store's floor. Their little claws clicked along the tile as they traipsed across it, ambling towards me. Chelsea followed after them. She stuck out her finger and poked me in the chest. "You punched me in my head!"

"Whoa, how about a thank you for saving your life," I countered in desperation. Simon and Hecubus wandered up to my feet indifferently, sniffing at them.

"Oh, do you mean after you broke into my car then instigated a fight with that psycho who almost killed me?"

This girl had some nerve, even if she was hotter than an imp's ass on taco night. I mean, yes, technically I broke into her car, but I wasn't trying to be creepy. Had I known Joliet was trying to shanghai her, I might have reacted a little differently. Though, as angry as I was, a guilty part of me could slightly see her point. To her, a gal who didn't know that I was trying to save her from a soulless toad, I was just some weirdo who'd been lurking in the backseat of her car. Since I'd saved her life, I was only slightly better than Joliet.

"Listen Ned," she said firmly, "I get that you helped me. I don't know what school of martial art you mastered that allowed you to block that bullet, but I appreciate it. However, not only were you hiding in the backseat of my car, but you also broke into my house, which means you know where I live. Please don't tell me I have to move?" she groaned.

"Oh come on. I'm not going to do anything. If you'd just give me a chance to explain myself-"

"Excuse me," said a customer from the rows of books behind us.

"What?" Chelsea hollered. The middle-aged man had a gray ponytail and was wearing stonewash jeans under a denim jacket with an outdated Frank Zappa patch on the front. His outfit screamed *forty and single*. He appeared taken aback by Chelsea's boorishness, but persisted, holding up a dog-eared copy of a Neopagan text.

"Is this an original Aradia," he asked, "or a reprint?" Chelsea studied the cover for a moment before answering.

"Neither. Can't you read? It's Starhawk's Spiral Dance. It's not for sale." The customer examined the back of the book where a brightly colored price tag was hanging.

"But it says here that-"

"I said it's not for sale." Chelsea turned her head back to me as the man retreated back into the rows of shelving like a frightened deer. "You were saying?"

I opened my mouth to speak, but the words sounded like I was just choking on a dull fishing hook. Finally I spit it out. *Time to come clean.* "Chelsea, it's true that I'd found my way in your back seat last night. Like I said before, I'd been waiting at the diner across the street because I just wanted to talk to you. When I saw you locking up the store, I paid my check and ran to meet you so I could apologize for acting like a loser. However, before I could make it all the way across the street, I saw someone come up and whisper in your ear. I thought that it was your boyfriend for sure, so before I could humiliate myself further, I hopped in the backseat of the nearest vehicle." Chelsea's grimace began to fade.

"I should have known that with my luck," I carried on, "the car would end up being yours." Chelsea cracked a guilty smile. "Then, when the two of you drove off, I had to come up with a new plan. I thought that I might just be able to go unnoticed long enough to runaway once you parked. But that didn't quite happen. Your boyfriend ended up being Joliet, a scumbag that I only know *vaguely* through an associate of mine. I'd run into him earlier at your store, but I didn't think much of it until I heard him in the car."

"Okay, go on," she insisted, her voice a bit more reasonable.

"Go on? Um, okay. Well, once I figured out that Joliet had a gun, I had to do something. Jabbing you in the head wasn't exactly how I planned it, but I'm just glad that I stopped the bullet. Once again, I didn't intend on punching you. That part can be blamed on physics." Chelsea chewed at her lip, pondering over my story.

"And how did I get into my bed? Did you do anything you weren't supposed to do? Because if so, I'm about to kick you in your balls."

"Whoa, wait, no! I'm not like that, scouts honor."

"Look me in the eyes and promise me Ned."

Chelsea wore a short sleeve Ramones shirt without a bra. I could see from my peripheral vision that her nipples were stiffened from the air conditioning. I tightened the muscles in my neck and balled my fists in an effort to keep my head from moving towards the glory waiting below. Instead, I managed to stare directly into her bright green eyes. *There'd be a time to mourn.*

"I promise. After I realized that you weren't dead, I just checked your driver's license. It showed me that your building was right next to where you parked." I scooped up Simon and Hecubus, and began to absentmindedly pet them. "So, along with the keys that were in your ignition, I gained entrance and locked you in. I even left my dogs to protect you."

"Wait, these sweet little guys are yours?"

"Don't trust their cute little puppy eyes," I said as I inspected the bow clipped over Simon's brows. "They'll bite your face off if you let your guard down. Anyhow, why do you ask?" Chelsea ogled the pups.

"Because I found those two pups on my front lawn—"

"See," I said, scratching at Hecubus' scrunched up maw with my index finger, "they did their job."

"With about a hundred dead birds and rats surrounding them."

"So, they did their job a little too well." Chelsea gave me a sober grimace. Apparently she didn't find my comment funny. "Oh, come on Chelsea, give me a little slack. Isn't what I did a little sweet?" Chelsea stared at me. I raised the hellhounds up so that all three of our heads were lined up, and gave my best puppy-dog face.

"I hear that antifreeze is sweet too," she said with a smirk, "but it doesn't mean that it's good for me."

"Ah ha," I hooted, "so that's what this is about. You're afraid that I might not be romantically healthy for you."

"Oh please."

"I knew it," I said playfully. "You've already put some thought to the possibility that I could be more than just some guy who you find waiting in your back seat. You've probably even considered my offer to take you out on a date?"

"You never even officially asked me," she said brusquely.

"Do you want to go out on a date?" I blurted. Chelsea pinched the bridge of her nose, mulling over my invite with a smile. I couldn't tell if I was driving her nuts or being charming, but I wasn't about to give up. "Remember, I did save your life. You kind of owe me." She sighed in frustration.

"Fine, tonight."

"Tonight?"

"Take it or leave it. That's when I'm open. And it's only because you saved my life."

"No, I mean…that's great. Tonight it is."

My mind began to race. I'd need champagne, a hotel room and a limousine in a hurry. Maybe I could get Billy to create some sort of light show or use his drones to deliver her the diamond necklace I'd have to purchase. If I was only getting one shot at this I was going to go all out.

"And don't make it anything big. I hate it when

guys try too hard."

Okay, clearly things had changed with women since the nineteenth century. "Oh, of course not. Come on its just two people hanging out and trying to get to know each other better," I lied, swallowing the lump in my throat.

"Meet me here at closing time," she added sternly. "I'll keep the dogs as collateral."

I couldn't believe it. I had completely transformed this disastrous situation into a date with Chelsea, the Cleopatra of the modern world. Now all I had to do was nail my exit scene. I gave a quick and carefree nod, and then started walking backwards.

"Well alright then. I'll see you tonight because, yeah, you have my dogs...and that's the time of our date." *Real smooth George Clooney.* "Okay, well...see you later." Chelsea watched as I stumbled on the threshold of the carpet. I tried playing it off by doing a little dance. "Maybe we'll go waltzing," I blabbered before escaping into the hallway that led to the exit.

I tried not to appear anxious as I made it outside, knowing that the store window looked out onto the sidewalk. But as I turned my head to give one last peak, I could see Chelsea's profile. She was back to work, collecting random books that customers left along the counter, Simon and Hecubus following behind her. My heart fluttered as I spotted a peculiar smile on her face. Heck, maybe she was excited after all. *Yeah, and maybe the Cubs would win the World Series.*

Chapter Eight

I had a lot of work to do before my date with Chelsea and not a lot of time to do it. First I'd need to race to the Sauganash neighborhood so that I could look into Thomas Elsberry. Depending on what I found, I would possibly have to make a couple more stops on my way back downtown. Afterwards, I'd need to drop by Billy's and bribe him and Stevie into evacuating their dorm. I needed somewhere for my date since I was technically homeless, and their stuffy rental was better than nothing. It wasn't that I thought I was going to get lucky. In fact, with Chelsea, I knew that wouldn't be the case, but I did want a backup in case we wanted to listen to music or watch a movie. You know, like the cool guy on television shows that always gets the chicks. Once I settled the dorm issue, I'd need to find a place to eat.

I had no idea where we could go. Like I said before, Hell loosely keeps up with human times, but we're pretty clueless when it comes to the fine details. From what I could tell from all the fat people now littering Chicago, there were a lot of options. I needed to find a laidback place where we could have a few drinks without interruption. It had to have a casual romantic atmosphere without feeling overdone. I was clueless where to start, but crossed my fingers that I could figure something out as the day went on.

I took the train as close to the Sauganash neighborhood as possible. The Blue Line track, which runs northbound towards the O'Hare Airport, appeared to be my best bet. Once I paid for my ticket and jumped on, I asked several reluctant passengers how to find Thomas Elsberry, but they rudely waved me off. Luckily, a kindly vagrant who confessed to being a robot from the future informed me that I'd need to get off at the Peterson exit and hike the rest of the way by foot. Technology is entirely too fascinating here on Earth. The homeless man, T-1000 as he liked to be called, told me that the CTA trains ran on an electric railway that powered the massive steel cabooses. T-1000 made it known that there was so much power within these rails in fact that they might be able to charge his demanding jaunt back to the future once he completed his mission. I wondered if the rail line could also be used to charge portals, as I had no idea how I was going to get home once I found Gethin.

Finally I arrived at my stop. I followed the directions T-1000 gave me and eventually found Thomas Elsberry's home. Sauganash had an interesting atmosphere. The old houses that tightly packed themselves closely next to one another were pleasant and welcoming. Large oak trees in every yard reached for the skies with their emerald covered branches, creating a canvas of shade throughout the neighborhood. Elsberry's apartment was a two-floor building with chocolate brick and egg-shaped windows. The lower floors were all commercial buildings and the upper levels were spaces for living. Thomas resided over a preschool that was then in session.

I rang his buzzer twice, waiting outside in the comfy air as children sang *Mary had a Little Lamb* in the background. As I'd expected, there was no answer and I was forced to take drastic measures. It was hard to try and rally any hate in me within my pleasant surroundings, but eventually I managed to melt the doorknob with a kiss of hellfire. I pushed the ruined handle open and gingerly walked up the stairs to the second floor. Although there was a pair of apartment entrances on each side of the hall, I quickly matched up the correct unit number with the directory I'd seen near the outside entrance's mailboxes, and knocked lightly. After a short wait, I repeated my strategy and melted away Thomas's door lock, slipping my way inside.

Elsberry's home was simple, but attractive. He had glossed wood floors, dark oak furniture and painted canvases along the flat. The entire apartment was tidy with a hint of chic in its wall design and fixtures. There were several blank canvases along his living room and a tackle box filled with unused paints. Everything seemed unmolested, like a model home for showing.

His dishes were clean, the garbage was taken out, and the bed was well made. There were no toothpaste tubes left near the sink or food in the fridge. It was as if no one really lived here, but only stopped by occasionally to dust. I wondered if I could find any clues that could verify the last time Elsberry was here, as Gethin had only recently disappeared. If the two times matched, I'd definitely have my lead suspect.

I pressed on, searching for timestamps or hints that would lead me to Thomas. I had nearly given up when something peculiar crossed my path. I'd opened up Elsberry's bedroom drawers and found that they were empty. There were no sweaters, pants or any other clothing. But as I looked under blankets and turned up furniture, I came across another clue. On top of the dresser was a smartphone. There were no phone numbers saved onto it, calendar notes, or anything that might say Gethin. The phone was cleared of any history or messages, but still had a signal. Perhaps I could take the device to Billy and Stevie in order to help me find more about it. Worst case scenario, I finally had a phone. *I was still pissed at Armen for that one.*

Next, I looked around and found that at Thomas's bedside was a single picture of a young man with blonde hair, blue eyes and a gentle face. He was on a boat floating atop of Lake Michigan with an older fellow who must have been his father. The man had long brown and gray hair tied in a ponytail, a trim beard with mustache and small gold studs in both ears. Both of them were dressed casually. At the bottom was an engraving with a date. It read, "The Chicago Sea-Pup Speedboat", with a time stamp from last month.

I tried to put the pieces together. Perhaps Thomas had found out what Gethin really was, and with the help of his father, who he was clearly still close to, had taken the Corruptor hostage. That would mean that one of the two mortals was either a powerful spooky or talented practitioner of the dark arts. If that were the case, then they could easily sell the very valuable fallen angel to the highest bidder. It would also mean that one of the Elsberry's were extremely smart, and very connected. It was likely they would no longer be coming back to the apartment. With nothing else standing out, I took the phone and framed photograph, placed them in my satchel, and left Thomas's apartment.

My hopes were to hit the ground running and race back downtown via cab so that I could prepare for my date. Unfortunately, Sauganash was far less lived in than most Chicago neighborhoods, so there weren't any cabs around. I was forced to take the Blue Line back, which tripled my intended time, and left me a half-mile walk to Billy and Stevie's dorm. Once the train had reached what locals called the Loop, I was running nearly an hour late. I started jogging my way to Billy's dormitory, using the less crowded Riverwalk that trailed alongside the Chicago River rather than try to fight my way through the busy streets. Regrettably, I wasn't still familiar with Chicago's modern cityscape, and the lower elevation of my shortcut caused me to pass up Michigan Avenue without initially realizing it. I was now under the Columbus Drive Bridge situated just next to lower Wacker Drive.

Lower Wacker was an underground road system

that stretched below the city. It was miles of dimly lit street tunnels that one could drive through in order to avoid the congestion on the city's surface. It was dark, secluded and pretty damn scary. I'd read about it back in hell, and was pretty positive that at least one or two serious spookies lived within its domain. Still, because it ran parallel to Lakeshore, and lead under the city, I debated cutting through it in order to make up for my current navigational errors. I peered along the shadowy streets, weighing my options. As I did, a sudden pang of pleasure rumbled through my belly. There must have been an evil spooky nearby.

Then, out of nowhere, a short man in a heavy long coat leapt on my back. It was Joliet. He had a rosary in his hand that he wrapped around my neck like a noose. I grabbed him by his highlighted hair and smashed him into the ground. The cement under him cracked and blood spurt from his mouth. I looked at the string of rose color beads looped around my collar with curiosity. It was old, with gold chain links and a gaudy cross. It had several inscriptions written in Latin. Louis began to chuckle.

"Louie, you maniac," I shouted. "What the Hell are you doing?"

"I have you now my lord," he gasped in victory between bloody coughs and giggles.

"You're an idiot," I said, removing the charm and throwing it at him. "I'm not a damn vampire. Holy symbols don't do anything to me." I paused for a moment, thinking about why he'd be mad enough as to try and hunt me down. "Oh God, is this about Chelsea?" Louie raised the rosary, clasping it awkwardly with his now broken and crooked fingers.

"This is about revenge. You stole her from my grasp, and then started me on fire. I can't sit down now because of how badly you burned my ass."

"Dude, you had that coming. If you would just talk

to a girl like a normal person instead of holding them at gunpoint, you might be the one who has a date with her tonight instead of me," I gloated.

"You lie," he squealed, his nose now fountaining with blood. "She would never go out with you. Besides, even if it's true, do you think she'll really ever be with you once you tell her what you really are? You disgust me."

I stared at the bloodied and broken body that made up Louis Joliet. He'd always been a weasel, making deals like the one he'd made with my predecessor in order to save his own skin. So why would he want to risk his own life, the one he'd been protecting since he could crawl, in order to get revenge? He either really did like Chelsea a lot, or perhaps having all of this time on his hands really was starting to mess with his head. Either way, I kind of felt sorry for him.

"Okay Louie, clearly you're having a bad day and I'm running late, so I'm going to let you off with a warning."

"Ha! You're the one who is about to have a bad day. I'm not a moron. I know holy symbols won't hurt you. *But* divine beings might. That necklace is a beacon. Place it on the neck of something purely evil and the holy hand of retribution will come forth to deliver justice to them." Joliet giggled again. "Prepare to be obliterated."

Just then a loud buzzing noise like the hum from a power line began to emanate behind me. I turned around towards the Riverwalk to see a swirling sapphire vortex forming above the river. The cyclone grew until it was man sized. A figure emerged from within. He was tall, muscular and completely naked. He had long flowing flaxen hair, gilt eyes and three pairs of wings made from golden fire. There was an ornate sword in his hand, bathed in the same holy flames as his feathers. The weapon pulsated as if excited. My guts began to twist in pain.

"May all those who are wicked fall by the righteous

blade gifted to me by the Lord," the angel's deep voice roared and he locked his gaze upon me.

"Shit, shit, shit," I muttered uncontrollably. My jaw unhinged as I shielded my eyes from holy flame's glow. I took a second to calm myself, taking a deep breath in order to stop panting, before looking back up at the divine who floated above the river. "Hello Michael."

Chapter Nine

Michael had always been a total kiss ass even before the war. He loved everything about being a servant of God. He never questioned his orders or wondered why humans were given so much more attention than us. It's probably why he earned his place within heaven's high rankings as the archangel. Well that, plus the dude totally knew how to smite the wicked.

I hadn't been fearful of being obliterated in centuries. Even here on Earth, there were very few practitioners of the magical arts or prominent spookies who had the kind of power to defeat an exiled. Michael was different. In addition to being one of the strongest angels in heaven, his blade, a sword forged from a hair plucked out of God's head, was pure holy righteousness. I'd seen it cut through leviathan and demons like butter, evaporating them into nothingness without breaking a sweat. To further exacerbate the situation, not only was I seconds away from being destroyed by archangel Michael, but he'd also be stark naked when he did it. *How degrading.*

Unlike humans, who learned the shame of who they were when Adam and Eve committed the first sin, Michael was undefiled. Since he was flawless, he never felt nude or exposed. He never experienced humiliation or indignity. So even though his hallowed penis flapped along the winds as he strode through the skies, Michael was never embarrassed. This made not being slain by him even more of a priority than it already was. No one wants, "Killed by a Naked Guy," on his or her tombstone.

"Ah," he said in his heavy voice, "is that you Nedonius? I almost didn't recognize you without the black wings. Come," he flaunted, "let me look upon you in your true form."

Michael raised his blade and a flash of light smothered me. I was blinded momentarily, but quickly regained my vision. I peered at my hands, which were now nearly twice as large as they'd once been. They were sturdy and able, as I'd always remembered. From the looks of things, so was the rest of me. My disguise had been torn from me. I was back to my real form, tall with sable hair and dark wings. I was wearing the grey suit that I'd met Armen in, and had the raggedy leather satchel hanging from my side.

"Damn it Michael," I said while dusting myself off, "not cool." Michael pointed the edge of his sword in my direction.

"Now Nedonius, let this traitorous life you forfeit long ago be reclaimed by my blade." I began to fall back and accidentally kicked into Joliet. The idiot gave one last raspy chuckle before dropping his bloody head and falling unconscious. Meanwhile, Michael slowly flapped his wings, hovering over to me, his eyes fixed and determined as he readied to lay me to waste. Only I had other plans. There was no way I was going to let him just have at me, especially since I had a date with Chelsea tonight. It was time to get ferocious.

"Sorry. Your plan sucks," I said as I focused my hate on his weapon bearing hand. Michael's bronze skin scorched with hellfire that caused him to drop his blade. Archangels were immune to pretty much everything in the book, except for a few select supernatural elements. Hellfire was one of them. Blisters began to bubble along his knuckles. He cradled his scorched fingers and glared at me.

"You'll pay for that," he said, lifting his charred hand. The seared skin quickly began to slurp back into its original form, reforming before my eyes. *Damn it.* He reached down to retrieve his holy sword, but I wasn't about to wait for him to rearm himself. I flapped my wings and soared into the depths of Lower Wacker Drive's tunneled streets, moving as quickly as my single set of wings would allow. The flapping stirred up street dust and garbage, forming a grey fog along the passageways behind me, masking my trail.

"Nedonius," Michael bellowed. "Don't make me chase you."

I weaved in and out of every winding subterranean street I came across in hopes to lose my tail. I'm a decent soldier, but I stood no chance with an archangel. My wings waved harder and harder until I was passing up speeding cars with ease. Turning became difficult and soon my eyes began to water from the sheer momentum. I tried to take a dive through a tight turn and immediately clipped one of my wings along a support beam, crashing onto the pavement.

I lifted my head to see if Michael was behind me. He wasn't. The secluded sublevel street was quiet, with only a smattering of dumpsters and loose trash nearby. I might have lost Michael for now, but there was no doubt in my mind that he was combing the streets. Only spookies and other high beings can see an angel in its true form, unless that is that the angel wants to be noticed, so I knew he could spend all day down here searching for me without drawing suspicion. I'd need to do something quick or I was screwed.

The pain in my guts from Michael's presence lightened, but still throbbed. I hopped to my feet and began taking a more in depth inspection of my surroundings. There was a television box decorated with trash bags and Christmas decorations next to me. Two feet with worn boots protruded from inside. I wasn't worried about the vagrant spotting me, as I was in my true form as well now, naked to the eyes of men. I became aware that there was only one way into this street section- the way that I'd come from. That meant I was cornered. A dim gold glow began to flicker along the concrete walls of Lower Wacker Drive. Michael was getting closer.

"Come out Nedonius," his voice called out, echoing throughout the passages. "Face the justice of the Lord."

"No!" I quietly pouted to myself as if I was a five-year-old child told to stand in the corner, "I don't want to face justice." The light from Michael's wings grew brighter. He must have picked up my trail.

I didn't want it to end like this. I'd always believed that there was something grander planned for me. I pondered, the way that only those about to be decimated ponder, about what I might have done differently had I been given a second chance. Obviously, I wouldn't have joined the rebellion or squandered so much time doing nothing. Maybe I'd have written a graphic novel or started a cult. You know, a legacy that lasts after your time is up.

I questioned whether things would have worked out with Chelsea. She'd been on my mind since meeting her, and as much as it pained me to admit it, I really liked the girl. I doubted that she would ever be able to accept me for what I really was, but hey, who knows. She seemed like an open-minded woman. Maybe I could have earned a permanent spot as a corruptor and stayed on Earth long enough to have a relationship. *Hey, a guy could dream.*

The street tunnel where I'd fled from was now a bright and brilliant yellow. Michael was very near. It wouldn't be long before he turned that corner and found me, sending me to eternal nothingness. I wasn't going to fight it any longer. It seemed obliteration was inevitable.

"Psst," hissed someone quietly behind me. It was the homeless man in the box. I narrowed my eyes to get a better look at him. He was a tall and emaciated black fellow with flowing crow colored hair and a crisp mustache. His weathered flesh was tightly wrapped around his bones with scars and scabs speckled across it. He had mismatched clothes covered in grime, and a button on his chest that said "Support Your Local Union". He lumbered his way out of the box, rising ominously like an old scarecrow. The streetlights above helped define his previously indiscernible features. Skin dangled from his neck and his skeletal hands clacked as he tapped the bone together. His eyes were sallow with dilated pupils, and his nose was grizzled, as if a dog had bitten it. I immediately recognized the spooky.

"DuSable?" I asked.

"Hurry Ned," he said with a heavy French accent, "there's no time to waste."

Jean Baptiste Point DuSable is regarded as the first resident of Chicago. He lived during the late seventeen hundreds and was respected as one of the most successful traders in Illinois. He was handsome in life, and well-liked by all, especially by the Potawatomi Indians who allowed him to marry one of their daughters. He owned land by the northern mouth of what is now the Chicago River and labored there for years until his eventual move to Missouri. He died in August of 1818 and was buried in an unmarked grave, but his spirit never seemed to rest.

I'd met him during my first tenure as a corruptor while he was leading a campaign against an old rival. He was a revenant, an animated corpse who'd returned from the grave in order to complete some unfinished business. Apparently, the British military had arrested Jean Baptiste when he was still alive for being an American sympathizer during the Revolutionary War and it really seemed to tick Jean off. To add injury to insult, the man responsible for his arrest had been an imported spooky, the son of an Irish witch named Collin Dain, who earned the rank of Colonel during the Revolution. The two had been battling it out in a secret war throughout Chicago's back alleys when we'd originally crossed paths, and I'd helped him burn down a few of Dain's elixir and fortune teller businesses in return for information.

"Come *mon ami*, you need to follow me if you want to live." DuSable went to his knees and began crawling back inside his open-faced box. He prodded his head inside the makeshift shelter and clambered forward. Suddenly, a flare of bright greens and oranges, like fireworks, went off within the cardboard and DuSable disappeared.

"I have you now Nedonius," a voice rumbled behind me. Michael flew into the tunnel and landed along the pavement. His flaccid penis dangled close to the flaming sword that he pointed at me accusingly. "Now, let that which should not be finally end." I ducked down awkwardly and began shuffling towards the box like a declawed cat. Michael tilted his head, watching as I gracelessly inched towards the cardboard shelter. "Is this how you wish to meet your end, crawling like cowardly vermin?"

Michael edged within striking distance, raising his gold flaming blade. I punched my head into the back of the box, taking in the aroma of pickles and feces. In front of me was nothing but the lining of the box. Kicking forward, I smashed my face along the back wall of the cardboard, hoping that something would happen.

"DuSable," I yelped, "save me!"

A clap of thunder and a pulse of light suddenly erupted from the box. My skin erupted into goosebumps as if I'd been thrown into cold water, and my body was thrust forward into what appeared to be a cloud of black smoke. I didn't know what was happening, but I was damn sure that it was better than what Michael had planned for me. *Saved by the creepy dead guy.*

Chapter Ten

I knew that I was on my back, and stretched across a hard cold surface, but because it was pitch black, I didn't know where or why. The smell of mildew permeated into my nostrils. I reached out my hands and felt cold granite in every direction. I was encased in stone. It was smooth, but sturdy. I was hesitant to push hard or punch through my encasing, but if someone didn't come soon, I'd have no choice but to go all Tasmanian devil in here.

A grinding sound reverberated throughout my tiny prison and suddenly the lid above me slid open. Soft amber light poured in the stonework container and I soon realized that I'd been deposited inside of a coffin- not just any coffin might I add, but a sarcophagus. The silhouette of a man entered my vision, though the brightness from the ceiling light bulb made him appear shadowy and indistinguishable. He lifted his hand and offered it to me.

"Ned," said DuSable's voice, "come out *mon ami*, and meet the gang."

I grabbed Jean Baptiste's scraggy forearm and used it to hoist myself up, crawling out of the tomb. There were gold artifacts and hieroglyphics strewn across the sandstone walls and ceiling. Standing behind Jean, like some kind of B-horror movie, was a gathering of assorted dead. There were several dried up mummies with putrid brown wrapping, a skeleton clasping onto a jarred brain, one ghastly beryl colored fellow in a top hat, and a stylish ashen man with a smooth pencil mustache. The group crowded inside the corridor, looking over Jean's shoulder with wide eyes and eager grins. *Shit, did the cardboard box whisk us away to Egypt?*

"Hey DuSable," I spouted doubtfully, "Are we in north Africa?"

The group of dead laughed in unison. Dry soil spurt from one of the chuckling mummy's mouths, and the skeleton's jarred brain began to fizz in its stew. Jean Baptiste gave me a sympathetic pat on my shoulder.

"No *mon ami,*" he said, "we're still in Chicago. This is the Field Museum's Ancient Egypt exhibit. It's where we call home."

"Oh," I said, "uh, neat."

One of the mummies, who sported turquoise jewelry, an elegant short cut wig and leopard skin cape, shambled up to me, poking at my chest with a pointy index finger.

"Not as neat as you my big burly angel," she said with a sensual female voice. "Ever been with an older woman before?" I tried not to gag, instead turning my attention to DuSable in hopes for an explanation.

"Ned my old friend," said Jean Baptiste, putting his hand between the cougar-mummy, and myself, "you have the honor of being in the presence of the first corporeal undead union. The *Negative-One Union* to be exact." Some of the group proudly puffed their chests.

"So," I cued, "do the disembodied undead have a union as well?" The assembly laughed in unison once more.

"Eh," said the elderly man with a top hat over a snort, "theirs is more of a club." I let the cadavers calm down their snickers before speaking again.

"Alright then Jean, who are all these nice folks?" I asked. DuSable beamed, waving his hand over to the mummies in introduction.

"Ned," he said, eyeing the eerily flirtatious female mummy, "this vixen was once known as Mukantagara, but now we just call her Mary." Mary extended her hand for me to kiss. I obliged her request, and could feel a dusty residue on my lips afterwards that I wasn't too excited about licking off. "And just behind her are her assistants Todd and Melvin." The two mummies following just behind Mary leisurely waved.

"Sup,'" said the one DuSable identified as Todd. He had long rope braids protruding from his bandages and a Megadeth t-shirt draped over his sunken chest. His partner Melvin, who was a poster child for the Chicago Board of Tourism with his "Untouchables Gangster Tour" t-shirt, Blackhawks baseball cap, and Windy City boxers, was a bit shyer, staring downward at his fluffy Chicago Bears slippers. He waved, but remained silent.

"And this," DuSable motioned, now showcasing the skeleton holding his jarred brain, "is German physicist James Franck." Franck held up his brain, which bubbled inside the glass jar. Along the bottom of the container's wood frame was a gold placard that read Dr. J. Franck. His bones were marked with neatly printed anatomic labels such as *spine of scapula* and *cora coid process*. Otherwise, the skeleton was very indistinct, with tea stained yellow bones that rattled when he walked. "As you can see, James donated his body to the museum decades ago. We're still trying to find a way for him to communicate with us beyond pen and paper. I think he said hi."

I gave a nod of acknowledgement and then moved along with DuSable. He sidestepped towards the blue skinned man with the top hat.

"This good sir," DuSable divulged, "is none other than Monsieur George Wellington Streeter. He's the madman that the Streeterville neighborhood is named after." Streeter removed his top hat and bowed. "George earned his fame by spinning lies to prospecting landowners in order to sell them property he didn't own along the shorelines."

"I did own them," Streeter hollered. "I ran my steamboat onto that sandbar fair and square. If you discover land, you get to claim it, and I claimed it as the independent U.S. District of Michigan, meaning it isn't subject to the laws of Illinois."

"Did I mention," DuSable added, "that he's a madman?"

"I think once or twice," I said as I returned Streeter's bow with one of my own. DuSable pushed me along, continuing to walk me along the introduction line.

The last in line was the smug gentleman in the trendy dress suit. The stranger kept his hands in his pants pockets, smirking as if he knew a funny secret. The man's pallid flesh was about the only thing off about him. Otherwise, his slicked back hair, thin mustache and devilish smirk conveyed the image of a sly businessman more than undead horror.

"This," DuSable purred, "is our local celebrity. Ned, meet Mr. Dillinger, infamous bank robber of the twenties and thirties."

"Call me John," said the man in a gruff voice.

"Though most people believe that John was gunned down near the Biograph Theatre, those who know the truth understand that he was changed days before the shooting in an attempt to cheat death."

"Changed?" I spouted.

"Oui," DuSable confirmed, "He's a child of the night." My face must have been dripping with bewilderment because Baptiste felt the need to quickly elaborate. "You know, as in Nosferatu or as Hollywood likes to call them, vampires."

"Oh, a vampire," I said with clarity. "Why didn't you just say that?" DuSable's face cringed in revolt. John gave a quick wink before taking a tiny step back, joining the crowd of ghouls.

"Anyhow Ned," said DuSable as he gestured his hand towards the crowd. The team gathered around Jean as if to take a team photo, some wrapping their arms around each other's shoulders. "We are the Negative One Union, an organization that protects the interests of our members here in Chicago."

I was delighted to meet the little band of undead, but a bit confused by DuSable's extensive efforts to ensure that I knew whom each and every member was. I'd been grateful for Jean's help, but the only things currently on my mind were getting to my date and not being killed by Michael.

"Well hey," I spoke up, "that's great and all, but I have to get going J.B. If you have a business card or flyer, I'd be glad to make a donation."

"Whoa now," DuSable objected, "You're not going to leave so early are you? We didn't even discuss why I decided to let you endanger our entire union by bringing you here."

"Endanger?" I argued, "When did I do that?"

"When you decided to follow me into that cardboard box, you made one of the most powerful entities in existence, God's personal hand of justice, Michael, aware of us -- Us, the creatures of this world who have cheated final judgment. I'm sure that the archangel doesn't appreciate people assisting his enemies, especially if they're swindlers of death."

I should have figured that DuSable wouldn't just help me for the sake of being nice. He was a businessman at heart after all. Jean Baptiste recognized that I was in a bind back on Lower Wacker Drive, and made a calculated decision to lend me aid in return for a favor. I contemplated walking away, but knew that ticking off a union of undead was probably unwise. Even if they didn't attack me outright, the chances that they might make a backhanded deal with Michael in order to save their own rotted skin was a distinct possibility.

"Okay DuSable," I said, "make it quick. I have a date to go on."

"Oh a date," Streeter sniggered, "how I miss courting. There's not much of a selection when you're dead."

"Speak for yourself," Dillinger said under his breath.

"Nedonius," DuSable cut in, "the Negative One Union needs you to help us with a little issue. You see, not much has changed since we last met. The child of Carman is growing even stronger in Chicago while we, the undead, are dwindling in number. That warlock Collin is making a killing on his new business venture. You see, he's stopped selling potions and tapped into the nightlife."

"Whoa," I shouted, "I can't burn down every nightclub and pub in Chicago. That's why I've been out of commission for so long."

"No, no," Mary gasped as she tightened the straps on her gold scarab belt over her decayed stomach, shrinking her waistline. "What we ask of you is much simpler. All we need from you is to rid us of Colonel Dane and his band of miscreants will follow. He's not only been bullying us, but all of the other spookies in Chicago for decades now, and it's about time someone stood up to him."

"Hey," I said reluctantly, "I'm not some sort of supernatural hitman."

"Of course you're not," said DuSable, "and we don't want you to be. We don't need him dead. We just want to send him packing his bags back for Ireland, or anywhere else that's not Chicago."

"So why can't you do it yourself?" I asked.

"Well," said DuSable, "we're outmanned for starters." Jean pinched at his rotted ear absentmindedly, slightly ripping the appendage from his head. "Plus, hex magic is quite formidable against undead. We don't stand a chance, especially when they're hiding in their main headquarters, the well protected nightclub known as The

Citadel."

Now it all made sense. DuSable and his deadheads needed me because I was an angel. Exiled, extensions of the almighty himself, tend to be unaffected by most spooky abilities, fallen or not. We are otherworldly, and hand crafted by God, whereas spookies are flukes from Earth. Their magic just isn't able to stand up to our raw divinity. It's like using a straw in order to try and blow out a fire. In other words, the Union were going to try use me as their invulnerable champion to scare off an otherwise very dangerous Dain, son of the ancient Irish witch, Carman.

DuSable *had* saved my life. And Michael would definitely be adding DuSable to his list of people to smite because of Jean's involvement in my rescue. I guess I kind of owed him. More importantly, because he had helped me, I now still had an opportunity to see Chelsea tonight, if only I could make it back to her bookstore in time. I was more than willing to stop at this son-of-a-witch's nightclub tomorrow to give the warlock a good scare and stop him from picking on the Union. Besides, I hated bullies.

"Okay," I agreed, "I'll help you, but I need something in return."

"Name it," Mary commanded.

"First of all, I use to look human. I need you to get me back to my mortal form. More importantly though, I'm late for my date and need to get there pronto. Think you can help?"

DuSable and Mary quietly stared at each other before the mummy diva turned her attention back to me. A devious grin erupted from her lipless face as she gently drew across my arm with her index finger.

"Oh," she said gaily, "I just might have the thing."

Chapter Eleven

The Egyptian *Book of the Dead* was a collection of mystical writings placed in ancient tombs to help guide the soul on its journey into the afterlife. The common versions were put inside of burial sites as more of courtesy, like Bibles in hotel rooms nowadays. However, some of the more influential individuals of Egypt, such as the pharaohs and high priests, received a much different version. The real *Book of the Dead*, had incantations and enchantments which assisted the deceased on the second part of their journey. It was rumored to have nearly two hundred different exotic spells that varied in purpose from empowerment spells to protective wards. Apparently, the Field Museum had recovered one of these ancient tomes during its scientific excavations, and Mary, a practitioner of the ancient magic, knew exactly how to use it.

The old mummy, along with her two cronies, Todd and Melvin, guided me to the basement where the book was safely stored. The museum had closed for the day, and the group used back halls to dodge what little staff still lingered. We passed a number of exhibits, including a massive taxidermy display with stuffed animals from around the world that'd been posed in fabricated habitats. There was everything from grizzly bears to elephants, as well as the infamous man eating lions of Tsavo, which coincidentally, were some of Lucifer's housecats. Finally, we reached the research facility located in the cellar.

An electronic, high-tech lock secured the curating vaults, but luckily, Mary had somehow acquired an employee key. She swiped the keycard into its slot, opening the automatic security doors. I followed the mummies and walked inside. The archaeologist lab was small and simple. It had a few scattered staff desks, computers, storage shelves, a small projector and a mini-fridge. Mary went to one of the labeled shelves and pulled open a long drawer. There in wait was a dry looking book, large and bound in brown leather and wrapped in clear plastic. She removed the volume from its shelf, and after removing the plastic covering, began flipping through the brittle pages.

"Let me see," she mumbled as her boney finger traced the hieroglyphics, "Ah, here we are- *Preservation of Parts*." Mary rested the book on a nearby computer desk, keeping her dehydrated brown eyes on the pages. "Come here Nedonius, and extend your hand."

I offered my palm to the old bat. Her index finger traced along my skin, tickling it as she began reading from the book, chanting incoherently. After a short time, my fingers began to tingle. Suddenly, my huge angelic hand began to pulsate and shrink. The process rippled up my arms and into the remainder of my body. I could feel static prickle across the surface of my skin, and watched as my angel body began to morph into something smaller, until finally I was once again the skinny guy with tattoos and the stupid grey t-shirt.

"Nice work," I complimented as I examined myself. "How'd you do it?"

"The ancient priests designed this spell so that the dead could remain exactly as they were in life. The principles of reversing time and matter apply to a great many circumstances. Think about that," she purred. "If things don't work out on your lady tonight I could look exactly as I did nearly three thousand years ago." I shivered and tried to keep the conversation moving along before things became awkward.

"Uh, anyway, how do you plan on getting me to my date? That psychopath angel Michael is out there looking for me, so I'm hoping you have a great plan."

"The same way you got here," she said as if the answer was obvious, "we'll just navigate you through the underworld. Now stand aside, and I'll open up the gates."

It only took Mary a few moments to prepare the spell. She'd procured a leftover McDonald's cheeseburger from the nearby mini-fridge that along with a can of coke would serve as an offering to Anubis in return for passage through the underworld. I wondered if she was talented enough to get me back to Hell when the time was right. Shortly after she placed her offerings on the floor a blue glow began to envelop the burger and soda, until finally a popping noise prompted the junk food to disappear altogether. The ground trembled as a flood of black water coursed in behind us. The onyx stream flowed from the entrance and into an abyss of nothingness before us. Soon after, a rickety long boat lifted from the depths and took to the surface. It was made of tattered whicker, and a single wooden oar rested on its seat.

"This isn't how I remember getting here," I protested.

"It's all relative," said Mary. "Now get in and start rowing. Once the boat ceases its movement, your journey will be complete." I climbed inside the wobbly boat, balancing myself at the tail end while taking a hold of the oar. "Here, take this," Mary removed a beetle shaped charmed necklace from around her neck and placed it over my head. "It will help make you undetectable to other spookies, including the archangel, Michael. And don't forget DuSable's deal- you need to stop that warlock before he gets any more powerful. Stop the tyrant, and our deal will be complete."

"I will, I will," I said as I concentrated on stabbing the water with my oar.

"Good." Mary nodded to Todd and Melvin. The two lesser mummies grabbed the side of the boat and gave it a push, kicking the boat forward. "We'll expect results immediately after your," Mary hummed, "*date.*"

I waved Mary off and looked towards the dark passageway before me. The nose of the raft drifted toward the large black hole. I began paddling the boat faster, moving with the current until I'd been swallowed by the gaping void. The neon lights of the curator's office quickly vanished behind me, snuffed out by the obscurity of the underworld. Somehow, I had floated into a spelunker's wet dream. The river's path was filled with winding caves and rocky passages. The soft eerie glimmer of green mushrooms and funguses lit up the otherwise murky caverns. The air was crisp and the atmosphere was cool and still.

Then suddenly, there came a sudden splash in the water next to me, and I could see the faint outline of a large serpent-like creature swimming below. It was massive-nearly five times the size of my boat. It skimmed the top of the water before submerging back into the river's depths.

"Damn underworld," I said aloud, "Why does it always have to be so dramatically bleak and creepy?"

Since I didn't bring my whaling hook, I decided to focus on rowing the ferryboat, pushing it through the calm oil colored waters. Boredom started to kick in, and it wasn't long before my thoughts took hold of me. I had no idea how I'd chase Collin Dane out of Chicago. Dane was a warlock and son of the famed Celtic witch, Carman. Along with his two brothers, Dub and Dother, he had been banished from Ireland after his mother's death, but luckily the Americas were accepting anyone who could get here. While his brothers settled in the east coast, Dane followed thousands of other Irish immigrants into Chicago, where he began his reign of terror. Even if his hex magic didn't have much dominion over the powers of hell, they'd be quite adept at manipulating men, which meant that he'd gained a lot of followers over the centuries. I'd have to be really careful not to harm his innocent servants or else Michael would be on me like vultures on a carcass.

I also wondered what in Lucifer's name was going on with Chelsea? Since we'd met, she'd had this silly way of creeping into my every thought, like a song you can't get out of your head. I've dated some of the most exquisite angels, erotic succubae, and even a spooky or two, yet none of them seemed to compare to Chelsea, the human bookstore owner from Chicago. I could hear it now. All of the other Forsaken would think I was mad if I came back down to Hell with a mortal as a girlfriend. *What was I thinking?* Nonetheless, the facts were in. Chelsea Zalenski had turned my heart upside down. I was willing to risk my career as a corruptor, and I was prepared for the Archangel Michael to smite me, in order to go on our date tonight.

I didn't know how long I'd been rowing when my ferryboat came to a sudden stop. I rocked back and forth a few times before stabbing my oar into the water in order to free myself from whatever the ferry may have been caught on. As I did, a sudden *thud* followed by a low moan resonated from under me. It was the leviathan. The thing must have been following me, and now I'd just jabbed it's who knows what with my oar. Bubbles started to fizz from under the ferryboat. I must have made it mad.

However, just before the beast swallowed me whole, a sudden shower of light poured from above me. There was a brilliant ring of orange glowing along the cave ceiling that, much like a bad U.F.O. reenactment on television, lifted me upward with its rays of light. I ascended to the top of the cave, which was a good thing, because as I looked down, I saw the massive head of the scaly river monster come up from the water's surface. Its narrow alligator-like snout opened up, snapping the boat into two before submerging back into the depths.

"That's right," I shouted as I floated upwards, "suck it Nessy!"

Before I could say another word, the bright circle

swallowed me up and spat me onto the sidewalk hugging Belmont Avenue, directly in front of *The Prologue*. The sun was setting and the pink sky was slipping into a dark purple. Cars zoomed back and forth behind me, and a red line train screeched its wheels along the rails nearby. I could see that the store lights were already off and the closed sign was hanging from the front door's glass. Chelsea had shut the place down.

I pressed the buzzer's ugly black button and could hear an electronic buzz echo from inside the store. Simon and Hecubus turned the corner and charged at the door, their tails wagging. I crossed my fingers that they wouldn't get too excited and try to break the door down. Luckily they stopped at the glass, moaning like wounded bears. Not a moment later Chelsea came into view from the hall and approached the store's entrance. She fidgeted with the lock and opened the door.

"You're five minutes late," she said, calmly. I sighed in relief, relieved that she wasn't upset.

"Sorry, I ran into some trouble," I apologized as the dogs leapt into my arms. Chelsea walked out onto the sidewalk and began to lock up the store. I balanced the hellhounds in one arm, opening up my satchel and placing them inside. The beasts fidgeted for a moment before a vacuum noise sucked them into the dimensional door. Chelsea didn't seem to notice as she finished turning the keys to the last lock.

"So," she said, turning to face me as she placed her keys in her purse, "where are we headed?"

Where were we headed? With all of the excitement today, I'd completely forgotten to plan our date. I needed to think quickly. What would a girl like Chelsea want to do? It had to be simple, interesting, and yet romantic. I wasn't too familiar with 21st century Chicago, but I *did* still remember 19th century Chicago. Maybe there'd still be something interesting from the old era lingering in the new age. Then, just like that, it hit me. I knew exactly where to take her.

"We're going somewhere a little different," I said with a smirk. "It'll be an adventure." Chelsea gave me a pleased smile. Hesitant -- but pleased.

"You've piqued my interest," she said with a devious wink.

Chicago has had a labyrinth of tunnels under its foundation since the city's early days. Early passageways were used to transport coal and ventilate buildings. In 1867, the city built an intake crib two miles out under Lake Michigan in order to bring more fresh water into the city. During my brief tenure as a corruptor, I used the underground highway in order to help some of my more *dishonest* souls smuggle illegal goods into town. It may have been over a century ago, but I knew that there had to be at least one or two of the tunnels left. All I had to do was head back to the heart of the city to find one. We took a taxi back downtown. I asked the driver to let us off just south of the river, near the Prudential Building. Once I paid the fare, I asked Chelsea to follow me as I guided us towards my intended location. Sure enough, as I checked the closest tunnel entrance, I found that the old Lake Street manhole was still around, rusted orange and locked by a simple metal cap.

Night had officially reared its ugly head, making the streets a little less busy. I waited for nearby pedestrians to clear out before giving a go at the underground entrance. Chelsea gave me a curious look as I played with the entrance's cap. It was engraved with the words *Chicago Water Management*.

"Ned, tell me where you are taking us," she demanded.

"A little place I like to call, *you'll* see."

I fidgeted with the lid, pretending to have an idea of what I was doing before prying the cap off with my hidden strength. Chelsea once again didn't seem to notice. Instead, she stood with her arms crossed, staring at the moon bathed in clouds. It wasn't until the musty odor I'd unearthed from below tore into our nostrils like angry hornets that she finally drew her attention back towards me. She turned and stared at me with a grimace. I was now kneeling down and inspecting the skinny opening. The hole wasn't too deep, and I could see the bottom from my vantage point. If I remembered correctly, a path below would lead to an assortment of tunnels.

"Ladies first," I said, waving Chelsea inside.

"Yeah, right. Do you honestly think I'm going to go into a dark tunnel before the guy that I found hiding in my backseat?"

"Can I just get a pass on that one?" I asked with an upbeat tone. "I mean I did save your life."

Chelsea gave an amused smiled, but said nothing.

"Fine, fine, I'll go first," I volunteered.

I used an old pipe-ladder built into the stone cavity and climbed down the hole. Chelsea followed behind me. Before long, the two of us were down at the bottom of a clearing that led to several lightless tunnels. Though I could still see because of what I was, I knew it would be an issue for Chelsea's mortal eyes. I contemplated using hellfire to make a torch, but didn't think she'd simply ignore fire spontaneously combusting from the tips of my fingers. Casually, before I could say a word, Chelsea had dug in her purse and plucked out a miniature flashlight, turning it on by twisting its head. She waved a weak beam of light down the damp corridors, fearlessly looking down their halls like a fortune hunter of old.

"Explore the underground much?" I asked in a lighthearted voice.

"When I'm not selling books," she said astutely, "I'm the head of the Chicago Paranormal Society's 'Soul Patrol'. A ghost hunter has to be ready for anything."

I gave an odd snort that sounded like a pig trying to

sing before covering my mouth. Chelsea looked me over, running the flashlight's beam in my direction. "Was that a laugh?" she chuckled.

"No," I said, embarrassed. "Let's not get into it."

"Are you sure you don't want to talk about it?" she asked sarcastically.

"No, I'm fine," I said hurriedly, trying to change the subject. "Wow, would you look at these tunnels, huh? I think the one we want is on the left. Would you mind shining the light in that direction so that I don't go blind?"

Chelsea snickered as she shined her flashlight down the left corridor. I took the lead, and began walking down. The low ceiling of the passageway was covered with mold and cobwebs, and we had to duck a bit to get through its drooping pathway. Slowly, we tramped our way through the obstacle course of puddles, rubble, and rusted pipes, but eventually made it to a massive iron door that I'd been looking for. There were old painted letters in crimson that read *storeroom* along the front.

"Okay," I announced, "I'm going in. Stay here for a moment, and I'll get the surprise ready."

"Sure Dr. Jones. Good luck."

I gave my best Harrison Ford smirk and winked. "Fortune and glory, kid. Fortune and glory."

I pried open the door, which gave a loud moan from its rusted hinges, and then quickly entered, hurrying to close the door behind me so that Chelsea couldn't see what was inside. The chamber was mostly as I'd remembered it. It was a massive quarry that had been carved out in order to store tools and mining equipment. There were primitively engraved stone steps that lead to a large pool of water. Moss clung to the ground, making the floor appear to be covered in squat grass. Old charred whiskey barrels and liquor crates lined the walls, standing amongst the room like sentries, and an antique mining rail with a single cart still attached leading into collapsed passageway.

I concentrated on some of the old whiskey barrels, and after recalling a few bad memories, stirred up enough anger to light the tops with hellfire. The orange glow glimmered across the coffee colored walls and emerald pond. The waters were clear enough to see through, and at the bottom was a large collection of discarded beer bottles of jade and amber. It was obvious that someone had been using this area as a drinking hole for some time, as the beer bottles were hundreds in number. However, instead of the beer containers being an eyesore, the shine of hellfire, and the ripples of water created an orchestra of reflected light onto the ceiling, producing a mosaic pattern throughout the quarry.

"Okay," I called out, inspecting my instant and accidental work of art. "You can come in now."

The creek of the door resonated throughout the cave as Chelsea entered. Her eyes squinted for a moment at the light, but soon they were wide open, along with her mouth.

"Well," I asked hopefully, "what do you think?"

"Wow," she said reflexively before unconsciously biting at the tips of her black manicured fingernails. "Ned, this is amazing."

Chelsea began to explore the cave, petting the walls as she made her way to the pond. She stared at the waters before looking up to see the light show above. She covered her mouth in awe, her eyes glistening. For one second, and not a moment longer, I caught a glimpse of the real Chelsea. It was an almost childlike expression that flashed before me, with her delicate eyes and big beautiful smile sprouting like winter flowers. Green, blue and brown colored her near perfect skin as she spun in a quick circle, hypnotized by the cave's magnificence.

But, as quickly as it came, the entire moment washed over, and soon her happy expression retreated, replaced by the protective frown that I'd become accustomed to. Chelsea stiffened up her posture and narrowed her eyes.

"You did this on purpose," she said heatedly.

"Uh, yeah, that's kind of what you do on a date isn't it? You take someone someplace nice."

"No," she said, squatting down towards the edge of the water, "what I mean is, you took me here because you knew my father was a glass artist. Ned, I thought you said you were going to stop being creepy."

"Whoa," I pleaded, "Chelsea, uh, honestly, I had no idea. I took you here because it's beautiful." Chelsea rubbed at her arm and looked down at a small crooked rock near her foot. The cave went quiet. I knelt down slowly and grabbed the rock, throwing it gently into the water. The splash caused the light on the cave surface to scatter like fireworks. Chelsea looked back up at me, her arms tightly crossed.

"So you're saying that you didn't take the time to research any of my family history in order to score points on our date?"

"Chelsea, come on- that's pretty harsh. Why would you even leap to something like that?"

"Well, I did find you in the backseat of my car before." There was a moment of silence. Chelsea chewed her lip before ashamedly turning to look at me. "I'm sorry," she said genuinely. "He died when I was very young and I'm a bit weird about it." The chamber went quiet again except for the occasional drip of water from the ceiling or crackle from the burning wood. I walked over to her, and gave her a short innocent hug with one arm. Chelsea squeezed back.

"So an artist huh?"

"Yeah," she said. "He was really good."

I don't see death the way mortals do, but it doesn't mean that I don't understand that it sucks. I've never really had anyone that close to me, but I could imagine the pain when someone you love goes away. I mean, I didn't even like my last girlfriend, but it still hurt when she walked out on me. You wonder if they're okay, what they're doing and all sorts of other painful stuff. I wonder if that's how God must have felt when we betrayed him.

"How'd he pass?"

"There was a fire in the school he taught at. He always thought doing the right thing was more important than anything else, so it was no surprise when Mom and I found out that he'd run back in to help.'

"And your mom?"

"She didn't last long without him." Her voice squeaked slightly. "She passed a few years later. I was already in my late teens by then, so I went away to live with my aunt for a few years before I headed off on my own." I heaved a small uncontrollable sigh, lowering my head in order to stare at my dirty shoes.

"Man," I said, rubbing the back of my neck, "that's heavy. I'm sorry." Chelsea shrugged.

"It is what it is. Anyhow, it made me tougher," she said before shaking her head, hard as if trying to fling something clinging from off her bangs. "I can't believe I'm burdening you with this stupid shit. I guess you can tell why I don't go on dates much. I'm no good at them."

"Yeah, about that. Can you please explain to me how is it that a woman like you doesn't go on hundreds of dates a year?" Her frown changed into a half grin.

"Oh boy, is this where you start coming at me hard with cheesy one-liners?"

"No!" I exclaimed, "Come on, I'm serious. Chelsea, I'm not sure if you know or not but you're amazing." She raised a doubtful brow. "Listen, even if we were to never go out again, you have to know what I'm about to say is not lip service. I've traveled a lot, and have met a lot of people. Never have I met anyone like you. You have a wickedly dry sense of humor that I adore; you're headstrong, and tenacious as hell." Chelsea gave a soundless laugh. "You may not be the common man's idea of a catch."

"Easy, Casanova."

"Wait. Let me finish," I objected. Chelsea smiled. "You may not be the common man's idea of a catch, *but* anyone with half a brain understands how remarkable you are. I mean seriously, how do you --"

Chelsea grabbed the collar of my shirt, pulled me close, and kissed me. A torrent of heat swirled in my stomach as she did. In all my millenniums, there had never been a kiss so sweet. I'd felt the soft mouth of a seraph, the provocative tongue of a succubus, and the passionate taste of numerous mortals, but none of my encounters could compare to this. My cheeks heated up and my eyes fluttered as her warm lips pressed against mine. Her skin was smooth and smelled of honey. My kneeling body melted into hers as my arms folded around her. I don't know how long it lasted, as my mind drifted off into nirvana, but after a steamy exchange of squeezing and caressing, we finally unlocked.

We stared at each other for a moment, innocent like children. Chelsea's mouth was pink from pressing against mine. I had nothing that I could say which would make this moment any better, so instead I picked up a nearby rock and offered it to her. She took it reluctantly, curious as to why I'd handed it to her. I pointed with my nose towards the waters. Chelsea gave a small laugh, and then threw the rock into the pond. It skipped a few times before sinking to the bottom, and then clanked onto the bed of glass.

I took a seat on the floor, watching as she found another stone and threw it. She stared at the water as it went calm again, and then sat down next to me. Without warning, she leaned her pretty head on my shoulder. I side armed one last stone, and together we watched the ripples dance across the surface. Time finally did me a favor and stayed still long enough for me to feel good again -- like I did before being exiled. It felt nice.

Chapter Twelve

After some time, the two of us finally decided to get going. Our legs were sore from sitting on the hard ground, and it was getting late. We hobbled to the exit hand-in-hand, our legs half asleep and feeling like jelly. It was almost midnight when we stumbled our way back to the surface. I knew Chelsea had to open up the store in the morning. And yet, as we walked towards Michigan Avenue to find her a cab, a certain thought crossed my mind. It wasn't so much of an idea, as a hope.

When God punished the Forsaken to the deep recesses of existence, he also cursed us for revolting against him. Along with the black wings and hair, he bequeathed us with the erratically frustrating seven deadly sins- the same ones he'd bestowed upon men in order to test their faith. It was his way of separating us from what we once were, flawless beings. We learned to hate, covet, and most tiresome, *lust* over anything enticing enough. So, even though I knew that my best next action was to simply put Chelsea into a cab and kiss her goodnight, a part of me strongly desired for something more. There was an itch that wanted to be scratched. It was now just a question of risk versus reward.

"So," I said with anticipation as Chelsea hailed a cab, "I guess you'll be heading home then? Funny, because the night is still young, you know?"

Chelsea stood still, digesting my meaning for a second before unleashing a wicked half smile -- a smile that let me know she knew exactly what I meant. Her brows perked up as she studied me from head to toe like art hanging up at a museum. She raised her hand, biting provocatively at her black painted thumbnail, slowly licking the top of it with the tip of her tongue. My groin began to pulsate. As she teased me, a yellow cab pulled up on the curb nearest to her and beeped. She ignored the driver when he motioned her over, and sauntered over to me, grabbing at my belt and pulling me in close to her. She dipped her nose onto my neck and exhaled hot breath along the surface. I was paralyzed.

"Do you want to come to my place?" she asked in a sensual whisper.

"Why yes," I tried to say in my most debonair voice. "Yes, I do." Chelsea pushed closer to me so that our chests were pressed together and fussed with my belt buckle. Then with a thrust of her hand…she forcefully pulled my pants down to my ankles.

"I'm sure you do lover boy," she said while walking towards the cab.

There I was on Michigan Avenue in my pitchfork pattern boxers, an erection the size of the Willis Tower swaying along for everyone to see. Chelsea slipped into the cab, shut the door behind her and gave directions to the driver. As I struggled to get my pants back up, an older couple who'd been studying a map of Chicago stopped what they were doing and pointed at me, smiles across their faces as they laughed at my shame. Not shortly after, a Porsche driving by beeped its horn and a lady passenger from inside whistled. I was humiliated. Once I'd finally managed to buckle my jeans back up, I looked to the street and saw that Chelsea's cab was slowly pulling away. *Wow, talk about ruining a great night Ned.* The brain between my legs had all but done me in.

But just as I thought all was lost, Chelsea rolled the backseat window down, stuck her head out, and blew me a kiss.

"Thanks for a great night," she shouted with a sincere smile smeared across her face. "Maybe next time I'll take you up on that offer Ned," she said sympathetically, "*maybe.*"

Little did she know, that for a guy like me, that was all I needed to hear. Although I tried my hardest to mess it all up, tonight was still a success. I'd need to form a plan for our next rendezvous, one that would make up for the last few minutes of our date. It would have to be sweet and genuine, with no connection to sex or any other shallow thoughts that might bubble up in my imbecilic brain- *a real beauty of a plan*. But first, I needed to rest. The day had been a long one, and almost being obliterated, rescued by the Undead Union, taking on a new job that involved me scaring a warlock out of town, plus having the date of my life, had taken something out of me.

Luckily, Billy's dormitory wasn't too far away. I felt bad crashing at his place again, so I first stopped to bring him an offering. I went to a twenty-four hour diner, *Capone's*, and picked up two of the menu's special, "The St. Valentine's Day Massacre." The massive meatball sandwiches were loaded with hot peppers, smothered in marinara sauce, and oozed with three types of melted cheese. I quickly understood why the mortals dubbed the submarine sandwich by its notorious name. It was a real killer.

I took the monster sandwiches over to Billy's, and after waiting for the security guard at the lobby to call up his dorm, his eyes studying my sack of sandwiches the entire time, I was finally given permission to go up to Billy's room. It was late, and Billy answered his dorm door with a bushel of bedhead and a pair of Stormtrooper pajamas. I could see Stevie was still glued to his computer in the background, the blue glow from the computer screen flickering in the otherwise dark living quarter.

"Ned," said Billy as he scratched at his backside, "what's up man?"

"Hey Billy, I'm sorry to bother you. It's just that I'm still having problems at my place. You think I could crash here again?" Billy looked at me reluctantly.

"I don't know man. I have-"

"Oh, I almost forgot," I raised the sack of sandwiches, their enticing aroma steaming from the paper bag. "I brought these for you and Stevie. They're from Capone's." Billy licked his lips and gawked at the bag.

"Well, I'm sure we can find someplace for you to sleep," Billy smiled, taking the bag from my hand. "Come on in, I'll get some extra blankets."

"Thanks," I said as I entered. There were several Giordano's pizza boxes strewn across the dorm room and a stockpile of potato chips, soda and Twinkies. Clearly, Stevie had taken advantage of my credit card. "Hey Stevie," I said. Stevie didn't flinch.

"Hey Ned," he replied in a welcoming voice, his eyes still locked on the computer. Billy looked shocked. Clearly I'd achieved some otherworldly goal by befriending Stevie. A half grin crept up Billy's face as he turned on the light and began to set up a makeshift bed on the floor for me. Afterwards, I handed Billy the greasy paper bag from Capone's. Billy took out the two sandwiches wrapped in wax paper and handed one to Stevie before unwrapping his own. His blue eyes sized up the submarine sandwich as his tongue slithered over his lips. Then, like some wild hyena, he attacked, devouring his sandwich in several gaping bites. I watched in awe as Billy wiped the oil from his lips before letting out a satisfied belch.

"So," said Billy as he gingerly wobbled his way to his bed, stepping over my makeshift bed and a few of his helicopter drone parts, "tomorrow is finally Friday. Do you have any good plans Ned? If not, Billy and I were going to put together one of my newest paintball drones, 'The Sky Shark.' You're welcome to help."

I squirmed along the ground, fighting to try and make myself as comfortable as I could on the hard cement floor. After slipping between the blankets and tucking myself in, I shifted several times so that my back was only slightly in pain. I'd have to remember the dorm room floor method as a solid form of torture if I ever went back to hell.

"Well," I said through a grimace as I fidgeted, "it's funny that you ask. I'm actually going to check out a nightclub called The Citadel. Have you ever heard of it?" Billy spit out a laugh that was a hybrid of a cough and chuckle. Stevie muted his computer. The two turned and stared at me simultaneously.

"Uh, Ned, how the heck do you plan on getting in there man?" asked Billy with doubt.

"What do you mean?"

"Well, for starters," Billy said throatily, now sitting up from his bed. "It's like a thousand dollars per person, and you need to be on their list. It's where all of the celebrities and hot shots go when they visit Chicago. The only way to get on *that* list is if you're beautiful or famous."

"Hey," I said with a laugh, "I'm good looking." Billy looked to Stevie, who shrugged.

"I mean," Billy shrugged, "yeah, but not that glamorous pretty that they look for. It's hard to describe."

"Well," I cut in, "even if I'm not their type of gorgeous, there's one thing that I have that makes the world go round…money."

"I don't think money will just work for this place," said Billy as he adjusted his pillow. "It's, uh, different."

"Nah, I'm sure it's fine. Money will work on anyone. It's been that way since before Christ."

"How would you know that?" asked Billy.

"Uh, I minor in history. Anyhow, if you two are interested in tagging along, I can pay for admission, as well as purchase some attire that will help get us in. All I need is a way to get us on that list." A wicked smile crept along Billy's face. Rebelling against his robotic nature, Stevie cracked his neck before rubbing his hands together animatedly.

"Leave that to Stevie," Billy gloated.

"No," cried Stevie. "Not me. Leave it to Vyrex."

"Vyrex?" I asked.

"Stevie's hacker name," said Billy.

"Sure," I shrugged. "Whatever it takes, just so long as we get in."

"Vyrex will handle everything," Stevie said confidently. He closed the game window on his computer and opened some odd program with a neon green background. He started typing wildly, and the icon image of the moon face from the 1902 movie, *A Trip to the Moon,* pulled up, only instead of a capsule in its eye, there was a massive keyboard-penis protruding from the socket. Gold lettering appeared above the photo that said, "Vyrex logged in," above it.

"Alright then. So to recap, come tomorrow the three of us will go downtown, pick up some night club apparel, and then, once Vyrex, prince of programs, gets us on the list, head to the Citadel."

"Sweet," said Billy. He noticed marinara sauce on his shirt and wiped it away. "But out of curiosity, why are you so eager to go to this place anyway?"

"There's someone I need to meet," I said casually. "It's a favor for an old friend."

The next day, I woke up to Stevie shouting into his computer headpiece. I must have been more exhausted then I knew because it was already early afternoon. I stood up and started folding up my blankets. Before I could finish, the front door opened, and Billy walked inside with a stack of books in his thick arms.

"Woohoo," he exclaimed, "final class of the week. And just in case anyone was curious, I aced my aeronautics exam."

I had no idea that Billy even had an exam, though

he most likely mentioned it several times. "Sweet," I offered a high five. Billy gave an awkward and uncoordinated slap onto my hand with his clammy palm.

"By the way Ned, how'd you sleep?"

I gave Billy a cross look while rubbing my aching back. It felt as if a CTA bus had hit me full on. I then limped off to the public bathroom located just outside the dormitory door, my satchel loosely hung over my shoulder. The stall was small, but large enough to use the trick that I'd learned from the manual in order to transform my clothes again. I was now wearing black jeans with matching sneakers, and a black hoodie that read, "Another day has passed and not once did I use algebra." Afterwards, I opened the satchel's flap and dug my hand into the dimensional door in order to wake up Simon and Hecubus. I could feel their fur with my fingers and pulled the pair of hellhounds like rabbits from a magician's hat. The two dogs leapt from my hands and onto the bathroom floor. They stretched out before sitting on their back legs, their tails wagging as they looked up at me.

"All right boys," I said, taking a piece of scrap paper and pen from the satchel. "I need you two to find Chelsea and protect her from that pervert I'd warned you about the other night. The idiot's name is Louie and he'll stink of cheap cologne, cigarettes and hair product." The two dogs growled as I scribbled a note on the piece of loose leaf. "I mean it. This is a serious job you two. That means no rampages or murder sprees." Hecubus barked. "Also," I tucked the note I'd written into Simon's collar, "make sure this note gets to Chelsea." The dogs whimpered. "I mean it!" Hecubus barked again and Simon snarled, which I hoped meant that they understood.

With that, I looked for the nearest window. There was a small tempered box of glass just above the stacks of toilet paper along the farthest wall. I went over to it and opened up the metal frame. The song of the city, which was made up of beeping horns and ambulance sirens, flooded into the washroom. Below was a sidewalk, which at the moment was absent of any pedestrians. I grabbed the dogs and held them out over the cityscape. The two pups leapt from my hands like soldiers on a mission, falling twenty stories downward. I could hear a boom and a crack from below, followed by a woman's scream, and then heavy barking. I looked down again and saw that the hellhounds had landed safely. Simon had leapt to his feet and was now growling at a frightened woman in a business suit who must have tried to run to the aid of the pup, while Hecubus carelessly licked one of his paws. They looked quite out of place on the city streets. I gave a quick whistle from above, and the two hellhounds stiffened up before scurrying up the avenue. Once I'd determined that they were on the right path to Lakeview, I shut the window and headed back to Billy's dormitory.

"So," I said as I reentered the room, "did Vyrex get us in tonight?" Billy looked to Stevie, who gave a stiff thumbs up. "Great, so now let's get some tails," Billy raised brow, "or whatever you call nice clothes nowadays."

"I know just the place," said Billy. "Every douchebag in my class who goes clubbing, goes to Saks beforehand. We could go there, pick out some threads, and then there's a cool little restaurant that we can eat at afterwards." Billy looked to Stevie, who was shaking his head, before turning to study me. Either my expression wasn't as neutral as I'd thought, or Billy had a heavy conscience because he immediately followed up. "I mean, if we're hungry cool. If not, no biggy."

We left shortly after, and as we did, I found two large cracks in the sidewalk where the hellhounds had landed. Neither of the guys seemed to notice. Billy was tremendously excited to be outside, like a dog about to get a ride in the car. Stevie on the other hand was quite the opposite. He glared at the sun as if they were mortal enemies, shielding his eyes with his hands as if he were Count Dracula. We strode through the busy downtown area to a nearby clothing store, and after slipping past an army of women spraying perfume on customers, made our way to the men's section of the store on the second floor. A strange short fellow with a pencil mustache and snug three-piece suit introduced himself as Esteban.

"So my friends," Esteban inquired, "tell me more about why you are dressing up?"

"We're planning on going to a nightclub," said Billy.

"*Oh*?" belted Esteban with large eyes.

"We're headed to The Citadel," Stevie blurted.

Esteban whistled. "Well, you must be *very* important people."

"Unfortunately we are," I said with a tired voice, combing my fingers through my hair. "It's a blessing and a curse, but we've learned to live with it."

"Oh my," said Esteban. "This is so exciting for me then."

"*Yeah*, it should be." I retorted. "Now Esteban," I put my arm around a manikin as I continued. "Price is no issue. So do whatever it is that you have to do to make us look like gods."

"It would be my pleasure," said Esteban as he pet Billy's shoulder. Billy's eyes bulged out of his head. "Come. Let Esteban do his magic. When I am done with you, even wired-jaws will drop.

Esteban did indeed work his magic. The guy was the Merlin of fashion. I watched as the strange little man ran from clothing rack to clothing rack like Dr. Frankenstein, frantically grabbing jackets, boots and accessories. One after another, Billy, Stevie and I took our turns in front of the giant three-piece mirror, trying on outfits until our skin chafed. Even if some of the apparel seemed as if it came straight from Siegfried and Roy's wardrobe, I have to admit, for the most part, we looked *damn* good.

It was just about the time when we were rapping things up near the cash register, and Esteban was telling us about the frequent shopper card that would save us a gazillion dollars on our next in store purchase, that I noticed we were being watched by one of the shoppers. A man, or what I thought was a man, stood on the balcony above the cash register, gawking at us. He wasn't discreet by any means, with his odd ensemble and broad pervert smile, yet no one in the store seemed to notice him. He was lean and androgynous with puke green hair wrought like rising flame, cat eyes and painted red lips. He wore a candy cane striped suit coat with matching tie, a gray kilt and high heels. There was a silver cord around his neck clasped to a flickering light bulb. The two of us made eye contact, and as we did, his smirk grew even larger until it all but consumed the lower half of his face. I grimaced, and as I did, he gave a short bow. Then he stepped out of my line of sight. I tried to follow him with my eyes, but he quickly moved along. Though his presence was strange, the fact that I didn't get any hits on my Spidey-senses quickly made him ignorable. Hopefully the guy was just another Chicago weirdo.

After our interesting shopping experience, Billy took us to his favorite restaurant, "Mi Amigo Diarrhea", where he gorged on his beloved platter, *The Burrito Bonanza*. Never in my life had I seen someone eat with such passion. He was like William Holman Hunt, splashing hot sauce and salsa onto his canvas before greedily eating it up. Gluttony was a rare sin during my first term as a corruptor. Only the rich could afford it. Nowadays, judging from the size of things, and more specifically, the size of people, it would be easy to get individuals to commit to the act once I officially became a corruptor again.

Once Billy had his fill, the three of us headed back

to the dorm where the mortals decided to rest. As they napped, I toyed with the phone I'd found in Elsberry's apartment. I went into the settings to see if I could restore any saved numbers, but came up empty. Just as I'd nearly given up, Stevie awoke. He watched as I tapped the buttons, trying to make a fun song with their beeps.

"What are you doing?" he asked, rolling out of bed.

"It's a phone I found. There are no names or numbers on it, and I'm trying to figure out how to return it," I lied.

"Well," said Stevie, "that's not how you do it. However, I *do* have a program that can help track the location of any new callers. Let me know if you receive any calls and I'll hunt down their home address so we can send the phone to them."

"Whoa, you can do that?" I asked. Stevie nodded. "You're remarkable," I said in an unusually high voice.

Stevie humbly shrugged. "I do what I can."

Just then Billy woke up, holding his stomach.

"Oh," he moaned, "too much burrito."

"Buck up amigo," I said encouraging before pulling out my new pair of pants. "The night is young. It's time to get dressed so we can go out and party."

Billy moaned before dragging himself out of bed. He then dove into our ocean of shopping bags and began sorting through them for his clothes. Soon, Stevie joined us, awkwardly hopping around on one foot as he put on his new socks. Before long, the three of us were fully clad and ready to go. Now suited up, it was time to meet with this Collin Dain, and along with my cronies, hopefully scare him out of town.

Chapter Thirteen

We looked like the cast of one of those bad teen dramas, but according to Esteban, what we were wearing made 1970's David Bowie appear boring. I'd been talked into buying dark dress pants, a white dress shirt, and a thin black tie with a form fitting leather jacket and boots. It was a mix between businessman and *Easy Rider*. As for Billy, he was donning a light blue V-neck t-shirt, blue jeans, and a white suit coat. Poor terrified Stevie was dressed in skinny jeans, a pink button-up shirt and a tweed vest with matching tie. Fashion had clearly changed since the nineteenth century, but it didn't stop us from strutting from our taxi. We headed straight to the club doors, bypassing a line of the youngest, most beautiful people in Chicago.

The doorman, a burly meathead with an odd Gaelic tattoo inked across his neck, placed his meaty hand on Steve's chest and pushed him backwards.

"Whoa, little man," he said in a tone that was cockier than a rooster in a henhouse. "Where do you three think you're going? The line starts back there."

Billy lowered his head, embarrassed. I contemplated the consequences of incinerating the big guy in front of a hundred or so witnesses. But Stevie refused to back down. The rail thin young man, nearly twice as small as the doorman, took a composed step forward and pointed his finger in the big man's face.

"Do you know who I am?" he said calmly. The doorman smirked, as if to say, *this should be rich.* "Check your list for reservation 247."

"Ha, we don't have numbered reservations you little twerp," he hooted, looking down at his clipboard. Then, as if a hornet had stung him directly in the softest part of his ass, the doorman's eyes widened. He looked up at Stevie, then back to his clipboard, clearly flabbergasted. "I mean," his voice lightened, "my deepest apologies sir. Of course you're on the list. Please," he said, unclipping the velvet rope behind him, "right this way my friends. Enjoy yourselves tonight."

Stevie's eyes seemed to twinkle as he dusted off imaginary dust from his shoulders. His eyes darted to the doorman, examining the guard with disgust.

"I can only say that we'll try, especially after the welcoming we received. I'm half tempted to have father speak with the owner of this club." The doorman lowered his head like a scolded dog.

"Sir, I'm so sorry about that," the security guard said regrettably. "If we could just forget about this little matter, I'd greatly appreciate it. I sometimes don't think before I open my mouth," he groveled.

"This is your one pass," Stevie warned. "Don't forget it." The guard nodded.

Whatever it was that Stevie had done, it worked. The beefy security guard kept his guilt-ridden gaze far from the moonlighting hacker, focusing instead on the next person in line, and waving them forward. Nonetheless, if there's one thing I learned about being sneaky, it's don't rub it in when you're cheating. It's a great way to get those who you've deceived to start asking questions. So, I pressed my hand upon Stevie's back and pushed him forward into the club.

We entered *The Citadel's* massive wood doors, which were fashioned to appear like a fortress entryway of old, with replica cannons and fake torch sconces posted along the walls. Just in front of us stood the hostess station, where a pair of provocative looking women awaited under an overhead black light. They wore tall white powdered wigs that nearly covered the communication headsets wired to an ear. Each was dressed in a similar corset and miniskirt, with clasped stocking along their thighs that protruded from their leather high boots. Their makeup, which colored their lips and eyes, glowed brightly in the dull light above them. The women batted their lashes and smiled at us as we approached, but Billy didn't seem to notice.

"Who in the Hell did that doorman think we were," he asked in a panic. "Don't tell me we just committed identity theft Stevie. I can't go to jail." Stevie straightened his tie, though his awkward posture and stiff mannerisms made him look more silly than suave.

"Relax," he said in his nasally voice. "No one would be bold enough to question the son of Bill Gates, especially if he's here trying to celebrate his birthday."

"But," Billy protested, "Bill Gates's son is --"

"Don't ruin the moment," I said, pushing the two forward. "Now," I announced in a boisterous voice so that the hostesses could hear. "I have someone important I need to find, so why don't the two of you go out and mingle?" Billy and Stevie's eyes bulged. The two huddled closer to onc another like frightened school children. "I'm sure these fine women here would be more than happy to help you both find ways to enjoy yourselves tonight."

"Uh," said Billy reluctantly, giving a polite smile to the hostesses. "I don't know if you're aware or not Ned, but we aren't the most socially adept individuals."

"Nonsense," I said. I plucked another credit card from my wallet and handed it to one of the hostesses. "Ladies, would one of you please make sure that these gentlemen get the best treatment this place can offer?"

One of the women, perhaps recognizing the unease in Billy and Stevie, went to the pair and pet at their chests in an attempt to calm them. She was a light skinned black woman with beautiful red lips and a set of killer legs.

"Are you sure?" she asked with a snake's grin as

she studied the credit card she pinched her gloved hand. "I have something in mind, but it's very expensive."

"Like what?" I asked in morbid curiosity.

"Bottle service in the V.I.P. area tends to attract all the pretty ladies around here. It's set aside for celebrities' months in advance, but lucky for you, the reservation for tonight cancelled. I'm sure we could arrange something for a few grand."

"Sure," I replied, "Go nuts. Money is no object. In fact, put your next month's rent on the card for each of you ladies as a tip for helping us out. Just make sure these boys have a great time," That said, I firmly slapped Billy and Stevie on their backsides. The two jumped forward, scampering closer to the hostess. The nightclub attendant gave me the slightest wink before taking Billy and Stevie by the hands and guiding them into the busy confines of the main dance floor. I stood near the coat check with the remaining hostess, watching as the guys took baby steps towards the fog fed dance floor with their delicious looking guide.

"Oh kids," I said to the remaining hostess, "they grow up so fast." She had a tattoo similar to the doorman's. Hers was across her naked shoulder, thinner, but similar in shape.

"So," she said curiously, with a delicate, but assertive voice, "I couldn't help but overhear that you were looking for someone important? Could I be of some assistance in finding them?"

"Well aren't you helpful," I complimented. "Yes, I'm actually here to see your boss, Collin Dane. Is he here by chance?" The young woman gave an obnoxiously dry giggle.

"Let me guess, you have a business proposal that will make him millions of dollars?" She didn't let me answer. "We get your kind all the time. He's not interested."

I shrugged. "I *am* here for business, but not the kind that involves money."

"Well Sir." she said with a false sympathy, patting me on the shoulder. "I'm sorry to disappoint you, but Mr. Dane doesn't speak business with people without an appointment."

"Even after my generous tip?"

"Even for those who tip well," she said coldly. "Sorry, it's his rules."

"I'll tell you what," I said with a flare of my nostrils. "Let Collin know that a representative for the Negative-One Union is finally here to speak with him about a proposal. If he still refuses, I'll leave this very minute." The woman gave me a puzzled look before sighing and pressing her finger to her earpiece. A red light flashed on the device as she began to speak.

"Hi sir," she said as she winced, "I'm sorry to bother you, but I have," her eyes wondered in my direction.

"Ned," I jumped in.

"I have a Mr. Ned here with me who's looking to see you. He says he's a representative of the Negative-One Union." She nodded a few times before looking up to a ball shaped camera that I hadn't previously noticed hanging from the ceiling above us. "Yes sir, immediately." Her expression looked surprised as she released her finger from her ear. "Ned," she said in a forced, but pleasant tone, "Mr. Dane would be happy to see you. Please follow me."

The nightlife had definitely had an upgrade since my first term as a corruptor. I followed the hostess through the doors to the main dance floor where scantily clad guests shaped like Greek statues, grinded on each other like animals. Waitresses in glowing body paint poured brightly colored drinks into visitors' mouths as music swam from massive speakers with a heavy but provocative electronic melody. The staff wore similar outfits as my hostess and all of them were stamped with Celtic tattoos. The male employees adorned themselves in white wigs that curtained the sides of their faces and tailored red military coats that were left open to show off their naked chests. The female employees wore high frosty hairpieces and garments that looked more like strips of cloth. Sodom and Gomorrah had nothing on this place.

The hostess guided me towards the back of the house, taking me to an employee door located near one of the bars. With the swipe of a key card, the doors opened, allowing us to enter. The hallway was filled with a white florescent light. It took my eyes a moment to adjust, but as they did, it occurred to me that my seductive beauty wasn't as flawless as she'd appeared in the club's dim fluctuating lights. She had light pockmarks across her cheeks that she had tried to hide with flesh colored makeup, and her nose was slightly crooked. *She was no Chelsea.* We finally reached a heavy steel door painted with a crimson pentagram. She typed a code into a keyboard next to the secure doors, triggering them to open. Inside was an industrial elevator that looked as if it could fit a small automobile. We took the smooth moving cart up, and when the doors opened up again, I was in the warm confines of a brown marble office, nearly twice the size of Chelsea's bookstore.

There was a crackling fire in the background and a massive library posted along the walls. A magnificent collection of old tomes were packed tightly in each shelf. Standing in the center of the office was an expensive looking leather couch, coffee colored, with a zebra hide stretched across the backrest. Near the spine of the room were floor to ceiling windows where a life size marble statue of Ares posed in a sentry position, his spear and shield in hand. As elegant as it all first appeared, I began to notice tacky posters and tawdry memorabilia that conflicted with the Bruce Wayne motif. Framed gold records, signed guitars and manikins with strange performer outfits were scattered throughout the room.

Most disturbing however was the stranger standing near the executive desk. She was grey like smoke, and drifted like it too. Her bleeding eyes flashed red when she saw me, giving me a spasm of pressure in my stomach. She had a mane of dried salt hair, taut skin and a silver dagger that pierced through her left cheek and protruded from out of the right. A crimson ribbon wrapped around her head as if to keep her jaw bound shut. She stared for a moment before floating backwards through the wall. *Damn spirits.*

"Um, Mr. Dain, sir," said the hostess over the faint thumps of base from music below.

"Leave us," commanded a man with a deep, but proper Irish accent from the far side of the room. I could feel a soothing rush bubble in my stomach as the hairs on the back of my neck began to rise. This man was a spooky. Of that I was certain. He sat behind a desk chair, its backrest facing me, blocking any chance of seeing who sat within it. The hostess scampered away into the elevator, hurriedly pressing its button numerous times until the doors finally shut. "Ned," said the voice welcomingly, "that wouldn't happen to be short for Nedonius would it?"

Finally, someone who knew a thing or two about what I really was. Unless you liked *Shakespeare in the Park*, continuously pretending to be someone you're not is exhausting. Luckily, I wouldn't have to hold back with Dain. He was on the level. Was I going to try and intimidate this man into leaving town? *Yes.* Was there a chance that this entire affair would end violently? *Maybe.* But still, I couldn't help but feel as if it was nice to have the opportunity to be frank with someone.

"That's the name Lucifer stitched into my underwear," I said while moving to the leather chair and rubbing at the black-and-white animal hide. The man in the desk chair remained silent for a moment, still facing the large windows that looked outward towards the city skyline.

"Ah the great Nedonius, the corruptor who nearly burned down all of Chicago. It's a pleasure to finally meet you."

"Sorry," I sat forward, further closing the distance between us. "I don't do autographs."

The man snickered. "Might I ask if you know who I am?"

"Let me guess. Bono?"

"No," he said with slight agitation. "I'm far older."

"Oscar Wilde?"

"No," he said more impatiently.

"William Wallace?"

"He wasn't even Irish," the man bit back.

"Alright, I give up."

The chair spun around. Hunkered within its seat was a little person with lengthy silver hair, dressed in a finely tailored grey pinstripe suit. He was squat with strapping arms and a broad chest. He placed his thick fingers on the oak desk, folding them over one another. They were decorated with gold rings.

"Well," he said matter-of-factly, "My name is Collin Dain, son of the great Irish witch, Carman. Congratulations, there are very few people who get the privilege of meeting me."

"Oh, I'm tickled pink," I said with absurdly over the top enthusiasm. Collin gave a short laugh.

"How do you like my nightclub," he asked.

"It's not bad," I complimented. "Definitely a step up from the potions shops and fortune telling booths that you owned last time I was in the city."

"The way to riches is arduous and cutthroat," he said in a cold voice, "but I managed."

I nodded, slipping onto the leather couch that angled towards both his desk and the fireplace. The circulating heat from the hearth made it warm and comforting to sit on. "That's a good one. I'll have to use it on the next corporate CEO I corrupt."

"Ah," Dane said, delighted, "so you plan on staying in Chicago a bit?"

"Well, yeah I hear there's an opening."

"Yes, I heard about your former successor. Too bad."

"Say Collin old boy, you wouldn't know anything about his whereabouts would you?"

"No," he said straight faced, "but then again, Gethin and I never really crossed paths. He was one of those," Dane sighed, "artsy types. I'm a businessman. The two don't mix."

"Uh, sorry Collin," I said hesitantly, staring at a signed photograph of Elvis hanging on the wall, "but you do know what an artist *is* don't you?"

Collin pursed his lips, taking a moment to shake off my insult. "You're referring to the music memorabilia. The parallels between music and business are quite uncanny. A person uses their natural talents in order to make a profit, creating an eternal legacy in the process. Your successor, Gethin, would disagree with that interpretation. Such is why his kind and mine could never work. It's not where he comes from, but what he is -- an expressionist without drive -- that makes him useless to me."

"And what about a former legionnaire?"

Dane grinned. "Now that is something entirely different. Have you ever contemplated having a partner Nedonius? You know, the two of us could work well together."

I laughed so hard that my eyes began to water. Dane waited patiently for me to finish before proceeding.

"Think about it, Nedonius. I own sixty-five Chicago restaurants, thirty-eight bars, and twelve nightclubs here in the Windy City. Not to mention, I possess countless stock on Wall Street. With my influence and your prowess, we can rule Chicago with an iron grip."

"Eh," I said tiredly, picking at my ear with a pinky finger, "power and sway don't really do it for me Dain-ster. I'm a simple creature," I flicked earwax onto his floor. "I like boobies and farts."

"I see," he seethed, pressing his hands down on his desk, the cigar being choked between his index and middle fingers.

"Which brings me to why I'm here."

"Ah," Dane exhaled. "Is it time for that already?" I nodded. "I must admit that at first, I thought to myself, who from the Negative-One Union has the audacity to come into my nightclub and demand an audience with me. But once I found out that it was the angel who accidentally burned down Chicago, or should I say the *devil* that accidentally burned down Chicago," I winced at the D-word, "I was as happy as a clam in high tide. Bravo on your demotion by the way."

"Former demotion," I corrected with my best poker voice. "I'm back baby."

"So," he said, pulling open a drawer and removing a cigar. "Why is it then that a devil who already has a job as a corruptor is in my office trying to negotiate for that fool and coward DuSable?"

"First of all," I said with scorn in my voice, "devil is *really* offensive. It implies a make-believe creature with horns and a pitchfork. We prefer fallen or Forsaken." Dane gave a grin, presumably proud of himself for finally sparking genuine emotion out of me. "And second of all, that *coward* DuSable sent me because it seems that you've been bullying all the spookies in Chicago for decades, and it's about time that someone put a stop to it. So he asked me to make your acquaintance." I shined my teeth with my shirt before smiling wide. "It's closing time Dainster."

Collin leaned his cigar over to a miniature guillotine placed on the corner of his desk and pushed its lever. The blade of the classical execution mechanism snapped down, chopping off the tip of his cigar with a quick whoosh and snap.

"And I suppose there is no negotiating is there?"

"Sorry pal," I leaned back in the sofa, my hands stretched behind my head. "This is an all or nothing offer. I'll give you a few days to leave Chicago or else."

"So, you're here ta' try and shake me down are ya'?" he asked, the polish now waning from his Irish brogue. "You want ta' shake down me, the most powerful warlock in Chicago?"

I stood up, opened my arms and gave a short bow before winking at him. "There's a new sheriff in town Danny Boy." Collin lit the end of his cigar and began puffing at it. "Come on Collin, we're getting off on the wrong foot. Look, you've had a good run," I said sympathetically. "Think of what you've done for the city. It's nearly two hundred years you've managed to make the Irish population a formidable force in Chicago. You've turned a community of rovers into something respectable. You've worked hard for that. Now it's about time you took a step back and had yourself a little vacation. Why not try Boston or Philadelphia?"

"If you're implying that I go bugger off to one of my brothers then you're mad," he said as he pounded on the desk. "One is a transgender lunatic and the other has no respect for business. On that note, if you think I'm going to take your pathetic offer, you're mistaken ya' damnable devil." His words struck me in the gut. I mean, come on and cut me some slack. I don't like to toot my own horn, but I do hone the powers of hell. All he had to do was show me a little bit of freaking respect and *not* call me devil. But here he was, all four-foot of him, insulting me like he was. Lava began to pulse through my veins. *Daddy was angry.*

"Oh Collin old boy," I said through my teeth as I cracked my neck. "I'm going to reiterate what I said before.

This isn't an offer."

Collin took another large puff of his cigar, and then without warning, blew an unnaturally large whirlwind of smoke in my direction. The cloud of gray quickly swirled several feet before reaching me. The force of the magical smoke took me by surprise, sending me backwards into a bookshelf. I was blind from smoldering ash that was now somehow pinning me down. I bent my legs so that both feet were firmly pressed against the bookshelf, and then with a furious push, kicked myself to the side of the smoke's swirling mass. I rolled on the ground and found that Collin had stopped blowing the remnants from his cigar, and removed a wicked looking knife from his desk. He raised the curved blade and cut open his palm before smearing a circle of blood on his desk.

"*Saighdear foirfe!*" he screamed. The bloody ring lit up with a golden charge of energy. Seven ethereal stags shrouded in spiraling electricity came speeding out of the loop, buzzing with power as they came to life. "Attack my friends."

The creatures lowered their heads and began stampeding in my direction. The lead buck crashed into me, sending paralyzing volts throughout my body. I could smell my hair burning as the beast evaporated into nothing. Moments later, a second buck smashed into me, sweeping me off my feet. I pulsated uncontrollably. But before the third could trample me with its electrical hooves, I glanced at the dancing flame in the fireplace and focused all of my anger. Nearly a dozen tendrils of fire stretched out like octopus tentacles from the hearth and pounded into the bucks. Small bolts of lightning showered throughout the room as the creatures dissipated, destroying bookshelves and furniture.

Collin began to recite more incantations, waving his fingers. His gigantic oak desk lifted into the air, hovering above him. Pointing in my direction, Collin screamed and the furniture came soaring towards me. *Now I was getting really upset.* I swung my skinny fist at the table's center of mass, smashing it into hundreds of wooden pieces. Collin's eyes grew wide. I raced towards him with an inextinguishable rage, leaping across the room and pouncing on top of him. I heard several bones crack and a whimper from the warlock as we collided. The two of us fell to the ground, me on top, causing spit to erupt from Collin's mouth. I could tell from his dazed expression that the warlock was stunned, and probably seeing double. I went to my feet, pulling him up with me by his collar, and raised him towards the ceiling. I balled my fist, and raised it, ready to strike.

"Are you going to leave town?" I barked. Collin shielded his face with his hands.

"Yes, yes," he said with blood stained teeth. "Please fella', just let me live."

"And will that be the last I hear of you?"

"Yes," he moaned, "I swear on my dead old mother. I surrender."

I let the warlock go, dropping him to the ground. He fell with a thump, and then rolled over to one side, cradling his ribs. His office was now in shambles, small fires and scorch marks littering the entire room. It felt good to let go, especially with a prick like Collin, but I'd need to wind down if I didn't want to murder any innocent bystanders downstairs on my way out.

"You have one week Collin," I said viciously. "If I see you in this town again, you're done for."

Collin continued to twitch in pain. I walked towards the elevator and pressed the button next to it. The steel doors opened and I walked inside. Once I'd made it to the ground level, I went to the dance floor. Crowds of oblivious guests mingled amongst each other, unaware of the supernatural battle that had just taken place above their heads. I searched for Billy and Stevie, but couldn't seem to find them. Finally, as I squeezed my way between the barely legal public orgy, and heavily inebriated dance-zombies, I heard my name being called.

"Ned!" Billy hollered from a moon shaped booth tucked in the corner. Steve and Billy were sitting behind a table full of liquor, surrounded by young and beautiful women. I couldn't believe my eyes. "Ned," Billy shouted, "come on man, join the fun." I walked over to them, and nodded to the group. Most of the young women were barely two decades old, and wearing attire that looked more like lingerie.

"Looks like you're having a good time," I said, staring at bottles of champagne.

"I'm sorry," said Billy, half ashamed. "We used your card again."

"No," I protested, "I told you to. I want you to have fun. Enjoy yourselves." The girls giggled as one of them poured a bit of bubbly down Billy's mouth.

"What happened to your hair?" asked Stevie. I looked up and felt at the top of my head. My hair felt singed, and was standing like tall grass.

"Ah, that," I said, patting my mane down, my heart still moving a hundred-miles-an-hour. "I tried something new. Do you like it?" Billy snickered. There was a short pause. I could tell that I was killing their fun. "Well guys, my business is done here. I'm going to call it an early night. You two enjoy yourselves though."

"Wait, are you sure?" asked Billy between a hiccup as a young woman in a red dress hopped on his lap. "We went through so much effort to get here, and now you're just going to go?"

"I came here to check up on some things for a friend," I tried to pat down my hair again. "But it appears that they don't have to worry any longer. This place is going to be under new management soon." Billy and Stevie looked at each other and shrugged.

"Well, alright then Ned," slurred Billy with dizzy eyes. "Thanks for showing us a great time. We'll see you tomorrow I guess."

I gave a small salute before starting to walk away. "Of course. Goodnight everyone."

The streets of Chicago were loud and surging with life when I stepped out of the club. There was still a long line of fools who were overly excited to waste their money at Collin's stupid club. I shook my head and started making my way north, walking beneath the street's canopy of neon signs. I was still wired from the fight, a side effect of having to hone your anger in order to stimulate your talents. I needed to walk a little in order to calm myself down.

I strolled out of downtown, through Lincoln Park and towards Lake View. It was a long walk, at least an hour, but I was up for it. While trotting along the Lincoln Park Zoo, a sudden buzzing vibration started tickling at my leg. It was the phone I'd found in Thomas Elsberry's apartment. I pulled the phone out and looked at the screen. The tiny monitor flashed with the words *Blocked Caller*. I pushed on the answer button and pressed the phone up to my ear.

"Hello?" I greeted curiously.

"Ned," said a soft male voice. Obviously, someone knew who had this phone.

"The one and only," I answered.

"Please stop looking for me," the voice demanded.

"Gethin?" The phone went silent for a moment.

"You won't find me, so please just leave me alone."

"Gethin damn you," I scolded, "I don't want to find you, but it's kind of my job. You're a corruptor. We need you back."

"You can be the Corruptor of Chicago again. Please, just leave me alone." His voice was shaky.

"Gethin, just tell me where you are? Armen needs

you back and Michael is in Chicago looking for me, so I need--" Gethin hung up. "Shit!" I hollered.

So it looked like Gethin was alive and well. If that were the case, then he'd most likely turned his back on hell. But why? I had to admit that I was slightly relieved that Gethin no longer wanted to be Chicago's corruptor, but it was still bad news. Hell would most definitely order his destruction. I needed to find out why the former corruptor had gone into hiding before returning to Armen with my report. I needed to understand if Gethin was being forced to betray us or if there was something else entirely. Besides, if I went all the way back to Hell with nothing more than a measly phone call as my proof Armen would castrate me for sure. Not to mention that I wasn't ready to go back yet.

I wanted to see Chelsea and figure out where she and I were going. It was the first time in what felt like forever that I had hope in me again. Don't get me wrong. I was no dummy. I saw the big picture. I knew that after I confessed that I'm a minion of hell, things would be a little awkward. There's always a period of adjustment. But that's what I love about Chelsea. She's very open-minded. I thought once the initial period of adjustment passed, she might be interested in hell. Heck, maybe she'd even be willing to come back with me.

Chelsea's store would have been closed, so I made my way to her apartment. It was almost midnight and my nerves were feeling much better. I arrived at her complex and could see that Chelsea's lights were still on. I gave my special whistle for Simon and Hecubus to see if they'd done as I'd ordered. The two hounds' faces popped up from Chelsea's apartment window. Simon, spotting me first, pushed at the screen covering the windowsill. The netted divider violently flew off into the street, creating a crash of tin on the hard gravel.

"Damn it Simon," I said as I picked up the screen. Shadow began to stir from Chelsea's apartment, and soon, my beautiful tattooed maiden was looking out from the window like a dark princess of old.

"Ned," she called out, looking at her window screen that was now in my hands. "What are you doing here so late, and why are you dressed like Don Johnson?"

"Hey Chelsea," I said, my voice cracking. "I um, was just taking a midnight walk and found this screen lying here. It looks like it might be yours. What are the odds, huh?" Chelsea gave her patented eye roll, though a small smile inched across her face.

"Come on up and get your dogs," she said, "I'll buzz you in. And bring the screen with you."

I scurried towards the building's main doors with screen in hand. Hurrying inside, I was hit by the smells of stale carpet and ethnic cooking. I made my way up to Chelsea's floor, transforming my speedy sprint into a dapper looking strut as I made it closer to her unit. Chelsea was waiting at her open apartment door with Simon and Hecubus at her ankles. Her hair was up in bobby pins, showing the sweet curvature of her neck. She was wearing a loose Metallica t-shirt and a pair of loose pajama bottoms decorated with skull heads. She looked amazing even in pajamas.

"Oh hello," I said with a shark toothed grin. "You look lovely."

"Ned, I don't know what you're up to, but that smile tells me it's no good."

"What? I was in the neighborhood?"

"And the dogs yesterday with their letter?"

"Hey, these dogs have a mind of their own. I can't help it if they want to scribe adorable love letters for you."

Chelsea tried to hide her smile and lightly slapped me on the arm. "Come in," she said.

Her place was how I remembered it from a couple of days ago, only now it had more life to it. Her television was playing the original silver screen version of *The Wolf*

Man, there were maroon candles flickering on her front room table, and the smell of vanilla permeated throughout her flat. She had a large red book resting face down on her couch with gold lettering. The language was unrecognizable.

"Looks like you're doing a little light reading. Is that some form or Aramaic?" I asked as she shut the door.

"It's Elvish," she replied. I responded with a blank expression. "You know, Tolkien?" I had no idea who she was talking about. "Oh dear God Ned, please tell me you know what Lord of the Rings is?"

"Oh, like the movies?" I asked innocently.

"Are you kidding me? You've never read Tolkien? You purchase rare gypsy summoning codices, but know nothing about nerd lore?"

"I had a sheltered upbringing."

"Cult?" she asked jokingly.

"The cult of all cults," I said bluntly.

"Yikes," she said sympathetically. "Tough gig."

"Eh, it wasn't so bad."

She invited me to sit while she removed a hot kettle for tea from off the stove. Although I was a coffee guy, she insisted that I join her for some green tea, apparently a favorite of hers since she was a little girl. *How could I say no?* As I'd come to find out, Chelsea was a bit of a night owl. She explained to me that she was just prepping up for an all-nighter with her newest book before I showed up unexpectedly. I tried bluffing, and apologized for my intrusion, insisting that I come back on another day, but Chelsea demanded that I stay.

For the next few hours, the two of us just sat and talked about whatever our hearts desired. We had a long conversation about some of the rare books in her store that I was familiar with, and I gave my opinion on how conventional magic has changed over the centuries. There was no reason to tell her how I knew, and she didn't care to ask. She mentioned that she hadn't seen Joliet since that bizarre night in the car, though she had a feeling that he was still out there. I hated the fact that I knew she was right.

Later, she tried reading me some Elvish, and explained to me the difference between *real* Tolkien-fans and posers. Apparently, I was a poser. I kept my words simple and short, as I mostly was enjoying just hearing about her interests and history. I told her about my new roommates Billy and Stevie, and joked about how the two were probably up to their ears in debauchery at the moment. I told a white little lie about being an art student, and dodged questions about where I was from, feeding her just enough to not start becoming suspicious. Our conversation was light, playful, and pleasant.

For some reason, maybe it was out of boredom or isolation, Chelsea wasn't as reserved as she usually could be. Her snarky comments and eye rolling were kept at a minimum, and I almost felt as if she generally enjoyed talking to me. She had lowered her guard, something that I wasn't used to. Most people I encounter either wanted something particular from me, or wanted nothing to do with me. Chelsea wanted neither. It felt good to have someone open up to me. I felt as if she'd gifted me with her trust, something that I'm sure most people rarely saw from the grumpy bookstore owner.

Nevertheless, night would come and go, and before I knew it, sunlight crept into the apartment. Chelsea yawned and stared at me with her gorgeous, but worn, eyes.

"Well Ned," she said as she stretched, "Tomorrow is Sunday. I have to open the store before noon. I think we'd better call it a night."

"Well, I mean, you do own the place. Take a sick day."

"Ha, I wish. I get most of my sales on Sundays. Besides, I'm sure you have plenty of studying to do."

"Yeah, you're right. I should head out." I stood up, combing my hand through my shaggy hair and started to make my way to the door. But before I could take a step forward, Chelsea grabbed my hand.

"*Stay*," she invited, curling her soft fingers along my palm. My heart began to pound and my stomach began to tickle.

"Yeah? I mean, are you sure?"

"Not like that Ned. I mean, no funny stuff," she said as she released my hand, "but, yeah."

"Oh," I said hesitantly, "Okay."

Chelsea stood up and took me to her room. She grabbed a few extra pillows from her closet and threw them at my head playfully before tossing them on the bed. The fight with Dane had drained me a bit, so I wasn't overly driven to try anything slick this time around. Still, I was in unchartered territory, and decided to feel out the situation.

"You get the wall side," she said. "So hop in." I removed my shoes and jumped onto the mattress, scooting until I was against the cool wall. Chelsea threw some blankets over me, and then slipped in under them. I froze, waiting for a sign as to what I should do. Chelsea turned off the light on her nightstand and rolled over onto her back.

"Goodnight Ned," she said as she made herself comfortable. But amazingly, instead of shutting her eyes and falling asleep, Chelsea moved over to me and rested her head on my chest. Her body was cold, but soft. "Whoa Ned, you're burning up."

"Sorry," I apologized, "but you're dealing with hot stuff here." Chelsea laughed before nestling her ear along my clavicle.

"Hey Ned."

"Yes?" The room went quiet for a moment.

"I'm about to be sincere for a second, so prepare yourself."

"Roger, preparing for impact."

Chelsea nudged me with her elbow. "No seriously. I just wanted to say that I wasn't lying when I told you that I like you. I know you're trying to be cool and mysterious, but I see right through you mister. I know you're not as much of a bad boy as you like to pretend."

"Thanks," I said with reluctant gratitude.

In all my days as a Fallen, never was there a time that I thought I'd be content with just lying next to a woman without, well…sex. At the moment though, just being next to Chelsea was perfect. Maybe I was like the tin man and had a heart after all. Maybe, even though I was considered one of the vilest types of creatures in the universe, there was still something left in me from when I used to be called an *angel*. Whatever the reason, all that I knew was that I was happy. So, it goes without saying that when Chelsea kissed me with her soft pillow lips and caressed me with her sweet gentle arms before falling asleep in my embrace, I had a new outlook on things. This girl was my heart's only desire, and I'd do anything, even defy the dark lord himself, in order to protect her.

Chapter Fourteen

A shriek came from outside the room, and I could smell the fresh aroma of smoldering meat. I leapt out of bed and into Chelsea's living area only to find her in the kitchen cooking bacon in a frying pan and dancing to the vocal solo of Dio. Simon and Hecubus were on the counter, staring at the sizzling strips of savory deliciousness.

"Good morning Ned," Chelsea greeted while poking at the cooking pork with a spatula. She was fully dressed for work, wearing a tight white AC/DC t-shirt, snug blue jeans and tall brown riding boots with buckles. Her hair flowed down and she had a tiny sparkling diamond stud protruding from her nose. I could smell her lovely vanilla scented perfume from where I stood. "There's coffee on if you want some. Breakfast should be ready shortly."

"Um…wow," I said, staring at the table covered with fruit and toast. Chelsea snickered and focused on the bacon. "I'm going to wash up really quick if you don't mind."

"Knock yourself out. There's an extra toothbrush in the bathroom that I haven't opened yet. Have at it."

I shuffled into the bathroom and took a look at myself. A skinny punk with shaggy hair and tattoos stared back at me. He wasn't unattractive by any means, with his narrow face and chiseled cheekbones, but he certainly wasn't Nedonius. It made me wonder what Chelsea would really think if she ever saw the true me. I turned on the tap so that I could splash water on my face, and as I did, a loud slurping noise poured from the faucet. Suddenly, a large jet of water shaped like a snake slithered upwards through the air. It hovered over me for a second before forming into Catherine O'Leary.

"Nedonius," she wailed with a hopeless and haunting cry.

"Shh," I hushed, putting my finger to my lips, "quiet it down you old bat. There's a mortal outside these doors." O'Leary frowned.

"Is this better?" she whispered.

"Much. What are you doing here?"

"You told me to find you if I have any news about Gethin."

"And?"

"Alas, he is *alive!*" she exclaimed boisterously.

"What did I just say?" I hissed as I listened at the door for Chelsea. Luckily, *Holy Diver* had just broken into the guitar solo part of the song, muffling O'Leary's voice.

"Apologies," she sighed in a low tone.

"Besides, I already knew that. He called me from the phone that I found in Thomas's apartment and told me to leave him alone. The nut bag has intentionally disappeared."

"Well Nedonius, according to one of my sources, a sweet young werewolf in Humble Park, Gethin is quite the enchanter himself, and was selling his services on the side."

"What type of services?" I asked before smothering my toothbrush in dental paste.

"Apparently, Gethin is a talented Evoker."

"A what?" I said through toothpaste foam as I scrubbed my teeth.

"One who revels in raw magic in order to produce new, unimaginable creations." I raised one of my brows. "In layman's terms Nedonius, if he has the appropriate resources, your friend can create minions for those willing to pay."

"I already knew that too. But why the heck would Gethin need money?"

"Not money Nedonius. Your hellish friend was looking for favors."

"What kind of favors?"

"Apparently those in which would hide him from the prying eyes of hell."

"So, he found a buyer then?"

"It would appear so."

"Is there any chance that you found out *where* he's hiding?"

"That," she said sadly, "I do not know. I did put out an alert with the other ghosts of Chicago, but to no avail."

"Bah, what good are you then?" O'Leary's dripping face frowned.

"Nedonius, I do not think you understand what I am trying to convey. I am a great and powerful spirit. I can find most anyone in Chicago. That is unless they're being concealed with powerful magic. And as you may or not know, there are very few spookies in Chicago that have such power."

"Collin, that bastard!" I hollered, spitting flecks of toothpaste.

"Ned, are you calling me?" Chelsea called out.

"No," I shouted back, "just singing to Dio." O'Leary gave a disapproving shake of her head.

"I too suspect that the warlock may be behind this masquerade," whispered O'Leary. "Though he has many wards cast on all of his properties. Ones that make it difficult for a spirit to enter."

"Well," I said after spitting out the last of the toothpaste, "I gave Collin a week to organize before hitting the road. Once he leaves the confines of his warded establishments, Gethin will most likely have to surface."

"One would presume," Catherine said, dripping over the sink.

"Alright Catherine," I said with a nod, "you did well. Unless you have anything to add, you can go now.

Keep me updated if anything develops and thank you for your valuable service." Mrs. O'Leary gave a look of surprise at my compliment.

"Of course," she said with a raised chin "I shall notify you if anything new comes about." With that, Mrs. O'Leary's form distorted again and swirled into a vine of water. The liquid swam back into the sink and squeezed up its faucet.

I wiped my face with a towel and then went to the kitchen to find a plate of steaming bacon and eggs waiting at the table beside a mug of black coffee. Chelsea gave me a smile.

"It's been forever since I cooked for someone," she said while pulling out a chair. "Forgive me if it sucks."

"Trust me," I said, making my way to her and petting her arm. "I guarantee it beats what they eat at Billy and Stevie's place."

Chelsea smiled, "Well then, sit down and dig in."

I boldly put my arms around her waist, pulling her in for a kiss. She jokingly resisted for a second before giving a shy smile and leaning in to softly kiss me. *Oh those lips*. After a minute she drew away and stared at me.

"Eat," she ordered as she pat me on the chest. "Or you'll be a skinny little hooligan forever."

"I wasn't always this skinny," I said.

"Sure Ned," she laughed as she wiped bacon grease from the stove's surface. I sat in the chair and scooped up a big forkful of eggs, serving it into my mouth. The cheese and avocado smashed between were a delight.

"You keep feeding me like this and I'll get fat on you very quickly."

"Ha, I can't imagine you big."

Oh, if only you knew.

I finished eating and soon collected the hellhounds. The three of us walked Chelsea to work. Chelsea and I made plans to see each other that night once she closed up shop. After I'd dropped her off, I used a nearby public restroom to transform out of the nightclub clothing. Now in dark blue jeans, sneakers, and a black hoodie with the Misfits skull across the chest, I hailed for a cab and took it back to Citadel.

The nightclub was locked up, with no signs of life. I tested the doors, but everything was secure. With mortals scurrying all over the busy streets, there was little to be done. I wouldn't be able to break it without catching someone's attention, which would lead to policemen, then harming mortals, until finally gaining the attention of Michael. Since I didn't want to get slain, I decided against breaking in, and instead resolved to wait out the week I'd given Collin.

While I waited, I thought that perhaps Stevie might still be able to take a look at the phone I'd found at Thomas's apartment. Maybe the great hacker would be able to track Gethin through the phone I'd recovered, or at the least, tell me a bit more about the owner. After a half-mile hike through the city, I made it to the dorm. I knocked on Billy's door, waited for a moment, and then tried the doorknob. The door opened, and the pungent smell of stale liquor and sweat permeated from the room. Billy and Stevie were both still in their nightclub attire, sprawled across their beds and snoring. There was lipstick on Billy's cheek, and a piece of paper with a phone number on his nightstand. Stevie was snuggling with a champagne bottle as large as his upper torso, cradling the glass container like a teddy bear, a gleeful smile spread across his face.

"Rise my minions," I called out. Stevie hopped up from bed, his giant bottle rolling on the ground. Billy cracked open a single bloodshot eye, blinking and staring at me before producing the sound that a cow might make when being branded. "Come on boys," I persisted, "lot's to do."

"Ned, I appreciate everything you've done for us so

far," said Billy calmly, "that's why I'm going to give you ten seconds to get out of the room before I scratch your eyes out."

"I'm glad to see you too," I chuckled. "Now seriously, I need you both to wake up. I have something for you to take care of."

"It's Sunday," Stevie whimpered in his nasally voice, "I have a castle war to fight in an hour."

"I'll tell you what," I said, pulling the blinds up, letting the sun pour in. The pair squealed in pain. "I'll scrounge up some breakfast, and won't give you any shit about the ungodly amounts of charges you put on my credit card last night, so long as the two of you get your butts up and help me. Stevie, I need you to trace a call for me." I threw the phone I'd found at Thomas's place on Steve's bed. His hand crawled like a spider, cradling the device and playing with its buttons. "The owner of this phone tried to call me last night, but we were disconnected before we could exchange information. I'd call them back, but the number is blocked."

Stevie opened his mouth to speak but, after grabbing his head in pain, simply nodded.

"Good boy," I said to him.

"And what do you need me to do?" asked Billy hesitantly.

"Oh Billy, your job is the most important of all. I need you to use your fancy computer," I said, pointing to the monitor on his desk, "and find out everything you can about Thomas Elsberry."

"Who?"

"He's a local artist in the area that I need to get a hold of. Find out anything you can about ex-girlfriends, his parents, or anything else that might help me find where he could be hiding."

"Uh, Ned, this is really weird. Are you a cop or something?" Billy made his way out of bed, shuffling afterwards to collect a bottle of water from his pantry.

"Yeah right," I laughed, "cops aren't this cool."
Billy tilted his head and gulped from a plastic water
container as if it was a baby's bottle. "Billy, I can't explain
now, but do this for me and I won't take away the Platinum
card just yet." Billy nodded, finished off the last of his
water, then lumbered to his computer and started it up.
"Perfect," I said as Billy stared at the loading screen across
his monitor. "I'll go get you two some food."

The minions needed breakfast, but with it being the
afternoon, I had no idea where to get it. I left the dorm
building and headed to the closest convenience store. After
searching for something suitable to eat, I gave up and
instead bought two frozen breakfast burritos. I heated up
the disgusting looking stuffed tortillas in the store's
microwave, paid the cashier, and headed back to the
dormitory. Steve and Billy were tapping away at their
keyboards when I returned, a symphony of clicks
resonating from their fingers. Billy turned to me with a
puzzled look.

"Um, Ned, I'm confused. I looked into everything
you were talking about and none of it makes sense."

"Do tell." I handed each of them a hot burrito. Billy
eagerly bit into his Mexican breakfast, eggs rolling off of
his lips and onto his chest.

"Well," he took a break from his burrito in order to
suck in cool air for his mouth, "Thomas Elsberry appears to
be an orphan. He doesn't have any family. He stayed at St.
Viator's Home for Boys and Girls, but was released by the
state when he turned eighteen, just before the orphanage
was shut down due to lack of funding." Billy took another
gooey bite of his breakfast before continuing with half a
mouthful. "Secondly, the guy doesn't seem to have any real
records besides the electronic lease he signed for a place up
north in the Sauganash neighborhood."

"Alright, that's strike two," I said while looking at

the hot bikini babe screen saver on Billy's computer.

"Strike three," Billy tapped the mouse and brought up a picture of Thomas that I'd never seen before. Thomas' skinny frame and blonde hair matched the photograph I'd found in his apartment. "Is that Thomas doesn't have any ex-girlfriends. Thomas Elsberry is an artist who gets his inspiration from the animosity he feels from society for being openly gay."

"I don't suppose you mean happy?"

"Grow up Ned," Billy challenged. "I think he's very happy about being gay."

"Ah, I see what you did with your words there," I complimented. "Besides, I could give two shits about someone's sexual preference. Where I come from, gender never gets in the way of good sex. What about a boyfriend then?"

"I tried searching all of the social media sites, but he's a pretty quiet dude. He doesn't have a Facebook, Twitter or Snapchat account, and his e-mail profile is as bland as it comes. The only thing that I came across that had any real significance was this article," he pulled up a web link from the Chicago Tribune. "It's not much, but let me know what you make of it?"

Billy hopped from his seat and let me sit down. The chair seat was warm from Billy's big ass. The article was short and basic, describing the early success that the artist, Thomas Elsberry had with his latest works, as well as the inspiration he drew upon from those who are prejudiced to his sexuality. *You mean the inspiration that Gethin bequeathed to you.* I scrolled through more of the web page before returning to the photograph at the top of the article. It was Thomas at his art exhibition, a flute of champagne in his hand. He was frozen in time, explaining a piece of art hanging on the wall behind him to some of the attendees. The older man I'd seen in the photo at Elsberry's apartment was in the background. He still had short brown hair, but now wore black-framed glasses with colored lenses that seemed more fashionable than functional. His trim beard came to a point and the studs in both ears were now glistening with diamonds. He was wearing a custom tailored slate suit and an expensive looking watch. He was looking at Thomas from afar, and seemed to have a small grin curling from the sides of his lips.

"Who is that guy in the background?" I mumbled to myself. Then it hit me. "Wait, that's him!" I shouted, standing up from the rolling desk chair. Billy licked the grease from his fingers, lazily staring at me as I examined the photo.

"That's who Ned? All I see is a middle-aged-"

"That's the man I've been looking for."

"Uh Ned, I thought you were looking for Thomas."

"Hey guys," Stevie butted in, "I got it." I gave him a quick glance to see what he meant. Flashing on his computer monitor was a map of the city from a bird's-eye view. "Ned, I traced the call."

"That's a good boy," I said as I looked over his shoulder. A red circle flashed over one of the buildings on the map. The place felt familiar.

"Ned, you're not going to believe this," Stevie snorted as he zoomed in on the building with the click of his mouse. "That call came from Citadel. We were probably rubbing elbows with your caller last night."

"Damn it I was right," I growled.

"Say," said Stevie, "this doesn't have anything to do with why you wanted to go to the club last night in the first place does it?"

"Yeah," said Billy, picking up a propeller from one of his drones and fondling it. "What gives man? You've been acting really strange."

"You got me," I confessed. "If I tell you what I've been up to, you both have to promise me that you won't tell a soul."

Billy and Stevie both stared at me with concern.

"Of course," said Billy. "Is everything okay man?"

I couldn't tell the guys the truth. Confessing that you're a servant of Hell who is looking for another one of your kin doesn't quite work on the surface. But I was desperate for their help; especially after realizing that it took me this long just to figure out whom Thomas's .dad was in the first place. The older man in all of the photographs wasn't family at all. It was Gethin, Thomas's agent, and more importantly, soul corrupting representative. Being a strange man in a strange land never works in the movies. I'd need Billy and Stevie to help get more answers, even if it meant deceiving them. I mean come on, what's the harm in a little white lie?

"Guys," I said in a sad voice, "It pains me to have to tell you both this, but the man I'm looking for…is my dad." Billy gasped like he'd been watching a Spanish Soap Opera, which was funny because at any moment I expected to hear the dramatic organ keys grind in the background. Stevie stared at me blankly, sipping from the contents of an old can of soda. "You see, my dad walked out on me and my mom when I was just a kid," I lied. "Ever since then, I've been trying to track him down."

"Whoa," said Billy. "Man, I'm sorry."

"It's not your fault Billy," I said solemnly. "Anyhow, I finally tracked him down, and discovered that he was a manager at The Citadel. Unfortunately, I wasn't able to find him there yesterday."

"That bastard," snarled Billy.

"Yeah, what a dipshit," added Stevie. "Is there anything we can do to help?"

"Well," I sighed, "That's what I'm getting at. Do you see the middle-aged man in background of this art exhibition photograph?" Billy and Stevie examined the photograph again. "That's my father. According to staff that I spoke with, he lives on the property with his boyfriend Thomas Elsberry, but the pair rarely comes out. He must be a workaholic or something. All I want is a chance to ask him why he left, but it seems that he may intentionally be hiding from his past. At this rate, I'll never see him again."

"Wait," said Billy. "I have an idea."

"What's that?" I asked with a fake frown.

"What if I set up a few of my surveillance drones around the place?"

"Yeah," added Stevie in an excited tone. Or, what some might consider a bored tone if they didn't know Stevie. "And I hack into nearby traffic cameras. Together, we could keep an eye on the nightclub until your dad finally leaves the place. We can have the place on lockdown, and call you right away if your dad or Thomas ever leave the place." *Now we're talking- technology and allies to the rescue.*

"You guys would do that for me?

"What are friends for?" said Billy, and with that, I immediately felt guilty. I'd lied to a lot of people in my lifetime, but it never really bothered me. Maybe it was because I was usually elbow deep in thieves, killers and lawyers. Now though, I was lying to good people. Nonetheless, it had to be done, and with Billy and Stevie's assistance, I might just be able to find Gethin after all.

"You guys are the best," I praised. And with that, as guilty as I felt, I was hopefully one step closer to finding my predecessor.

Chapter Fifteen

Maybe it was a mistake to give Collin an entire week to evacuate. With the amount of property he owned, I thought seven days was a respectable amount of time for the warlock to try tying up any loose ends before hitting the road. But now that I knew Gethin was inside with him, a week seemed far too long. Nevertheless, if I wanted to pay back my favor to DuSable for saving me form Michael, I'd just have to wait. Pressing further might cause the warlock to go from a state of defeat to insult, and possibly cause him to change his mind about leaving. Besides, I had Billy and Stevie pulling surveillance on the place. If Gethin reared his ugly head, they would call me so that I could swing into action like Spiderman, and capture the bad guy before he could get away. One way or another, Gethin's days were numbered.

I imagined that Gethin was shaking in his boots if he'd learned that I'd evicted Dain. Collin's wards might protect the former corruptor at the moment, but they wouldn't keep Gethin safe once the warlock left. And with Collin being as survival of the fittest *Charles Darwin* about things as he was, I couldn't see him taking the risk of bringing Gethin with him, especially after our little scuffle. Just in case though, I spent any free time that I had stalking the alleys nearby, watching from afar. And when I wasn't there, you bet your ass that Catherine O'Leary was. Between the eyes of Billy, Stevie, O'Leary and myself, nothing could get by.

With time to kill, I thought what better opportunity to be with Chelsea. For the following few days, I did everything in my power to juggle my schedule between stalking The Citadel and hanging out with the girl. So that I didn't miss the chance of confronting Gethin, I tried making as many arrangements as I could in the downtown area. I sent dozens of taxis to pick Chelsea up at the bookstore so that the two of us could enjoy picnics at Grant Park and dinner by the Lake. I even once arranged for another midnight visit to the underground pond where we had our first date. Chelsea didn't seem to mind traveling back and forth, confessing during one of our dates that although she never finished school herself, she knew how demanding a student's schedule could be. Who was I to argue with her assumptions? Besides, it gave me a chance to put my mind at ease while enjoying her company. Every time we were together seemed to be better than the last, and as our relationship blossomed, I realized that I felt more like myself than I ever had before.

But on one of our dates later in the week, just as Chelsea and I had finished having lunch near the Chicago Art Museum, Billy tried reaching me by calling Thomas's cellphone.

"Ned," he said in a panic.

"Billy, what's up man?" I asked as I chewed on a chicken salad sandwich Chelsea had hand made for me. Chelsea gave me my distance, taking a moment with Simon and Hecubus in order to admire the massive bronze lions positioned along the museum's steps.

"Hey, I'm at my dorm with Stevie. You have to get here right away."

"Why what's up?" I said in a calm voice, trying not to alarm Chelsea.

"It looks like someone is moving out of The Citadel. The staff is packing tons of boxes into cars parked in the club's back alley."

"Is *he* there?" I said nonchalantly. Chelsea didn't seem to notice. "Should I go?"

"Yeah, he's there," said Billy. "But you're going to

need to look at this before you head off to confront your old man. Trust me, you'll have to see it to believe it."

"Alright, I'm just a few blocks away. Give me five minutes."

I hung up Thomas's phone and gave Chelsea an innocent smile.

"All well?" she asked while petting under Simon's head. The demon-dog's leg twitched from excitement.

"Yeah, Billy's dad came to visit him unexpectedly, and he needs my help stashing some unmentionables."

"Ah," said Chelsea, standing up from the museum's steps. "Don't worry, I've had to stash porn and drugs for my friends too."

"Aw," I said sincerely, giving her a peck on the cheek, "You're such a good friend." I looked down at Hecubus, who was licking his chops while staring at a policeman's patrol horse. "Hey, mind if I take the pups with me for the night?"

"Wow," she said while handing me Simon, "custody battles already?"

"Don't hate," I said while scooping up Hecubus. "I'd make a great weekend father." Chelsea laughed.

After throwing the hellhounds in my satchel, I waved down a cab, paying the driver ahead of time in order to get Chelsea back to the bookstore. That done, I raced to Billy's dorm, which was less than a mile away. I hurried to get to his room, fearful that my opportunity to catch Gethin was shrinking, only to find the drone builder and hacker huddled over Billy's computer.

"What's going on?" I asked, catching my breath. "What do I need to see before I go get this bastard?"

Billy moved his big ginger head in order for me to take a look. His computer screen used the view of a traffic camera just across the street from The Citadel to spy on the nightclub. On top of the display, white lettering blinked the current time and date. From the camera's vantage point several white sedans were parked in the alley, their caution lights flashing. There were packs of security guards and bar staff. And Gethin, the Gethin I'd seen previously in Thomas's photos. But something was different about him. His face was now downtrodden and fearful as he packed a few cardboard boxes into one of the vehicles. His clothes were fashionable, but a bit unkempt with dirt marks around his knees and elbows. Around his wrists was an odd pair of manacles with glowing inscriptions etched into the metal.

"Dude," said Billy, looking up at my reaction, "you weren't kidding. Your dad is a total workaholic- to the point of slave work. They have him in chains."

I gave Billy a cross look before planting my face in my palm, unsure of what to do next. *If Gethin was purposely trying to hide by his own will, what was with the manacles?* Maybe he was an unwilling participant after all? If that was the case, this had gone from a manhunt to a rescue operation. I needed to get him out.

"Well boys," I said, cracking my neck. "You did well. Now, it looks as if I'm going to have to go confront my dear old dad, even if he's part of some freaky masochistic sex-cult. Why don't the two of you celebrate helping me find him by taking my credit card and going out to lunch?"

Billy shrugged. "Are you sure man? We could watch to make sure you're okay? You know, call the cops if things get weird or something."

"Nah, I'll be fine. Besides, that will only draw attention. If I wanted to be on television when I confronted my long last dad, I'd go on Maury Povich." Billy smiled, but managed to hold back any laughter.

"Alright," added Stevie excitedly while retrieving my card from his desk. "You're the boss."

I gave a wry smile. "And boys," The two looked at me curiously as I went for the door. "Don't wait up for me. This might get weird."

Just then the white wooden door I'd been approaching exploded open as if destroyed by dynamite. The blast sent the three of us sailing backward onto the floor. Wood chips rained down, and I could see a light stream of blood trickle from Stevie's ears. The level-fifty Paladin lay motionless, his eyes rolling along his head dizzily. Billy crawled like a worm towards his desk, taking cover behind it. I stood up, a bit dazed, but still lucid. Standing in the hallway were two scraggly men along with two matching grimy women. They had long dirty dreadlocks, tie-dye shirts with Grateful Dead emblems on them, and hemp necklaces. The men wore corduroy pants and the women sported long colorful sarongs, all of them adorned in socks with sandals. Each of the four had a polished wooden wand in their hand, covered in vines and moss. Their eyes squinted at us, and one of the men who had a nappy beard and glasses, gnashed his yellowed teeth.

"Well, brothers and sisters," said a recognizable voice from behind the group. Three figures emerged from behind the crowd of hippies. Two of them were massive with Celtic tattoos inked across their necks. I quickly recognized them as Citadel doormen. The third figure, who pushed past everyone and boldly entered the room, wore a fine white dress suit, and smoked a bulbous cigar. His silvery hair was drawn in a ponytail and he gripped a short black staff made of polished steel. Collin Dane was now looking down at me like a bug to be squashed. From the looks of things he hadn't taken too kindly to my threat. "Here lays the cause of all that is foul with this world," he said, pointing to me. "He is an unnatural blight. It is his kind that has created sin, disease, and *pollution* throughout Mother Earth."

"Oh, hello," I said through a happy smile. "Dain, you didn't tell me you knew Edward Sharpe and the Magnetic Zeros? I love that one song you have."

The four tie-dye druids hurried into the room, ready

for a fight. The bearded man in glasses pointed his handheld rod at Stevie and hollered.

"Herba-funis little dude." A cluster of cord-like vines sprouted from the carpet. The roots wrapped around Stevie, tightening until he was fastened in their grips. Stevie, who was already a bit out of it, gasped as the vegetation constricted him. One of the female druids with dark hair down to her knees and thick-framed glasses stepped forward. She thrust her wand, and a thick wooly fur as dark as her mane, and thicker than her leg hair, began to rise from her skin. She fell on all fours, allowing her glasses to tumble next to her. Claws sprouted from her fingers, causing her wand to fall to the ground, and large fangs protruded from her mouth. In seconds she had changed from a grimy but harmless looking woman who needed deodorant to a feral grey wolf with foam oozing from its mouth. The wolf leapt onto Billy's back- opening its maw, ready to devour its fat prey. As the wolf attacked, the other two druids pointed their wands at me, the tips now glowing green and ready to fire.

"Nedonius, my devilish friend," said Dane vindictively, "I give you the Druids of Franklin's Tower. Druids of Franklin's Tower," Collin added as he puffed on his cigar, "kill Nedonius."

Great, just what I needed. Druids. As Billy and Stevie were quickly learning, though these grungy looking deadbeats appeared harmless, they tended to have a trick or two up their sleeve, compliments of Gaia. I looked to Billy and Stevie, who were beyond terrified. Your first brush with the supernatural will do that to you, especially when it's threatening to squeeze the life out of your lungs or rip your throat out. Ideally, I'd like to contain a fight like this, keeping it low key as to not draw public attention. But unfortunately for the Druids of Franklin's Tower, I take it very personal when someone threatens my minions. So, although there were mortals looming nearby, I had little choice but to take action. I quickly opened up my man-purse and woke up the hellhounds.

Simon and Hecubus hurled out of my satchel as if shot from a cannon towards the pair of druids who were pointing sticks at me. The dogs each aimed at separate targets, tackling their victims like linebackers and clamping down on flesh with their mustached jaws. The druids rolled around the room, screaming in terror as they slapped at the hellhounds with their wands. The little beasts thrashed and twisted the larger humans in the air with their clamped mouths, rending flesh and bone in the process. It was disturbingly cartoonish.

With everyone distracted, I leapt to my feet and ran towards Billy. I grabbed the she-wolf by the tail and swung her at her partner attacking Stevie. The she-beast let out a yelp as the pair violently collided, before both went limp. Stevie's vegetative-coils released him, twisting back into the carpet before disappearing altogether. He rolled over in a gasping panic before crawling behind his bed and using it as a bunker. Billy, who now had small claw marks raked through his *Count Chocula* t-shirt, hurried to his side of the room and removed his Captain America shield from the wall. He held it up over his head, protecting himself from the flailing druids that Simon and Hecubus flung around the dorm.

"That's it!" shouted Collin as he raised his staff and pointed it towards the hellhounds. "Back to Hell with you." A bright red mystical rune appeared under Simon and Hecubus, and soon the little dogs were locked in place. Though the animals whined and whimpered, they couldn't seem to move. Collin was using his hex magic to thwart, and possibly destroy, my hellhounds. *How dare he.*

Outrage poured over me. It was a type of indignation reserved only for my worst enemies. This warlock was not only bold enough to try to expel my dogs, but overturn the very powers of Hell itself. It was insulting.

Flames dispersed outward from my hands and eyes, soaring upwards towards the ceiling. Collin recognized my anger, and motioned towards me with his head. He looked back to his goons and grunted.

"Handle him and I'll take care of these beasts," he ordered. The two security goons ran towards me, arms extended in an attempt to grab me. I centered my anger at them, lifting my hands in their direction. A barrage of flames poured from each of my palms, drowning the beefy henchmen in orange and devouring them. The blaze instantly disintegrated the pair, turning them into ash and embers. All at once, an alarm began to ring above us, and water from the sprinkler systems showered downward. *So much for my cover.* Collin watched from the doorway, shaking his head in disgust. "If you want something done right, it looks like you need to do it yourself."

With that, he waved his hands at Simon and Hecubus, and the two beasts lifted up into the air. He gestured again, and the hellhounds flung backwards and out the dorm window near Stevie's desk. Glass smashed outward as the pups soared down to street level. Watching my poor animals being helplessly pitched out the window was beyond infuriating. A scream from inside me bubbled up to the surface. I opened up my jaws wide and gave what I thought would be a ferocious roar, but the rage was so tremendous, that instead, a burst of hellfire shot from my mouth towards Collin. Unfortunately, he was ready. The little sorcerer quickly held up his staff, mumbling incantations that covered him in a globe of ice. Though the protective frost steamed and bubbled, its unearthly coolness slowed down the fire until I was out of breath. Collin glanced over the battered druids and piles of ash as the ice disappeared, assessing the situation.

"I'll never leave Chicago, Nedonius," he snarled as he removed a gold bird's feather from his pocket. I readied for his attack. He thumbed the spine of the quill, and suddenly, his body, and all the bodies of his underlings, began to glow a brilliant white. "But the same can't be said for your precious bookstore owner. I may have to pay her a visit soon." *Chelsea.* Fuming, I lifted Billy's nearby computer chair and hurled it at the warlock. But it was too late. Collin and his cronies swiftly vanished, subjects of some type of traveling charm. The chair, now spiraling midair, smashed into the wall behind him.

I stood with my fists clenched, glaring at the spot where Dane had once been. Smoke plumed from my eyes, hands, and mouth as water trickled down over me. Billy lowered his Captain America shield and nervously walked over to within arm's reach. There was a moment of silence as I tried to calm myself. Billy looked me up and down. I offered up a weak smile. Billy smiled back. He then held out his hand, and with his index finger poked at my arm. A spark of flame, like that from a lighter, spurt from where he'd made contact.

"Cool," he said simply. Stevie popped his wet head out from behind the bed like a wary gopher.

"Is it safe?" he squeaked.

"Yeah," I said hoarsely. "It's safe for now."

Billy circled me like a vulture, eyeballing my smoking exterior. "What are you man?" he asked. I took a deep breath and let the last of the smoldering fumes die out. When I'd calmed myself enough, I turned and faced the two.

"Well boys," I said with hesitation, "I don't know how else to say it. I'm a fallen angel from hell."

Billy turned to Stevie for explanation, but the skinny hacker looked just as baffled. The two vacantly stared at each other, seemingly trying to read the other's thoughts. Finally, Stevie made it to his feet and limped next to Billy. They turned back to me, gawping like I was a lion at the zoo. They ignored the occasional panicked student running past the dorm room from the hallway and towards the fire exit.

"Um, Ned," hummed Billy, "Are you saying that you're a demon?"

"Demon, *no*. Those are unclean spirits. I'm the real deal- an angel who rebelled against God and was evicted from heaven for doing so."

"You mean a devil?" asked Stevie. I winced.

"We don't really like that word Stevie. It's kind of offensive."

"Sorry," he apologized as he crossed his arms.

"So, why are you here?" asked Billy.

"Well," I sighed, running my hands through my wet hair. "That guy that I said was my dad, well, he's actually a colleague of mine. You see I'm trying to be a corruptor again."

"A what?" Billy blurted out.

"A fallen angel that comes up to Earth and helps sinners sin. I basically make sure that naughty people are continuing to do naughty things so that when they die, they go to where they belong."

"Dude," said Billy, "that doesn't seem very nice."

"There are a lot of ins-and-outs Billy. Believe it or not, the good guys can't exist without us. It's a Yin needs Yang sort of thing. We, the Forsaken, are kind of obligated to do everything in our power to stick it to the man -- in this case, the Big Man, while they do everything in their power to thwart us."

"So," Stevie asked with a blank stare, "is there going to be some epic end of world battle someday like it says in the Bible?"

"Maybe. *But*, we totally don't have the manpower at the moment. Heaven is built like Fort Knox so in order to even the odds, we've been recruiting; damning souls, and then taking the really nasty ones and implementing them into our army. Maybe someday when we're ready, we'll attack, but for now, trust me, we ain't ready for a fight."

Billy and Stevie's eyes grew wide.

"I have another question," said Stevie. He looked up at the irksome sprinkler spraying cold water down on him. "Who is your colleague?"

"His name is Gethin, and he's the Corruptor in charge of Chicago. He disappeared a few weeks ago without any good reason. Since I use to work the area back in the 19th century," Billy gasped at the comment, which I tried to ignore, "the people in charge felt I was best suited to find him. Hence why I've been asking you guys to help me hunt the guy down."

"What about that Thomas guy?" asked Billy. "What does he have to do with it?"

"From my guess, Thomas was Gethin's last project. It's the classic soul for fame scenario. Gethin promised Thomas a great life as a famous artist in exchange for eternal damnation. The only reason I was looking for the guy in the first place was because he disappeared along with Gethin. But thanks to you guys, I don't need to find Thomas. I know Gethin is hiding in that miserable little puke Collin's basement."

"I'm guessing Collin is the little wizard," Stevie speculated.

"Warlock," I corrected, "but good enough. Like I said, there's a lot of ins-and-outs, but long story short, that little shit is hiding my man."

"Now that we know the truth," Billy began with a meek shrug, "are you going to kill us or something?"

"Ha," I chuckled, "not bloody likely. You two are too nice to be damned souls. Contrary to what the Bible says, it takes a lot to be on the dickhead list. Besides, I need you guys. You know things about the 21st century that I can only dream of."

"Hey," said Billy in awe, "you weren't kidding when you called us your minions. We're literally the servants of hell." I watched as reality dissolved into Billy's mind.

"Wow," Billy said. Overhead the fire alarm went mute and the sprinklers turned off. "This is serious."

"Listen guys," I spoke up, "I'm in a hurry to save my girlfriend's life, so how about we make a deal. You two help me find Gethin, and I'll move you both out of this dump." Stevie took in what was left of the dormitory. Parts of the wallpaper were singed and nearly all of the furniture was destroyed. He then walked over to his computer, which was dripping with water, and patted it like a fallen comrade. I jumped in right away. "I'll even get you new computers."

"Will it require our souls?" asked Billy.

"Damn it Billy," I flailed my arms, "It's not like that. I'm not going to trick you two into damning your souls. You two are my buddies now, believe it or not."

Billy stared at me with an uneasy half grin, cracking his thick knuckles while Stevie prodded at his hard drive. "Okay, deal," shouted Stevie. Billy gave Stevie a cross look.

"Whoa," spat Billy in a panic. "Stevie, you just made a deal with the dev-" he paused, "with a fallen angel."

"Meh," Stevie shrugged, "I'm comfortable with it so long as he fixes my computer."

"Fine," Billy conceded. Suddenly, cries of a fire truck rang from outside. "I'll be your minion, but I still have a lot of questions Ned."

"Right," I said. "And I promise to answer them, but for now, girlfriend time."

"Ned," Billy said reluctantly while rubbing the fat part of his neck, "Are you sure it can't wait? We're kind of in trouble here. The police and fire departments are downstairs. Even if my dad is a cop, Stevie and I are probably going to be getting expelled, and possibly arrested for this."

"Nonsense," I said as I picked up a shard of glass. I grabbed Billy firmly by the collar. Billy looked horrorstricken. "It's not your fault that some pyromaniac broke into your room and took you hostage." As if on cue, a squadron of policemen came pouring into the hallway outside Billy and Stevie's dormitory. A handful of firefighters stumbled in after them, portable extinguishers and axes in hand. I spun Billy around and hugged him tightly, holding the pointy end of the glass to his throat, using him as a giant meat shield. Slowly, I crept backwards towards the broken window near Stevie's desk.

"Police," shouted one of the lead officers. "Let the fat kid go."

"Oh come on," Billy complained. The policemen held out their pistols, ignoring him.

"You'll never take me alive," I said in my best crazy person voice. "Mom didn't love me. Escape the matrix! Escape the matrix!"

I released Billy, pushing him at the policemen like a ginger battering ram. Billy's big body landed on the lead officers, forcing them to the ground. I aimed at the window behind me and leapt out.

Falling is an interesting thing. It's not like flying with wings. There's not a lot of freedom to it. The air gets sucked out of your lungs as gravity violently pulls you downward. I fell for a good five seconds or so, studying the beautiful Chicago skyline before smashing into the pavement. Concrete exploded as I crashed face down, but my body held together. Everything was dark. My body was slightly lodged inside the walkway, but I could hear people jabbering around me.

"Oh my Lord," a woman shrieked. "Is he dead?"

I could hear footsteps as someone ran up to me. Hands that felt like they were covered in latex grabbed my arm, pressing two fingers onto my wrist.

"I don't have a pulse," said a man's voice. "Hurry,

let's get him in the ambulance. Mark, you get the pads ready."

A pair of thick hands lifted me up, causing rubble to roll off of me. I pretended to be lifeless, keeping my eyes shut. I could smell cheap aftershave as I listened to the emergency radio crackling from one of the men carrying me off. A static filled voice rained from the speaker.

"Suspect has leapt out of the window. I repeat-suspect has leapt out of the window. We have a jumper. Do you have visual?"

"We have him now," one of the men shouted into his radio as they dragged me onto a steel slab that I could only assume was a gurney. "No signs of life. We're going to try and resuscitate him, but it's not looking good. We're headed to Northwestern hospital." An electrical voice came back from the other side of the walkie-talkie.

"I have the victims here. They say it was another one of those homicidal art students. Be careful." *Good job minions.*

I felt the cart under me being wheeled into a vehicle, and afterwards, two metallic doors slammed. The air-conditioned automobile I was now in kicked forward. Sirens shrieked from outside the ambulance, and I heard shuffling from inside the van. Judging from the sounds nearby, I assumed that there were at least two people in the back of the ambulance with me. One placed his rubber-covered fingers on my neck while breathing like a cow.

"Mark," said a deep voice as the stranger pulled up my shirt, "Is that defibrillator ready?"

"Got it here," said another man, "Charging." The light hum of energy sang above me. Suddenly, cold metal touched my chest, and a shot of prickly electricity pulsated through my body. Like I've said before, it takes something special to kill Forsaken, but that doesn't mean that nothing bothers us. The raw energy sent a surge so strong that I opened up my eyes involuntarily and frenziedly sat up.

There were two heavy set men sandwiching me, one with blonde frizzy hair and a mustache, and the other one, a bald dark man with glasses.

"Ouch, you sick shit," I cried, slapping the defibrillator paddles out of the blonde man's hands. "That freaking hurt." The men stared at me with open mouths. Then, as if reality hit them, the dark man rubbed his eyes with his fingers and the bald guy placed his hand on my chest, trying to push me back down.

"Sir, I need you to remain calm. You fell from a window. We're taking you to the hospital."

"Like Hell you are," I said, pushing them both away from me. The electricity must have had my body on edge, because the shove was overpowering, causing both paramedics to go flying into the ambulance walls behind them. "Sorry boys, I've gotta go see my baby." I stood up, banging my head on the short ceiling, before moving to the back doors of the ambulance and opening them. A car behind us slammed on its brakes. "Gentleman," I said with confidence, "have a nice-" Just then, the ambulance hit a large pothole and I went flying out of the back. I rolled for several feet before finally stopping. Horns beeped as cars whizzed past. I dusted myself off as traffic swerved around me. "Damn it. I can't even get off a cool one liner."

I hurried through the lanes of cars, avoiding the ambulance that had swiftly pulled over. Quickly, I made it to the sidewalk, and cut in between a set of buildings. My legs kicked in, and before long, I was sprinting faster than any mortal ever could through the Chicago alleyways and side streets. *Well Ned, you sure know how to draw attention.* If I wasn't burning the city down, then I was jumping through skyscraper windows and escaping authorities. This wouldn't bode well for my future.

Block after block, I raced through downtown, weaving between bike paths and under bridges. It was midafternoon, so most people were still stuffed in their offices, worrying about reports and payroll. Those who were out seemed to mostly be tourists, staring upwards at the thousand foot towers soaring above them. I didn't know how I was going to evade authorities *and* check up on Chelsea, but it wasn't going to stop me from trying. Then, as if my guardian angel was calling me- *yes I see the irony and redundancy*, the distinct sound of scraping metal grabbed my attention from above.

Hovering overhead was the elevated train system, riding north on its raised tracks towards Chelsea's bookstore. I'd completely forgotten about the Red Line. I didn't think that I could sprint the rest of the way without running into another police officer or two, so, I made my way towards the large steel stilts holding up the train's bridge. Since using my wings could only attract more attention, I instead began climbing the inside beams of the train tracks, trying to hide myself from onlookers as much as I could. The iron rafters were tightly welded together, so scaling the rail system by using large bolts and thick edges wasn't too difficult.

Just after a large silver train with a red stripe passed by over me, I clambered to the top of the rails. The passing train was only a hundred feet or so away, so I made sure to dodge the center beam as T-1000 had warned, and chased after the caboose. Before long, I was at the back door of the redline train, and after conjuring up a bit of anger, prying open the lock with my hands. Once the latch snapped, the metallic door swung open easily, and I climbed inside. There was no one within the back cart, so after jamming the door shut, I took a seat and caught my breath.

The sun shone brightly through the dusty glass. I watched as people below walked briskly through the streets, rushing past the potted bright flowers, public artwork, and awe inspiring buildings that clung near the sidewalks. *Some things never change.* My first term had the same problem. Mortals were so excited to make something of their lives that they forgot why they were doing it in the first place. Conquest, success, achievement, these are the things that mortals value. *Oh, the irony.* If only they knew that this was completely the opposite of what the *Big Guy* wanted for them.

As the train beat its metal lullaby over the track's joints, it speedily took me through the cityscape, past the parks and into underground tunnels. Maybe I was in a mood, but as I listened to street musicians at the loading stations and passengers talking about what they would cook their family for dinner, I became a little jealous. You don't get this in hell. Things are more sterile, less civilized. No one is excited to go home to their family because in hell, no one loves anyone as much as they love themselves.

After ten minutes or so, the train came back up from the tunnels and we were back in Lakeview. Pedestrians changed from hurried businesspeople to casual locals, and the buildings shrunk by ten sizes. I kept looking through the windows, nervous of what I'd find once I made it to The Prologue, when a twinkle in the blue sky caught my attention. I was hypnotized by white flame that sparkled above the soft fluffy clouds. *Wait, why is white flame twinkling above the clouds?* My chest began to sting as if I'd been stabbed in the heart. Grimacing, I wiped my hand across the window in order to smear off some of the filth, peering through the clean spot.

Michael flew through the air, his wings flapping while his penis dangled through the winds. His sword shone brightly, gouts of holy flame blazing from its steel. Though he was some distance away, I could see from his posture that the archangel was locked onto the train. He soared downward, closing the distance between us with the speed of a hurricane. *Shit, I must have gained his attention with all of my earlier dramatics.* Now was not the time. I needed to get to Chelsea before that idiot Collin did. Then, without warning, the train began to slow. We were reaching the next stop, allowing Michael to catch up with us easily. Michael grasped the rear of the train, prying open the already broken door and swinging it inward. He hovered just outside the opening, refusing to come in.

"Greetings, Nedonius," he said in his boisterous voice. "It's time to continue that conversation of ours. I hope that you've learned to accept your fate. Now come out and die honorably."

"Yeah right," I said sarcastically, trying not to sound as terrified as I was, "when Hell freezes over."

Chapter Sixteen

I'll be the first to admit that I'm as stubborn as a cockroach in nuclear fallout. I've had some close calls in my days, but managed to survive each and every one of them due to my sheer grit and thick headedness. Nonetheless, I couldn't think of anything as bleak as my current circumstances. Michael had me cornered, and would be ready for me this time around if I tried to disarm or distract him. There was no place for me to run. With fight and flight off the menu, there was only one other option. I'd have to live up to my name and be devilish.

"Nedonius," he exclaimed, placing his massive hand along the doorframe. His body was nearly too large to fit through the train's backdoor, but odds were that he was determined enough to manage. "I wish I could admire your unrelenting attitude, but the truth is, I can't possibly respect anything as lowly as you. Now, come out here and face me. Don't make me go into this metallic dragon in order to get you." I gave an exhausted sigh and raised both of my hands in surrender.

"Fine, Michael. You win," I said sadly. Michael's platinum eyebrows lifted curiously above his brow. "I can't stand running anymore. It's finally time for my reckoning."

"Oh?" He flew backwards and hovered over the tracks. "Are you being sincere?" He gave a short pause, and then smiled. "Well, that's wonderful. Come out then so I can obliterate you," he said casually. He said it as if we were about to share a cab together or get a cup of coffee. I nodded and followed him out, balancing along the edge of the moving train before hopping down onto the wooden beams connected to the railway. There was another train behind us, only a stop or so away, but it was catching up quickly. "Honestly Nedonius, this is for the best," he said cheerfully, whirling his burning blade. "Perhaps you will even feel God once more before I disperse your wretched energy into oblivion. You never know."

"One could hope," I said with melancholy as I knelt down. I lowered my head over the center rail. Michael stretched his arms before raising his sword above his head and clearing his throat.

"Nedonius," he called out in an authoritative tone, "I, Michael, Archangel of Heaven, banish you to your final death. Be gone you tainted fiend."

The sword's crackling flame became louder, and I could hear the archangel grunt as his blade descended. Quickly, I pulled my head backwards. A rush of air and heat blew past my cheek as Michael's sword narrowly missed me, instead kissing the center rail with its blazing metal edge. A popping noise followed by an electrical hissing cried from the center beam. Brilliant blue bolts of energy traveled up Michael's weapon and into his strapping arms. Michael's bloodshot eyes bulged wide as his hair stood up and his body stiffened.

"Nedonius," he cursed through his ground teeth with a shudder, "you are truly a fiend of the worse kind." The train behind us blew its deafening horn. It was much closer now. Though Michael was invisible, I was not. I needed to get out of the train's path before it stopped and ruined my plan.

"Well, Michael. I wish I could stay and talk more, but it looks like you have a train to catch. *Ciao* old friend!"

I leapt from the tracks and crashed down onto a dumpster. I bounced off of it with a thud and rolled into an alleyway. Luckily, the front of buildings constructed near the raised tracks faced away from the bridged L-tracks, putting the tail ends of their structures under the railway. So, save for a few rats, there was no one around the back of the buildings to see me fall nearly twenty meters. I made it to my feet just in time to hear the thump of the train as it collided with Michael. It was hard not to giggle.

Nevertheless, though it would take him a moment to gather his wits, the archangel was still looming nearby. I started to race through the alleyway under the tracks until it met with one of the main streets. From there, I hopped in the nearest taxi and had the driver take me to Chelsea's bookstore.

To my relief, the store wasn't on fire or surrounded by wannabe spell casters, and I could see Chelsea at the register from the storefront window. I'd hoped that Simon and Hecubus had found their way back to *the Prologue* and would be waiting for me at the door, but they were nowhere in sight. I wasn't so much fearful for their safety, as I was of the mayhem they could create without direct supervision. Hopefully, they'd sniff their way back to Chelsea's store without incident.

I opened the store door, inadvertently jingling the bells tied to the entrance. The store's speakers were blaring some sort of heavy metal, which meant that Chelsea was still in a good mood. I walked into the main storefront, scanning the library for anyone who looked suspicious. The store was empty. Chelsea's nose was deep in a book. She twirled a lock of her black hair in her finger while biting at her bottom lip. Her eyes glanced up at me and her eyelashes fluttered.

"Hey killer," she said with a half-smile. "I thought you had to help Billy?"

"Hey, um…more important matters came up."

"Oh really?" she said flirtatiously. "Well, I know that I'm completely irresistible, but don't you have school or something that you need to go to?"

"School-Shmool," I said as I scanned the streets for any of Collin's goons, my head bobbing and weaving between bookshelves. Chelsea gave me a curious look.

"Hey, on a serious note, have there been any weirdoes in the store today?"

"I'm looking at one right now."

"Nice, but seriously."

"No. I mean," she hesitated, "I don't think so. I haven't seen Louie since the last time we had a car party. I reported him to the local police, but they said they don't have anyone like that on file. They're going to keep an eye on my store, but you know how that goes in Chicago."

"Are you sure?" I said as I reached the register. I leaned over the counter and examined near her feet. "No new age hippies or men with security painted onto their t-shirts?"

"Uh, no," said Chelsea, placing her book on the table. "Why do you ask?"

"No reason" I said innocently.

"What's going on Ned?"

"Chelsea, it's kind of complicated, but I have something I've been meaning to tell you."

"Oh God, please don't tell me you're wanted by the FBI or something? I can't date another guy who's serving time."

"Whoa," my head cocked back. "So we *are* dating? Like, we're a couple?" Chelsea raised her fist as if she was going to punch me. I winced and took a step back with a half-smile pinned onto my face. "Cool," I reflected, "I have a girlfriend."

"Easy lover boy. There's a difference between dating and being boyfriend-girlfriend."

"What? Since when?"

"Since always. Anyways," she waved her hand in a rolling motion. "You were about to confess something awful that would make me change my mind about everything weren't you?" *Oh boy, it was now or never.* I needed to just come clean already, not just to clear my conscience, but also to protect her. She needed to know what she had accidentally fallen into, even if it meant that she'd hate me in the process.

"Ah, yes, about that. It's just, we've been having such a great time this week and I didn't want to spoil it."

"Ned!" she hissed. "Just spit it out."

"Um, okay, well Chelsea, remember how you said that you see right through my mysterious act?"

"Yes," she said nervously. "Oh, no Ned. Please don't tell me you're going to say something that makes me want to file a restraining order on you. So help me God, if you do, I'm going to cut off your balls and wear them like a necklace."

"Geez, that's a bit much, don't you think?"

"Just get to the point already," she said while shaking her head.

"Okay," I said before taking a deep breath. "The truth is Chelsea that I really do like you a lot, I mean more than I've ever liked anyone before," Chelsea smiled briefly before squinting her eyes in suspicion, seemingly more apprehensive about what I'd say next. "But I have been holding back. You see I'm not like other guys." Chelsea gave her patented eye roll.

"Seriously?"

"Let me finish," I begged. "I'm not like other guys, because well, here it goes," I rubbed the nape of my neck. "I'm not human at all."

Chelsea stared at me, her expression barren. After a moment, she rubbed her temples in frustration.

"Ned, if you don't want to see me anymore, all you had to do is say that you don't see us working out."

"No!" I shouted. "That's the exact opposite of what I want Chelsea." I closed the distance between us and grabbed onto her soft hands, squeezing them with mine. "I've never been so happy. That's why I want to come clean with you." I went down to one knee, my hands still gripped on hers. "Chelsea, I'm absolutely mad about you, and I need to be truthful. I'm not human, and because of it, I think I've endangered your life."

Chelsea pulled away one of her hands and poked down at my chest, as if testing to see if I were real. I looked down at her black painted nails before staring back up into her eyes.

"So then Ned," she said tiredly, "what are you then?"

"Well," I sighed, "I'm a fallen angel, or as we like to call ourselves, Forsaken."

"You mean like, a devil?"

"Dang it. Please don't use that word."

"Oh sorry Ned," she said sarcastically. "I'm so sorry that I offended you by calling you a devil. I'm sorry that I thought I'd finally met a decent guy, and it turns out that he's just another wacko." Chelsea jabbed me on my arm, her face now frozen with anger. "For that matter, I'm sorry you're a freaking asshole Ned."

"No, Chelsea, it's true. I really am a fallen angel. I can prove it." I jumped over the counter and looked through the shelves below the register. There were pads of papers, a stack of plastic bags, and a collection of other useless office supplies scattered throughout the shelves. "Don't you keep a gun or anything around here for security?"

"No Ned. This is Chicago. As violent as the city can be, we still are sane enough to know that guns are stupid."

"Fine," I said, picking up a stapler. "Then hit me in the head with this."

"Are you nuts?" she asked as she stared suspiciously at the staple dispenser. "Why would I want to do that?"

"Because you can't kill me Chelsea. I'm immortal. You could hit me in the head as hard as you'd like, as many times as you'd like, and it won't make a lick of difference because I'm a divine being, created by the hands of God and outcast into the depths of hell. Only other divine beings can kill me. Well, that, and the occasional spooky."

"Spooky?"

"Um, yeah, they're supernatural creatures spawned by your world. You know, like ogres and skin changers."

"No, I don't know and I'm certainly not hitting you on the head Ned."

"You have to, because there's a powerful warlock who's after me, and he knows all about us. I need you to believe me so we can get the heck out of here."

Chelsea took a deep breath and crossed her arms. "What do you mean?"

"I'm not exactly sure myself. His name is Collin, and he's been keeping tabs on me since I threatened to kill him."

"Kill him?" Chelsea groaned before shifting her weight. She seemed antsy to get away from me.

"It's a long story. I didn't actually want to kill him, just scare him away for some friends of mine at the Undead Union. Anyhow, I think he must have been using his magic to spy on me, and knows all about us."

"Ned, I'm not hitting you on the head," she said as she left the register area and backed away from me. "You need help. Maybe we can still see each other after a nice psychological evaluation. Heck, they might even prescribe you some pills that will have us on another date in no time. For now though, I'm going to have to ask you to go home."

I was just about to deliver a zinger about not needing any penis pills for our next date when several white sedans pulled up in front of the bookstore, followed by a jet-black sports car. Their wheels screeched as they parked along the curb, and I knew almost immediately that these were the vehicles I had seen in the alley of The Citadel on Billy's computer. Nearly a dozen men and women began pouring out of the cars, all of them wearing powdered wigs, sunglasses and dressed as if they'd just left a morning rave. Some of them were familiar faces, including the hostess with the crooked nose who'd originally taken me up to see Collin. They wore obnoxiously tight patent leather body suits with ammunition bandoleers along their hips and shoulders. The group of colonial-era fashion models was armed and dangerous. Each of them held a submachine gun at their side. They sashayed up to the sidewalk with puckered faces and narrowed eyes, staring into the store.

As if on cue, the group parted so that the ebony sports car was in view. The door opened, and Collin Dane hopped out, a form fitting black-and-white chessboard pattern trench coat wrapped around him tightly. His right hand gripped onto his staff, while his left hand adjusted a pair of sunglasses over his eyes. Just then, the passenger side door opened and Louis Joliet, bandaged and leaning on a crutch, stumbled out. He scowled as he gazed into the store, his bruised and blackened eyes focusing on Chelsea and me. In his good arm was some sort of rocket launcher, its primer green shell gleaming in the late afternoon sunlight.

Collin nodded to Joliet before digging into his pocket in order to remove a chained pocket watch. He began swinging it like a pendulum. Without warning, the traffic in the streets, walking pedestrians, and anything else in motion began to slow down until coming to a complete halt. The sounds of beeping horns and sirens went completely mute. Only Dain's cronies, Joliet and Collin himself were still stirring. The goons lined up and aimed their weapons inside the Prologue.

"You've got to be joking me?" I said aloud. "Since when did the Legion of Doom get such cool cars?"

"Hey Ned?" Chelsea said fretfully.

"Yes?" I said slowly.

"Are these the people you were talking about?"

"Uh huh," I said, swallowing a lump in my throat.

"Okay, in light of Peter Dinklage being able to stop time, I'm going to believe you now."

"Thanks," I said nervously. Just then, Collin motioned with his hand, and shouted something incoherently. All at once, the group opened fire, shattering The Prologue's large window, and spraying bullets into the store.

Chapter Sixteen

Splintered wood chips, shreds of paper, and tangerine sparks erupted from the storefront. A spray of bullets landed in my chest, knocking me backwards. *Geez, I'm really a magnet for these things.* I fell onto my back, violently knocking my head against the store's linoleum floor. I was dazed and out of breath, but still conscious. Chelsea had fallen prone, and was now doing her best military crawl towards me.

"Ned," she said over the piercing gunfire, "Oh God, please don't be dead." She wrapped her arms around me, cradling me, tears swelled in her eyes. I could feel the hot lead sizzling in my skin. "Please Ned, talk to me?" she cried out as a vase fell from the countertop next to us, smashing on the tile.

"I don't suppose you have insurance on the bookstore that covers evil warlock attacks do you?" I asked between gasps.

"No," she said with a sad smile. Wet eyeliner ran down her cheeks, "I don't think I do."

"Chelsea," I coughed, "could you ever have ever have seen us working out?" Chelsea paused momentarily, ignoring the lights above us as they twitched on and off. She nodded with certainty. "Yes Ned," she said between sniffles. I could feel my devilish body rapidly repairing my wounds. "You're as weird as they come, but I think we had a shot."

"Great," I said cheerfully as I sat upright, my wounds now fully healed. "That's all I needed to know."

Chelsea looked up at me, astonished. "But...but how?"

"I told you already. I'm not human babe. Now," I said as I cracked my fingers together, "let's get you to safety so that I can handle these knuckleheads."

Chelsea glared at me. Then, out of nowhere, she raised her hand and began slapping my arm.

"You asshole. What is wrong with you?"

"Chelsea, I understand you're pissed, but now is not the best time." Chelsea gave me one last swat on my cheek.

"Everything you've told me is a lie Ned. You're a dick."

"You're right," I said while taking cover behind what was left of the counter that held up the register. Slowly, I peered out from the corner, watching as the last of the goons unloaded their remaining bullets into the store. For a moment, the firing died down, as the goons were fidgeting with their weapon clips, giving me an opportunity to strike. "For now though, let's focus on the problem at hand."

I stood up, ignoring Chelsea's reaction to my proposition, and took in my surroundings. The Prologue was trashed. There were shredded books and shattered pieces of glass all throughout the store. It seemed like anywhere I went, destruction followed. Outside, time persistently stood still. It was like looking at the backdrop of a cheap movie set. Though the main actors, being the maniacs with machineguns, were in motion, the rest of the scene was frozen. I searched for Dain, but alarmingly, he was nowhere in sight. His thugs, however, rushed to strip their magazines from their smoking machineguns.

"Hurry, he's coming," shouted a man with a George Washington wig, grey jacket and wired sunglasses. "Get those clips in and fire."

My mind raced as the group tried to reload their weapons. Collin was smart enough to know that bullets couldn't hurt me, so why would he risk sending his flunkies after me with only mundane weaponry? Then it dawned on me. Collin wasn't trying to kill me. He was trying to kill Chelsea. For him, a warlock who was used to getting what he wanted, murdering an innocent girl was the perfect pay back. *That bastard.*

A storm began to brew inside me. These goons were intentionally risking their lives in order to try and take the most precious thing I had here on Earth away from me. My heart began to beat out of my chest and the blood in my veins rushed throughout my body like a freight train. The smell of brimstone fermented in my mouth and smoke billowed from my nostrils. Soon, my hands were ablaze with hellfire, lighting up the room with a tiger glow. I concentrated on the line of attackers in front of me. The majority of them, frightened by the hellfire, retreated for their vehicles. What few remained aimed their compact machineguns and began to unload. Spurts of fire spat from the holes on my chest where the bullets landed, but I kept on my feet. All at once, I let out a formidable howl that shook the foundation of the bookstore. A tempest of flame poured from my hands, dancing across the room before raining down on the remaining shooters. The firing squad instantly smoldered into ash, their remains peppering along Belmont Avenue.

Car ignitions started, and soon the caravan of sedans was hastily backing away from The Prologue. I gathered all of my hate into a large sphere of fire between my fingers, raising it over my shoulders like Atlas. With all the strength that I had left in me, I hurled the flaming globe towards the convoy. The bright sphere broke up, spreading a tidal wave of flames across the streets and onto the vehicles. The heat was so intense that the front of the bookstore crumbled and collapsed into a pile of ash. I half expected the cars to dramatically explode like they do in Hollywood, but instead they just made an odd crackling noise before evaporating into powder and smoke.

A singed and disheveled Joliet, the only remaining

bozo around, hobbled from behind a steel mailbox, his rocket launcher in tow. He lifted the large weapon, resting it on his shoulder as he took aim.

"I will have satisfaction," he said fearfully, yet defiantly. I shot him a dark glare, which caused him to shudder.

"Louie," I growled, "what makes you think that your stupid rocket launcher will be any different?" Louie shakily adjusted his sights.

"Because," he said boldly, "Master Dane enchanted the ammunition with holy magic you bastard." My eyes widened in fear, causing the aura of heat around me to die down. Louie had a wild card again. I wasn't certain if it would work, but I was too damn frightened to find out. I tried to take cover, but the only thing near me that was still standing was the register's counter, which Chelsea was hiding behind.

"Whoa, Louie, hold on. If you shoot me, you risk hurting Chelsea as well. Don't you want to take her on the rebound after you destroy me?"

Louie gave a sour face. "Frankly, I don't give a shit any longer," he shouted. "Now die!" His index finger lowered towards the trigger. It looked as if I were a goner. But, just before he could fire, Chelsea hopped up from the register, a sawed off shotgun raised at her shoulder. With one eye squinted, she aimed and fired. The buckshot sent Louie flying back.

Now I don't want to get too graphic, but when Joliet's cranium exploded like a firecracker in a pumpkin, I didn't worry too much about him getting back up. The Forsaken are a pretty tricky bunch. Yes, Louie had sold his soul for immortality, but we didn't offer him the top shelf deal. Louie received the discounted version, the one that keeps his ticker going so long as he keeps himself preserved. Disease, starvation or drowning might not do him in, but serious trauma, like, I don't know, a buckshot to the head, still does the trick.

I turned to Chelsea in awe. "I thought you said you didn't have a gun?"

"Let's not argue over the value of being honest right now Ned."

"I completely agree," echoed a ghostly voice from within the store. It was Collin. I couldn't see him, but the pulse in my gut told me that he was close. I ran to Chelsea, stepping in front of her and shielding her as much as I could. "I mean, after all Ned, you haven't been very honest with any of us. For example, I thought you were specifically here to run me out of Chicago, but apparently, that's just a side job of yours. If only you'd have known that I have been harboring your precious fallen brother, Gethin, this entire time. You might not have decided to side with those imbeciles who call themselves the *Negative-One Union*. Then again, you've never been a very good corruptor." I tightened my fists and clenched my teeth, ready to strike at the little puke if he'd show himself.

"Come out Collin," I shouted into the air, "and I won't piss on your corpse after I kill you."

A laugh reverberated throughout the bookstore. "Oh, isn't that precious? You still think that you have the upper hand. If only you were smart enough to comprehend that a warlock of my caliber doesn't just show up to his enemy's doorstep without a plan."

"Ha," I laughed, "You mean like Louie and his rocket launcher? Swell plan."

"Oh, are you referring to Mr. Joliet?" asked Dane in a composed voice. "Don't worry, he didn't have an enchanted rocket launcher. I lied to him in order to gain his allegiance. On that note, you sure know how to make enemies in the city. Mr. Joliet was fixed on being the one who delivered you the killing blow. All I had to do was give him your little gothic girl if she survived."

"Hey buddy," shouted Chelsea, "I don't know who

you are, but I can tell already that I don't like you. So why don't you do me a favor and make a fist, then jam it up your ass."

"Well said," I complimented, but Chelsea just shot me a dirty look. *Obviously, she was still mad.*

"My dear," said Collin, "Your time on this Earth is getting ever shorter. One more outburst like that and I'll flay you alive young lady."

"Dain," I hollered, "why don't you just leave the girl out of this and tell me what you want already?"

"Absolutely," said Collin in an astute voice. "I want revenge. I'd rather it be against the Union, but I'm perfectly comfortable with punishing you instead, especially after you threatened my life inside my own nightclub. I'll start by picking apart your sweetheart there as if she were a dandelion. Then, I'll use a little spell I've concocted to obliterate you. It seemed to work on that annoying quasit."

Dane was a liar, cheat, and all around evil bastard. Of that I was certain. But just like with Louie, I couldn't be sure if he were bluffing this time. I've never heard of a witch's spell that could obliterate Forsaken, but I did recall Armen mentioning something about a missing quasit. Plus, my instincts told me that Collin wasn't the kind of warlock who would make such a claim unless he could back it up. I couldn't risk him hurting Chelsea, but I didn't want to betray DuSable. I quickly scanned the room, desperate to find some sort of miracle that could get me out of this mess. You know, like one of those emergency boxes hanging on the wall that says, *Break in case of Evil Genius.* At first, I didn't see anything, but then, as if by miracle, my eye caught a glimpse of a plastic "Ever-Fresh" water bottle standing on a partially destroyed book counter.

The water inside appeared to be boiling; yet the plastic container remained intact. As I looked closer, I saw the watery outline of a nose, two eyes and a mouth. Catherine O'Leary, or at least, the watery face of Catherine, was inside. She had gathered her spirit within the confines of an *Ever-Fresh* water bottle, and was spying on us. I locked eyes with her bubbly pupils as I began to speak.

"All right Dain, well played," I called out. "I'll give you what you want, just don't hurt us. I surrender."

"Excellent," his voice reverberated. "Now, where is the Negative-One Union?"

"They're hiding in the Egyptian exhibit at the Field Museum," I confessed. "They are using an ancient Book of the Dead, and have a few wards up that have kept them magically concealed, just like you've been doing at The Citadel in order to hide Gethin." I raised the volume of my voice, my glare still pinpointed at O'Leary. "They don't expect anyone to ever find them, so if you act soon, you'll definitely catch them with their pants down."

Catherine frowned. I gave the bottled ghost the quickest of winks before turning my attention back to the room. It must have finally dawned on the old bat that I was trying to get her to warn DuSable because I could see from the corner of my eye that O'Leary's grimace had transformed into a grin. She gave a quick wink back before her liquid face dissipated into a fizz of bubbles and disappeared altogether.

"Very good Ned," said Collin as he appeared in front of me from a puff of smoke. He was still wearing his sunglasses, though his timepiece had been placed into his pants pocket, the chain still dangling along the front. His staff was pointed at my head with one hand, and a police Taser was firmly gripped in his other. He had a pair of headphones around his neck whose wire winded down into his jacket pocket. "However, I'm afraid I was lying about letting you go."

Suddenly, a brilliant flash of light poured from the tip of Collin's black staff. My eyes burned, and I quickly felt dizzy. I tried to focus, but all I could see was the white radiance of whatever spell Dane had cast upon me.

"It hurts doesn't it?" Collin asked rhetorically. "I call it the *Manfred Mann's Earth Band* spell. Do you get it? Any targets that are under the spell's effects become…blinded by the light." Collin snickered under his breath, entertained by his own shitty sense of humor. "On a side note," Dane said calmly, "did you know that it was Bruce Springsteen that originally recorded the song, yet the remix that Manfred made in 1976 is the version that made the melody incredibly popular?"

"Screw you Collin," I said while scratching at my throbbing eyes. The pain didn't go away, so I swung my fists blindly. "What's your point you two-timing bastard?"

"I believe that *is* the point Ned. God made angels, who betrayed him and became Forsaken. Lucifer and his servants quickly became the world's source of evil, but to be honest, if you really look around and see all of the nasty things this world has to offer, you realize that it is man who does evil best." I could hear Collin's feet crunching on broken glass as he approached me. "That's because man," he said near my ear, "does it with style."

I felt a jab in my gut, followed by a surge of electricity. My body locked up, and a buzzing hummed in my ear. I was so disorientated that I couldn't tell up from down, cold from hot, and light from darkness. I was in a world of chaos. Volts of energy made my body convulse, and before long, my brain was mush. Then suddenly, the brutal currents stopped, and something small and hard was shoved into each of my ears. I could hear music. It was the sound of an electric guitar, with a drum beat in the background. A pair of men's voices sang in harmony, their words regrettably familiar.

"*But she was blinded by the light, Revved up like a deuce, another runner in the night- Blinded by the light, revved up like a deuce, another runner in the night.*"

Collin had managed to take my senses from me. I'll give it to the bastard, what he lacked in ability, he made up for in resourcefulness. I wasn't dead just yet, but I'd condemned Chelsea and myself to the furnace for sure. *Shit.*

Chapter Seventeen

I listened to that same damn song on repeat nearly a hundred times. My wits were mostly fried, but I could tell that Collin had levitated me into a car's trunk. It wasn't difficult to figure out. There was a sense of weightlessness followed by a sudden drop into a confined, but carpeted space, then, just after something heavy slammed over me, which I could only assume was a trunk door, a rumbling engine purred underneath me. The drive felt short, no more than ten minutes or so, and shortly after the engine stopped, I was removed by two pair of large hands, most likely more of Collin's goons. They dragged me up a set of stairs, my feet bouncing off of each step, until at last, I was thrown into a cold room and the headphones were removed.

I couldn't hear what they were doing with Chelsea, but the fear of it overcame my blind anger. Collin was probably capable of a great many evil deeds by the looks of things. He'd managed to outsmart not just one, but two separate Forsaken. That definitely gave room for concern. If I were lucky, he'd use Chelsea as a bartering tool, but that was more of a hope than a reality. I'd obviously pissed him off by threatening him within his own domain, and may have cost both Chelsea and myself our lives.

"Well Ned," said Collin, penetrating the ringing in my ears, "home sweet home. Please don't get too comfortable though. Tonight, after I destroy the Union, I'm going to banish you." I was still blind, but it didn't stop me from feeling around desperately along the floor. It was cold, most likely cement, chipped and covered in a layer of filth.

"Why don't you just kill me already?"

"Come now Ned," said Collin dryly. "We must keep to the itinerary. Besides, you can't just kill Forsaken. Everyone knows that." There was a short pause. "*However*, you can definitely send them someplace where others can do the job for you. I'm going to do to you what I did to that nosey little quasit who was looking for Gethin. That's right, you have a one-way ticket through a portal back to heaven. Won't it be nice to be back where it all started? Although, I hear they really don't like your kind in that neck of the woods anymore. My guess is that you won't last more than a minute before some sweet cherub bashes your brains in with her harp."

There's no way Collin possessed that kind of magic, *was there*? That would take a very serious understanding of divine power. Then again, if anyone could figure out a way to open up a portal from Earth to the Holy Gate, it was the asshole that was holding me hostage. Collin was the kind of guy who crossed magic with physics. He dissected each ritual and spell, using his abilities in ways I'd never seen before in order to further his cause. Plus, if Satan could figure out a way to get us corruptors back-and-forth from Hell to Earth after we'd been imprisoned there, I'm sure there were loopholes for getting into heaven from Earth as well. I didn't want to believe it, but then again, what choice did I have? I mean, he had Chelsea, so even if he couldn't send me up to heaven, he sure as Hell could do something terrible to her. *Oh my God, Chelsea.* I had to save her.

"Where is she?" I snapped, escaping my inner thoughts.

"Who? Your little tattooed girlfriend? Oh, she's alive. At least, she's alive for now. The ritual tonight calls for the blood of an innocent, and your girlfriend is the perfect specimen. How poetic, don't you think? We have two star-crossed lovers, one a rare bookstore owner from Chicago and the other a devil from the depths of hell, both dying at nearly the same time in order to preserve their eternal love. It's like Romeo and Juliet." His voice sobered. "Isn't love grand?"

I lifted my arm up in the air and extended my middle finger towards where I thought Collin's voice was coming from, but he didn't seem to care. He chuckled softly before tapping his shoes together and walking away slowly.

"Come boys," he ordered. "Let's leave old Ned here to his thoughts. I'm sure he has a lot to think about. Besides, the undead need killing again. It appears that you just can't keep a good dog down."

I heard a few pairs of feet march behind Collin's lighter footsteps, followed by the heavy slamming of a metallic door just feet in front of me. It appeared that I was locked in like a rat in a cage- a cage that was most likely guarded by armed men and warded by Collin's hex magic.

"Oh, and Ned?" Collin's muffled voice called out from behind my prison door. I stayed quiet. "Too bad you're out of sorts or else I could have arranged for you to meet Gethin. He's here too you know?" I clamped my teeth and gave a low growl. "He tried to make a deal with me as well in order to save his human lover. It appears that you devils have a real affinity for falling in love with mortals. How silly. No worries, I'll invite him to your ritual so he can say hi. I think he's going to get a real kick out of watching you get sucked up into heaven. I mean after all, it was him who helped me design the ritual in the first place." Dane laughed like a hyena before walking completely out of earshot.

I was doomed. Even if I somehow managed to get my sight back, I had no idea how I was going to get out of that cement room, find Chelsea, and then break us both out. A man like Dane probably had all sorts of guards, gadgets, and dangerous tricks throughout the building. I might have survived the war against heaven and endured the torture of hell, but this was different. The odds were stacked terribly against me. A simple warlock had outfoxed me. *Weak.*

I crawled until I found the nearest wall, and then leaned up against it, resting my head atop my knees. With my vision still absent, there was little to do but contemplate all that I'd done to get me here. I replayed some of my most unforgettable moments, like the time Azazel and I dared those Greek guys into making a giant horse in order to sneak into an enemy city. Man, were those dudes totally gullible or what? But every memory, as fond as it might be, always had a way of being interrupted by the thought of Chelsea. For one golden week, I had the opportunity to spend time with her, and for one week, all I wanted to do was figure out how I could find a way to be with her longer. She was dark humored, weird, and above all else, the most caring and lovable person I'd ever met. She deserved poems written about her and portraits created in honor of her beauty. And *I* had sentenced her to death.

The thought burned deep inside me, and to keep from going bonkers, I made myself as comfortable as possible, balling up along the cold stone in order to get some rest. I was too flustered to sleep, but I needed to recuperate from my bookstore brawl if I were going to try to make a last desperate stand before being sent back to heaven. I sat in a huddled position, unsure of what to do next. With boredom now at the helm, I tried focusing on my fried senses. The flashing colors in my irises weakened as I squeezed my eyes shut, which was a small relief. But I still didn't know how long it would be until I completely regained my sight. So, I waited. I don't know how long I sat like that, curled up all miserable like, but it felt like an eternity. Then something caught my attention.

"Nedonius," said a raspy low voice. "Nedonius you fool, wake up."

I lifted my head. My vision was blurred, but I could at least make out shapes and colors. Collin's magic was beginning to wear off. I could see the outline of my surroundings. I was in a bare room with a single door and no windows. There was a small drain, no bigger than a tea saucer, where water could be bled just a few feet in front of me.

"Nedonius say something," the voice whispered from the drain. I crawled towards the dimple in the ground, putting my lips over the hole.

"Who is this?" I whispered.

"It is I Nedonius, Catherine O'Leary."

"Cat," I shouted before looking over my shoulder. "Thank hell." There was a camera along the ceiling staring in my direction. I tried to act natural, and lay down as if I were simply resting my head near the drain. *Very smooth Ned.* "Catherine, you beautiful dead woman," I said in a hushed tone, "you have to get me out of here."

"We are trying," she said in a low voice, "However, Mr. Collin Dain's nightclub is heavily secured."

"We?"

"Yes, *we*. After the incident at the bookstore, I hurried to the museum and reported to the Negative-One Union as I assumed you desired. They have quite the setup might I add," she merrily complimented. "I've always been quite fond of Egyptian culture. Perhaps it's because-"

"Cat," I hissed, "not now."

"Apologies Nedonius. As I was saying, they felt dreadful about what had happened to you, and blamed themselves for their part in your captivity. So, we have abandoned the museum, setting up a trap for Collin if he shows, and united in order to free you. However, this saloon of ill repute that Mr. Dane calls *The Cathedral* is built like a fortress. You are in the sublevel of a maze-like basement. I have found a backdoor through the drains in order to get past the protective wards, but we still are unsure of how to get inside. Besides the wards, there are guards everywhere, technological doohickeys along each corridor, and a few of Mr. Dain's bizarre creatures protecting the inner sanctum. It won't be easy."

"And Chelsea? Cat, did you find Chelsea?"

"Yes Nedonius, of course I did. I knew you wouldn't shut up about her if I didn't find her first." A sigh of relief went through me. Collin hadn't been lying about keeping her alive, which I was momentarily grateful for. "She is unharmed, and in a room very similar to yours just down the hall."

"Okay," I whispered, "So what's the plan then?"

"First, do you promise to keep your word and help me gain vengeance upon that wretched reporter, Michael Ahern?"

"Yes, yes, of course," I said, pressing my fingers down on my eyes in an attempt to gain more of my sight, "I promise. That reporter will have more worries than Hitler when I get back to hell."

"Very well then. I shall help you escape from this cell, while the Union conducts their assault from above."

"Assault?"

"Well, how else do you plan on them penetrating The Citadel? True to its name, this building is an impenetrable fortress. DuSable and his team have deliberated, and due to the time constraints, they have little other choice but to attack through the front doors. As long as they can gain your assistance, the Union feels that they may have the edge to finally put a stop to the warlock tyrant Collin. We haven't much time though before the warlock figures out that the museum has been abandoned and the Egyptian exhibit is rigged to collapse upon itself if Collin enters."

"Wait, but didn't you say that there were guards everywhere here? The Union doesn't stand a chance."

"Do not be so doubtful Nedonius, the undead are more capable then you think. The Pharaoh Queen has something special at hand in order to even the odds. Let's just have you and I focus on getting you free for now.

Stand back."

I lifted my head, and crawled back towards the wall, trying to look as casual as I could. A spout of grey murky water began to gush from out of the drain. The dirty puddle crept across the cell's floor, rolling slowly towards and then under the steel door. I tried focusing on the camera in my cell as O'Leary poured through the break under the egress, but even with my recovered eyesight, it was hard to read the motives of a faceless monitoring device. All remained quiet for a moment, and then suddenly, there was a violent thrashing and clanging along the prison door. I heard a heavy male voice trying to speak, but his words were hushed by coughing and gagging. There were a few more desperate gasping noises before finally a loud thump returned the silence.

The lock on the door snapped, and the large gate swung open. There on the floor was a single guard, his black security shirt drenched in water. A grey stream leaked from his clamped mouth, and his dead hands, which had let go of a nearby Taser, were locked onto his neck. Then all at once, his jaw drew open, and a flood of liquid teemed out. The resulting puddle collected together before floating upward, forming into a humanoid shape. The watery figure of Catherine O'Leary slowly materialized before me, unpolluted by my blood any longer.

"Come now Nedonius," she said, gesturing to me. "Let us get your bookstore friend. There's no ward on your cell, but we'll have to figure something out for the main vault door. It's hexed with frighteningly powerful wards."

"One thing at a time Cat. Now show me where Chelsea is." Catherine gave a sigh.

"As you wish," Catherine said with a bow. "Though I feel she may be safer locked up. You would not believe what kind of creatures this man has created."

I stepped over the security guard's body, and found myself in a narrow brick hallway with dozens of doors along each wall. Collin could imprison an army in here if he wanted. Catherine led the way, taking me to the last door on the left. I fidgeted with the lock, drawing the bolt backwards. The catch released, breaking the door from its seal. I tugged at the metal barrier. The hinges let out a loud squeal before opening. Catherine wafted her way inside, stopping above a figure that was huddled in the corner. It was Chelsea. She was shivering in a ball, and winced as the hallway light poured over her. She seemed unharmed, as Catherine had said. Black mascara mixed with tear tracks ran down her cheeks. Even with her swollen eyes, she was still more beautiful than ever.

I rubbed the back of my neck nervously and smiled as innocently as possible. Chelsea's gaze drew over me. "Don't worry," I said with a lightly playful voice, "Your knight in shining armor is here." Chelsea stood up, wiped the black from her cheeks, and then ran up to me. I opened up my arms for a passionate embrace, but instead of a hug, Chelsea balled her fist, wound back her arm, and punched me square in the bridge of my nose. Snot shot from my nostrils and my still weary eyes began to water once more.

"Son of a bitch," I shouted, grabbing at my nose. "Why did you do that? I'm just now getting my vision back."

"Ned, if you think that I'm excited to see you then you're more idiotic than I'd previously assumed," she hissed. "You're a piece of shit, and like a fool, I opened myself up to you." My sight slowly returned, and as it did, I could see the lion's grimace on Chelsea's face. Pissed didn't quite describe how infuriated the woman appeared at the moment. I'd met cinder-spawn with far calmer demeanors. O'Leary looked at me and frowned. I put my hands up in surrender, ready for Chelsea to swing at me again with one of her haymakers.

"Chelsea," I begged, "Please, this is hardly the time. Let's get to safety first."

"You said that at the bookstore. It's never the time is it Ned?"

"Seriously? You want to do this in the middle of a rescue operation? Come on, don't act like this."

"I don't care," she hollered. "In fact, I don't think I want to go with you." Chelsea took a step back and entered the cell again. "Let me be, Ned. Clearly, betrayal's engrained in you." My gut clenched and my heart dropped. Chelsea was trying to wound me, and she had.

"Ouch," I said gloomily, "harsh." Chelsea shrugged uncaringly, crossing her arms in defiance. I wanted to try to invoke reason in her, but suddenly…

-Boom!

The main door at the end of the hall, a large steel contraption, beat with authority. The cement walls around it shed rubble and dust from the impact. It was as if a battering ram had smashed into its center. Chelsea, Catherine and myself paused, listening intently. There was heavy clanking on the other side of the doorway, as if someone was banging pots and pans along the floor. I glanced at the exit, and then back to Chelsea.

"What the shit was that?"

"Unfortunately, it's one of my creations," announced a calm male voice from the cell across from Chelsea's. It was low, smooth and had a slight eastern European accent, as if Barry White and Vlad the Impaler had had a baby. I shuffled over to the cell door, still holding onto my throbbing nose, and looked inside the cell through a small eyelevel slit. No more than a foot away was the familiar face of an older Forsaken. He was tall, with strong, but handsome features, long hair tied in a ponytail, and a tidy beard. Both of his ears were pierced and shined with small polished diamonds. He wore a custom fit buttoned white shirt with a loosened black tie. I could feel a twang of pleasure quiver inside my gut. "That monster trying to get in here protects the prison."

"Wait." The door slammed again as if a rhino had charged. "Gethin, is that you?"

Gethin looked surprise. "How do you know my true name?"

"Gethin, it's me Nedonius. You know, the guy you replaced a hundred or so years ago?"

"Oh great," he groaned, "out of the frying pan and into hell's fires. Nedonius, I told you to back off. I knew this would happen."

"You knew that I'd come to rescue you? That makes no sense."

"Nedonius, you truly live up to your reputation- all muscle, no brains. You can't save us. The only thing keeping us alive right now is the fact that the beast outside those doors was never taught to use a door handle. Once he gets through that door, he'll rip us apart."

"Not on my watch pal," I said confidently. Another bashing hit the door, creating a hairline crack in the middle of the steel, just above a set of drawn runes painted in blood. It wouldn't be long before whatever this thing made it inside. "By the way, why are you working for Dane anyhow? He's a total ass-hat."

"Does it look like I'm working for him under my own will? Come now Nedonius, the man is a notorious scoundrel. He double-crossed me, and now I am his prisoner. He's taken my Thomas, and forces me to help him create demon spawn or else."

"Um," I hummed over another crack at the door, "Isn't Thomas just another mark?"

Gethin blinked a few times before getting closer to the eye slit and focusing his gaze towards Chelsea. "Is *she* just another mark?"

How could I be so thickheaded? Thomas may have started off as just another soul for Gethin to corrupt, but soon the men became intimate. Gethin had fallen for Elsberry while helping the young artist start his career. That explained the phone at Thomas's place, the framed picture on the dresser, and a slew of other details I'd neglected to give any real thought to. *Typical Ned.* And if that were the case, Gethin was willing to do anything to help save Thomas, including making an army of demon spawn for Collin.

"Gethin," I said through the door bars, "I can help get Thomas if he's here."

"Sir," howled Catherine, "that's not part of the plan."

"Cat," I spat, keeping my eyes on Gethin, "it is now. Go find the others and tell them we're in danger." Catherine rubbed her liquid temples and moaned. "Please," I begged. She nodded and then whirled into a miniature cyclone, oozing back into a small puddle. She slid into a drain located along Chelsea's cell floor and trickled down inside.

"What makes you think I'll help you?" asked Gethin. "Even if we don't get murdered by my creature, you're going to take me back to hell."

"Dude, isn't it obvious? What do you think Collin will do with you once you've created enough demon spawn for him? He's already told me that he knows how to ship us back to heaven. Guys like you and I don't do well in places like that. Besides, I'm not one hundred percent sure that I'm taking you back to Hell just yet." Gethin pressed his face across the cell window. The exit thumped hard again, and metal moaned from the main door's hinges. One more hit like that and the steel barrier would collapse entirely.

"Why wouldn't you take me back?"

"Because you're in love with Thomas, like I am with that woman," I protested, turning and pointing to Chelsea. Chelsea staggered back as if hit by some invisible blow. I was too embarrassed to keep looking at her, so I concentrated on Gethin. He glanced at Chelsea before staring back to me. "Alright, hurry, let me out. I have an idea."

I hastily tugged at the lock and opened the large door. Gethin was wearing the same outfit I'd seen him in on Billy's computer. Some type of European style suit, covered in smears of dirt with small tears in the knees and shoulders. His human disguise was taller than mine, better built, and more handsome. Coolly, he stepped out into the hall. As if there wasn't some mysterious beast trying to break into the prison in order to kill us. He tightened his tie knot like a man walking into a business meeting and gently cracked his neck. He was about to say something when the hinges of the main door finally gave way. The steel door fell to the ground with a heavy *thud*.

Dust from the impact fogged the entryway, but quickly settled to give us a better view of what was about to murder us. A gargantuan jellyfish monster hovered in midair as if it were floating in water. Its neon blue body pulsated with fluttering gleams of bioluminescent light. Dangling under its belly were fifty or sixty long serrated tentacles. On each end of the feelers were separate torture devices, screwed and stitched into the creature's flesh. There were knives, chainsaws, and spikey flails dangling from the ends, ready to rip us into bits. Most peculiarly, along with the intimidating arsenal, was a set of less conventional weapons fastened to the limbs. Items like a coffee maker, microphone, and one large and extra scary purple dildo.

Gethin looked at me with a less poised expression then he'd been wearing before. "By the way," he said reluctantly, "Dane personally customized this one. It's nearly indestructible."

The beast raised its microphone up to a large pair of lips along the center of its body. The rubbery mouth opened, revealing a perfect pair of gleaming pearly whites, like the ones in toothpaste commercials. The monster cleared its throat before jingling a tambourine connected to another one of its appendages.

"Ladies and gentleman," it announced in a recognizably lively and somewhat maniacal voice. "Thanks for having me in your city. I'm Screamin' Jay Hawkins." Its tone was identical to the famous artist's. "And I'm here to rip you to pieces."

"Uh," Gethin added. "It also thinks its Collin's favorite musician, Jalacy Hawkins. That's to say if Screamin' Jay Hawkins was a homicidal maniac."

Oh great.

Chapter Eighteen

Chelsea's eyes bulged widely as she took in the creature. Without a second thought, I shoved her back into her cell, causing her to fall on her back, and slammed the door shut. Just as I did, Screamin' Jay Hawkins let out a high note while jolting all of his tentacles forward. A swarm of slimy snake-like arms, nearly fifty-feet long, hurled through the narrow hallway towards Gethin and I. I shielded my face, taking a boxing glove, frying pan, and backscratcher to my arms and gut. Gethin wasn't as lucky.

A board with one long iron nail pierced into his shoulder, while the purple dildo hit him straight in the forehead. Gethin winced, pulling the board-and-nail out of him before pushing back at the bundle of other tentacles shoving forward. He began retreating into the back hall near the dead security guard's body. The strength of one of the monster's arms alone was frighteningly powerful. Teamed up with twenty others it was overwhelming. I joined Gethin, hurrying backwards towards my old cell.

"Gethin," I hollered as a vacuum hit me across the head. "You said that this thing is nearly indestructible. Is there anything that we can do to at least put it on ice?" I asked as I slapped away a tentacle with a feather duster. The voice of the Jellyfish monster began to sing.

"I put a spell on you because you're mine. You better stop the things that you do. I ain't lyin', no, I ain't lyin'."

Tentacles felt along the walls, clanking vicious looking swords and axes along the surface. A few of its less occupied arms grabbed at the dead security guard near our feet, dragged him towards the door, and cut the body cleanly in half with what looked to be an industrial saw blade. It pulled the corpse towards its mouth, and then in one large bite, swallowed him whole. Gethin whipped his head to me.

"The monster was originally created to guard the place," he shouted as he swung open my old prison door, taking cover behind it. I ran behind him, helping him hold the door in place as a waffle iron and dagger covered tentacle pushed against it. "However, the cost to feed this thing was getting to be too much for us to let sit around idly all day. So we made it multi-purposeful. Hence the vacuums and cooking utensils."

Just then the massive purple dildo flew over the door's barrier and slapped me across the cheek. The drum of the rubbery sex toy rumbled across the cell door before drawing back onto the other side.

"Don't forget the dildos."

Gethin smiled. "How could I?"

"*I just can't stand it babe,*" sang Jellyfish Screamin' Jay Hawkins. "*The way you're always runnin' 'round. I just can't stand it, the way you always put me down. I put a spell on you because you're mine.*"

"Anyhow," Gethin carried on, "what I'm trying to say is although this creature doesn't have any real weaknesses, it was made to guard and clean. It isn't the smartest monster you've ever met. Unless Collin commands otherwise, it has direct orders to protect the prison while also keeping the lower levels spotless."

"So," I said while a saw began to cut through the cell door, "after it rips us into pieces, it's going to clean it all up. Effective and efficient," I said sarcastically.

"Just shut up a second and let me do the talking." Gethin stepped out from the safety of the door. I watched through the peek hole as the jellyfish floated towards us. "Mr. Hawkins, Sir!" Gethin called out. "I have a request please."

The creature paused, retracting its appendages so that Gethin could speak without distraction, as it raised the microphone closer to its mouth.

"Oh goody," said the beast, "A song request. Would you like to hear about real pain as I take you apart? Perhaps 'Constipation Blues' is in order?"

"That's a good tune Mr. Hawkins," Gethin said sincerely. "The request I had however was more aesthetic based."

"Hmm," the monster contemplated, "whatever do you mean?"

"Well Sir, if you're going to pick us apart like daisies, I was hoping that it would at least be in a more respectful environment. I mean, to be blunt, I know that Mr. Dane ordered you to keep things clean and the state of these cells is a bit appalling Sir." The Jellyfish frowned at the mention of Collin. "Don't we deserve the dignity of a clean death Mr. Hawkins?"

Though eyeless, the jellyfish shuffled its head back and forth as if taking in the corridor's condition.

"My oh my, you're right. This place is absolutely repulsive," said Jellyfish Hawkins as he raised his duster, broom, and vacuum. "We can't have that. Mr. Dane would be so disappointed. Let me clean up first, and then we'll get back to the killing. Hmm, maybe I should put some plastic down first. I don't want to have to tidy up twice now do I?"

"That's a fine point," Gethin complimented. "We'll wait by the main entrance while you clean up and prepare ourselves for the massacre.

"Yes," Jellyfish Hawkins said enthusiastically, "Please do. It's gonna be a good one." The monster began sweeping at the floor and dusting the walls. "And try not to track any filth from the hall into the waiting room. I just cleaned it."

"Absolutely," said Gethin politely. "I'm just going to collect the other prisoner so you can clean her cell too.

It's filthy."

Gethin began walking forward with a bold confidence. I tiptoed behind him, trying not to track any dirt along the corridor floor. The jellyfish ignored us as we opened up Chelsea's cell and waved her to follow us. She did so reluctantly, but as she crossed the threshold into the hallway, her eyes went big. Jellyfish Hawkins, a creature that was part H.P. Lovecraft, part janitor, was humming along as he scrubbed at the ceiling with a brush, paying no attention to us as we walked out of the prison area and into the waiting room.

I could tell that it had hit her, the same way it had hit Billy and Stevie when Collin came to visit. Being exposed to the supernatural is a game changer, even if you do run an occult bookstore. The pages of Chelsea's favorite stories were coming to life right in front of her. Enamored, she tilted her head and examined the creature as if it were a crossword puzzle; callous to the fact that the Jellyfish Hawkins planned on tearing us limb from limb once it had finished cleaning.

Fortunately, Gethin had outsmarted the monster, though our window of escaping the dungeons alive was quickly shrinking. So, with little time to spare, I grabbed Chelsea by the hand and began to tug her towards the exit. She clumsily followed, her eyes still fixed on Screamin' Jay. The green painted walls of the cement chamber we were now in were polished to perfection, and the single mirrored elevator, the same elevator I'd been escorted into during my first meeting with Collin, shone brilliantly. The fragrance of potpourri and scented candles permeated through my nostrils, sickening me with its flowery delight.

I kept an eye on the prison archway as Gethin tapped at the elevator button with conviction. Luckily, it wasn't long before the elevator bell rang and the doors opened. While the monster mopped blood from the security guard's innards, we quickly ran inside. Hawkins' humming resonated throughout the lower level. I pushed at the ground floor button several times. Finally the doors shut and the elevator kicked upwards.

"Are you okay," I inquired, placing my hands over Chelsea's shoulders. She looked confused, but after a brief nod, opened her mouth to speak.

"Yeah," she said stunned, "but I don't think I'll ever be able to listen to Screamin' Jay Hawkins again."

Chapter Nineteen

Gethin stroked his facial hair, staring at the elevator's buttons like they were a math problem. Chelsea, who in lieu of almost being murdered by a tentacle monster must have temporarily pardoned me, pet my head as if she were comforting a sick child. I nodded and smiled. She returned my gesture with a weak smile of her own.

"Are you still angry?" I asked quietly.

"I'm trying not to be Ned," she said through a sigh, "but you lied to me."

I nodded. "I know, but would you understand, even just a little, if I told you it was because I didn't want to lose you?"

"Maybe a little," she said reluctantly. "Yes. I suppose I would."

"Sweet," I said in relief, "because that's honestly the truth."

Gethin looked at us and shook his head. "Sorry to interrupt, but we'll still need a code to go directly to Collin's office. I don't have it." Gethin played fretfully with the elevator's security system. "But that's where he's keeping Thomas."

"Okay, what are you thinking then?" Chelsea seemed to have gathered her wits.

"Whoa Sigourney Weaver, you're not coming with us," I barked.

"Like Hell I'm not," she bit back before taking a deep breath. "Ned, you don't get to drag me into your world, a world that gets my business destroyed, me captured, and my reality shaken, without expecting me to want some payback."

"Chelsea, you may hate me even more for what I'm about to say, but that's exactly what I get to do. You're not going anywhere but home."

"Ned, Collin is a dick. He needs to get what's coming to him. I might not be able to take bullets like you," she argued, "or trick squid monsters into cleaning up basements like Gethin, but I'm smart. You need me. Besides, I can't go back to *The Prologue* after knowing that everything I've read about in my bookstore is true. And another thing-" Chelsea yelled, but before she could finish, Gethin interrupted.

"Wait, did you say *The Prologue*? As in the occult bookstore on Belmont?"

Chelsea and I gave Gethin a blank stare. Without looking, Gethin reached back and pressed a button, which kicked the elevator's brakes on just before we reached ground level.

"Gethin, what the Hell are you doing?"

"Ned," Gethin said calmly, "I understand that you are head-over-heels for this woman, but we can't save my Thomas unless we have her."

"What?" I cocked my head back. "What are you talking about?"

"Madam," Gethin addressed Chelsea, "Is it safe to say that through the years of owning your bookstore you have learned to read magical incantations?"

Chelsea gave a smug half grin. "Which do you need, Aramaic, Egyptian, Latin or Hebrew?"

Gethin mirrored Chelsea's smile. "My apologies Nedonius, but we *do* need her. In order to release Thomas, we need her to read from a specific tome. I know which book it is, but I don't understand human incantations." I punched at the elevator wall, leaving a large dent. Gethin took a loud breath before shaking his head. "Very mature."

"Ned," Chelsea called out to me, her voice now calmer than a moment ago. She took her soft hands and placed them on each of my cheeks, guiding my eyes towards hers. "Ned, listen to me. I know you don't want me to be put in harm's way, and I appreciate that, but listen. I've finally been introduced to a world that I always prayed existed, and if I ever want to live with myself, I need to help put this asshole in the ground."

I digested her words for a moment. Chelsea wanted revenge. The thought saddened me. "Wrath is a sin," I sighed, "I'm rubbing off on you."

"*Ned,*" Chelsea said my name slowly and clearly, "I know I've given you a hard time for lying to me, but in this last week, I've met a man who cares for me more than anyone else has since my father. I met a guy who is funny, kind hearted, and above all else, loyal to those closest to him. I get that you must have done some bad shit a long time ago, but there's nothing wrathful about you. Nor is there any reason that you can't be the person you started as. Ned, you're a cool guy. I think you still belong in Cloud City."

"Do you really think that the Almighty Lando Calrissian would have me?"

Chelsea snorted. "Did you just call God Lando Calrissian?"

"Did you just call heaven Cloud City?"

Chelsea squeezed my hand and planted her lips on mine. When she drew back she was smiling. "Yes, I think *He'd* have you back. And I think I'd have you back too if we live through this. For now though, let's worry about Chicago."

Fire surged in my heart. Not that pissed off hellfire, but the good stuff. Pure and clean flames, like the kind that surround Michael's blade. My frown flipped upright, becoming a beaming smile. I raised my scrawny human fists and held out my chest proudly like Hercules.

"Ready to kick some warlock butt now big guy?" Chelsea asked.

"Hulk Smash!" I said in a deep, primitive voice.

Gethin thumbed at his glistening eye. I looked up at him, tilting my head curiously.

"Dude," I inquired, "are you crying?"

"What you two have," he said in a shaky voice, "Is exactly why I made a deal with Collin. Hell has no love, and Heaven is boring, but on Earth, one can find the right person."

"Wow," snickered Chelsea, "We should put that on a Hallmark card."

Gethin quickly sobered up, shaking his head in disgust.

"Yeah," I added, "you never know when you'll need a card that says, 'For That Special Mortal, From Your Loving Dark Angel.'"

Gethin frowned. "Oh, the two of you belong together," he snarled as he pressed the release button on the brakes. Chelsea and I continued to snicker like a couple of school kids. "By the way, once this door opens, there will most likely be a plethora of armed staff, as well as some of my grizzlier demon spawn waiting for us at the lobby. We'll need to fight through them in order to get to the east stairwell, climb up three floors, and break down Collin's security door. Are the two of you up to it?"

"Bring it on," I snapped my finger, sparking a flash between them.

Bing. The elevator bell announced that we had reached the main floor of the nightclub. I took the front, using myself as a shield for anything outside. The doors drew open, and to no surprise, we were greeted by countless sets of anticipating eyes. There was a gaggle of human bouncers at the front in matching black security t-shirts and plastic earpieces. They were armed with stun batons, ready to strike. Near the main entrance stood a dozen or so powdered wig goons in patent leather, gripping machine guns. They were exact clones of the goons we'd fought off at Chelsea's store. Perhaps most frightening of all however were three monsters on the dance floor. The creatures looked as if they'd been taken directly out of the pages of a *Dungeons & Dragons* Monster Manual.

There was a hulking olive-scaled creature with a long nose, horns, razor talons, and sunglasses standing upright near the D.J.'s booth. The monster had a long cottony beard hanging under its metallic bear trap jaws. Beside the brute was a tiny green man, no larger than an infant, with feathered black hair and a penciled in goatee. The little man had wolfish teeth, burning red eyes and wore a purple jump suit. He gripped a wand with an odd symbol on top that looked like a mix between a cross and tattoo gun. Next to him, near the stairwell, a ten-foot tall granite statue of Michael Jackson with a vehicle sized mini-gun duct taped to his arm waited.

"Shit," said Gethin under his breath, "It's Z.Z. Chops, The Artist Formerly Known as Mince, and Michael "Stonewall" Jackson. They're some of my best work."

"Well, hi everyone," I greeted with false enthusiasm, waving hello. "Are you here for Collin's Dungeon-Crawl?"

Chapter Twenty

Almost immediately the security guards charged, stun batons in hand. *Collin learns quickly.* I was having none of it though, especially with Chelsea ducking behind me. With a wave of my hand I called forth a tide of hellfire from my fingertips, which blanketed over them. The extreme heat of the supernatural element did what it has so many times before and turned the small unit of steroid addicted guards into ash. I ran out of the elevator with flame in hand, trying to draw attention away from Chelsea and Gethin. As I did, the powder wig goons in leather began unloading on me with their submachine guns.

Bullet after bullet plunged into my chest, spitting small tendrils of fire and black blood from their entrance wounds. The momentum piercing into me caused me to slide backwards, though I fought in order to stay afoot. I didn't know how long I could remain like this, but before I could guess, the Mozart wannabes suddenly stopped firing. There was an extraordinary tune, ghostly and beautiful, being whistled from inside the elevator. The melody, far too loud to be made with a natural pair of human lips, was a seductively low and sweeter than wine. Rubies could have sung the notes. I was enthralled with the tune. But if I thought for a second that the whistle had a profound effect on me, I was more fascinated to see what it had done to the humans.

The wigs had dropped their firearms and begun ripping at each other's clothes, shredding the material to bits as they threw the garments over their shoulders onto the ground. Men tattooed with Gaelic runes rubbed their sculpted bare chests along the naked breasts of women painted in body glitter. Accessories like hairpieces and sunglasses were tossed to the side, undergarments were hastily removed, and mouths devoured exposed flesh, sucking onto any part they could get their lips on. I would have remained in awe of what I was seeing if not for a sharp tap at the back of my shoulder. I spun around, ready for the enemy, but found only Chelsea panting behind me, her eyes wild with desire.

She grabbed at me, raking her black fingernails through my hair as she jabbed her tongue into my mouth. Her skin was pink, and I could feel the heat emanating from her as she grabbed between my legs. She tugged up on her shirt, exposing milky breasts, which she pressed up against me, then worked her tongue down to my neck, licking it with intense fervor. Chelsea moaned with desire, ready for more. But before things could get any kinkier, the party pooper Gethin interjected.

He pulled Chelsea and I apart, his eyes still locked on the wigs as he kept up his whistle. He wrapped his arms around Chelsea from behind, holding her in place. Chelsea tried to lick upwards at Gethin's chin, but he pulled his head back just in time.

He stopped whistling. "No, no darling. I'm afraid you're not my type."

"Well, well, well," I said over the groans coming from the pleasure mound above us, "aren't you just a barrel of surprises. I wish I would have known that you could do that. It could have helped in the planning process."

"We have a plan?" Gethin asked facetiously before returning to his whistle. I grinned. He hadn't gotten far into the melody before he stopped blowing air again. "Nedonius, if you would, I'd appreciate it if you handled the beasties creeping up behind you, as my influence does little against them." I turned to look, and saw the hulking bearded troll approaching, its iron jaw clanking in anticipation. "And do hurry," he said over a panting

Chelsea. "My little song's effect is very temporary."

I nodded, and then spun around to meet the long nosed beast. The troll slathered drool along the floor while looking me up and down. Little did I know, the green little bugger behind him had hatched a plan of its own. Using Z.Z. Chops as cover, the goblin looking squirt spun its wand in the air and barked some unknown language. Twinkling sparks showered down onto the little shit, and before I knew it, there were hundreds of little Artists Formerly Known as Mince running throughout the club. The little green demons chattered their teeth together as they circled around Z.Z. and myself, creating a sort of fight club ring for the two of us to duke it out inside. The giant and I studied each other like a pair of Tijuana roosters about to rumble. Though the goblins probably wanted a fair fight, all of the damn cleverness had inspired me to think outside the box.

Focusing anger upon myself, I called forth hellfire to ignite my skin. Flames sweat out of my pores, and before long I was completely engulfed in fire. *Flame on!* I charged the giant. Not sure what to do, Z.Z. began to lumber backwards, but I caught up to the beast and clobbered it in the mouth. The demon not only fell back, but its face and beard charred into a black husk before caving in upon itself. I turned to the little green shits, who were now beginning to panic. A few of them tried to create some sort of Spartan line, while the others took refuge behind chairs and tables. I stomped my feet as I closed in on the brave ones, my flaming footprints scorching the smooth wood floor. One by one, I picked up the little monsters as they swatted at me, and began to hug them, turning them into ash.

"Come here little guys. You're so damn cute," I hollered over their screams.

But before I could celebrate my morbid and creative victory, a spray of thunder and lightning sent hundreds of bullets from Michael Jackson's mini-gun into my body. The force sent me flying into a glass table that rested behind me. The table shattered, driving me to the floor with a hard thump. The sheer magnitude of the mini-gun had caused me to lose my train of thought, extinguishing the hellfire along my skin. I was stunned, and the blurriness in my eyes, which had only recently gone away, came back with a vengeance.

Fresh gunpowder permeated the air as Michael "Stonewall" Jackson began to clumsily thump his feet towards me. He was most likely lining up for another shot. Meanwhile, the excitement must have snapped the powdered wigs out of their trance, because the half-naked band of freaks were now staring at me from the balcony as they rearmed themselves. *This was going poorly.* I tried to stand, but my vision was all over the place. The blurry forms of Michael Jackson, the wigs, and an army of remaining goblins closed in on me. I wondered what would happen if all the machinegun fire turned me into paste. I mean, a few bullets can't kill me, but a torrent downpour might.

Then, as if by some miracle, all the windows and doors within the dance club imploded as dozens of shadowy creatures poured inside. From my viewpoint on the ground, I could see that these infiltrators weren't on Team Dain, in part because they began pouncing on the goblins and powdered wigs scattered throughout The Citadel. Michael Jackson began raining gunfire at them, while a few of the naked wig goons tried to reload. *Why does it always seem like I'm on the floor and nearly unconscious when fun things happen?*

I stared up at the club lights wired throughout the ceiling rafters as glass, blood and bullets whizzed over me. Suddenly, Gethin's big bearded head jumped into view. Chelsea was behind him, nervously tossing her head back-and-forth between the ensuing chaos.

"Is he going to be alright?" she asked over the gunfire. "I've never seen him like this."

"Oh, he's quite alright," said Gethin as he reached behind me, tucking his arms under my shoulders so that I was sitting upright. "It just takes a bit for our kind to get their heads straight once they've been clobbered like he has. He'll have his wits back in no time." Gethin began dragging me backwards towards the bar. "Now my dear, if you would be so kind as to start making your way towards the stairwell, I'll meet you there with Ned."

Gethin hauled me through the freshly broken glass, navigating me around the combat. I watched like a drunk as the battle ensued. A small army of what appeared to be wild safari animals had made their way into the club. The beasts were mostly of flesh and fur, with exposed bone protruding along certain parts of their bodies. There were undead rhinoceroses, bears, alligators, elephants, and a recognizable pair of man eating Tsavo lions. Most of the animals had been riddled with bullets, but still they persisted in their reign of terror, biting the heads off of goblins, clawing at powdered hair goons, and leaping onto stone Michael Jackson. It wasn't just them either.

In the background, the great Mukantagara, better known as Mary the Mummy, held up the Book of the Dead, using it like a guide to give orders to zombie monkeys and skeletal wolverines. Beside her were her two lackeys, Todd and Melvin. Both of the mummies brandished bronze swords that they used to hack up goblins. Near the entrance was the skeleton of scientist James Franck, his jarred brain in one hand, and some sort of cattle prod in the other. Franck jabbed the prod at the wigs, jolting them with electricity. He fought shoulder-to-shoulder with George Streeter, who had a cane sword in hand that he used to skewer goblins.

Then there was Mr. Dillinger, who no longer looked like the traditional John Dillinger in history books. His eyes now shone a lightning green, he had long claws on his fingers, and a menacing pair of fangs protruded from his mouth. He zipped from goon to goon, tearing into their necks and feasting on their blood. One of Dain's henchmen, whose white hairpiece hung off the side of his head, opened fire on Dillinger, but the vampire was too quick. He bolted behind a table before charging the gunman at alarming speeds. The goon attempted to raise his hands in surrender, but it was too late. Dillinger stretched out his arm and swiped at the man with his claws, removing the goon's head in a single blow.

Finally, there was Jean Baptiste DuSable, who charged through the battlefield and towards Michael "Stonewall" Jackson with a rattle tail held in the air. Everyone in the spooky community knew that DuSable was a *houngan*, also known as a voodoo priest, but it wasn't until this moment that I realized how talented DuSable really was.

The revenant, armed with only his rattle, shook an angry fist at Michael Jackson as he mumbled under his breath in some form of French. The stone statue ignored DuSable's threatening gesture, aiming at the emaciated Undead Union leader with its machine gun. DuSable hurled his rattler at Michael's smoking firearm. The rattle seemingly bounced off without harming the statue, but before M.J. could shoot, the long barreled weapon suddenly disassembled, falling onto the floor in pieces. Although it was hard to read the expression of a statue, I didn't think it liked the spell too much. The golem lifted its heavy hand and swung hard at DuSable. Jean Baptiste desperately leapt backwards, narrowly missing the statue's sparkly-gloved hand as it smashed into a table.

"Nedonius my friend," shouted DuSable as he ran a circle around Michael Jackson, "Are you alright?"

"He's fine my good man," answered Gethin. "He just needs a minute. We're headed up to Collin's office in order to free my Thomas."

DuSable jumped out of the way of another one of Michael's slow moving blows.

"Gethin, is that you?"

"It is DuSable, though I've seen better days." Gethin grumbled as he struggled to drag me backwards. "Say, any chance that you can help me with Nedonius? He's heavier than he looks." DuSable examined Gethin for a moment, sidestepping another one of the golem's fists as he did. "Sure, I guess I can help." DuSable looked up to the balcony, which was now fountaining red.

"John," Jean called out, "take over for me." Dillinger nodded, leaping from the balcony and onto the dance floor. He spun around Michael Jackson, taking swipes at the statue whenever opportunities presented themselves, chipping away small chunks of stone. At that same moment, DuSable shambled over to me. He grabbed me by my shirt and pulled me towards the stairwell. He looked to Chelsea and smiled. "Oh, so you must be the girl Nedonius has been talking about. Aren't you lovely?"

Chelsea, slightly taken off guard by DuSable's less than fresh appearance, smiled reluctantly at the ghoul. "Oh, um…thank you."

"Jean Baptiste Point DuSable," said Jean as he stopped tugging me in order to bow. "It's a pleasure to make your acquaintance."

Chelsea's jaw dropped. "Like, *the* Jean Baptiste DuSable?"

DuSable gave an eerie skeletal grin and then forcefully grabbed hold of me again. The group, however unintentional as it was, used me as a giant broom to sweep up all of the glass, gore and bullet casings along the way to the east stairwell. I could feel the pricks of shards and heat from hot lead all across my ass, and the lukewarm sensation of fresh blood on my palms. Just as they reached the door to the stairs, my fingers began to twitch and my eyes blinked hard, as my senses returned. I shook my head violently, trying to recover from my dizziness so that I could get back to kicking butt.

"That a boy," said Gethin as he helped me to my feet. I wobbled at first but then stood on my own. "Come now, we're almost to Thomas. I need you for this part." Gethin was nervous to be sure, and I couldn't blame him. I didn't know how long it had been since he'd last seen Elsberry, but I'm sure it was agonizing to not know how he was. I gave the skirmish one last look, and seeing that we were on the brink of victory, nodded and took to the front of the line.

"Okay," I said, patting DuSable on the shoulder. "Good work." Jean winked with his rotted eyelid. "Oh, and thanks for saving me." Jean nodded like a bobble head.

"What are friends for?" he shrugged. I looked at him suspiciously.

"Well, if we truly are friends, then you won't mind helping us with something that's not part of the plan. Gethin's lover Thomas is in Collin's office, and we need to grab him before Collin gets back from the museum. You're not obligated to come."

"Ned," said DuSable as he removed a burlap voodoo doll from his coat pocket. The figure had white long hair stitched in its head and a black business suit painted on its body. "Of course I'm in. Let's hurry though. This doll would have turned to ash if Dane had fallen for the deadly trap we set for him at the museum, so he must still be lurking about."

"Understood," I grabbed at the stairwell door. "I'll go first."

The group formed a line behind me, and together, we rushed through the entrance. It was drab and quite ordinary, used only for emergencies and clandestine cigarette breaks. The handrail was a bright yellow. Above it, the wall was littered with obnoxiously vivid signs that gave directions in case of a fire. Step by step we huffed up the stairs, ready for anything. Finally, after a few hundred steps, we'd reached the top. A single door, similar to the one that we entered, greeted us as we caught our breath.

"Now everyone pay attention to the emergency signs," I announced, "because before this night is through, I definitely intend on burning this shit hole down."

Chapter Twenty-One

DuSable volunteered to check the third floor door of the stairwell. The undead voodoo practitioner stepped in front, moving his long coat flap from his side as if he were about to quick draw a revolver from the imaginary holster on his hip. But instead of clapping his hands together and humming or summoning a great spirit, the revenant simply tapped at the handle with his fingers several times as if to check its temperature, before pushing on the lever and exiting.

"Wow Jean," I said dryly, "way to mystify us with your insight into the arcane arts." DuSable gave a ghoulish smile with his rotten lips, oblivious to my sarcasm. I wondered if anyone in the Undead Union had a sense of humor.

We followed Jean Baptiste through the exit. Once we did, the four of us found ourselves in a short ceilinged hall that stretched to the front of the building. At the end was a single black door of solid oak. The chessboard floor, bleach white ceiling and neatly framed pictures littering the walls were mesmerizing, creating a funhouse pattern effect that made it hard to focus. Cautiously, we edged our way to the end. The majority of the photos along the wall were all very dated, mostly colorless, each of them with two things in common. First, every photograph was in some iconic landmark in Chicago. Second, they all had Collin in them. *Alas, the Museum of Dain.*

The older photographs tended to be of the warlock in the 19th century. He posed near the old Water Tower, along Lake Michigan, and on the Magnificent Mile. His face was always solemn and dangerous, and his hands were always tucked in the pockets of whatever business suit was popular at the time. Some of the photos had Collin posing with famous celebrities, from Al Capone to Mayor Richard Daley. Clearly, anyone who wanted power in this great city needed Collin's approval first. No wonder DuSable and his union wanted Collin gone. He was the ultimate tyrant.

We reached the big black door, engraved with the name, *Professor Collin Dane* in gold painted letters along center. The four of us looked each other over inquisitively.

"Professor of what?" I said aloud as a joke came to mind. "Jerk-anomics?" I looked to the group for approval. Chelsea shook her head in disbelief. Gethin and Jean gave blank stares.

"Oh Ned," Chelsea said sympathetically, "That was terrible."

"Well, Queen of Comedy," I replied, "what do you got?"

"He's an instructor for gastroenterologists," she said bluntly.

"Wait," I interjected, "how is that funny?"

"Because he teaches the art of assholes," she said as if it were obvious. DuSable chuckled wildly, clinking his yellowed teeth together.

"Nice," I complimented, giving Chelsea the gun-finger gesture.

"Children," hissed Gethin, his cheeks now flush. "Can we save Thomas now?"

"Oh, yeah," I shrugged guiltily. "Sorry."

The door was thick and heavy, but surprisingly, it was merely wood. There were no steel reinforcement, high tech gadgets, or trap doors beneath the walk space that we could see. There were also no obvious runes or wards along the threshold, which made sense with Collin. He was one of those clean and calculated types. Why warn intruders when you can surprise them? Just because there was no wolf's bane hanging over the threshold didn't mean that the entrance wasn't magically protected in some way or form. It just meant that the enchantments were camouflaged. I looked between DuSable and Gethin, hoping one of them knew some sort of spell that would help. Gethin ashamedly looked down at his feet, and DuSable started to whistle, pretending to inspect the ceiling.

"Seriously?" I said. "No one knows how to get in?"

"I could tap it a few times like I did with the last one," DuSable offered. "If I melt like wax, you'll know it was warded."

"No Jean," I said, shaking my head, "we need you just in case someone has to die in the next room." DuSable's posture went slack as if he'd just lost a checkers match. Then, in a moment of clarity, he winked to me, clearly impressed with my generosity. "Well, I did say that I intended to burn this shithole down," I said while holding my hands out. "Everyone back up. Things are about to heat up."

"Wait," shouted Chelsea as she stared at the engraving. "Would you just give me a minute you pyromaniac?" She pressed on, ogling the door, specifically the title along the surface. The gold lettering was scribed in some antiquated font, etched deeply into the wood. She mouthed each letter, pinching subconsciously at her chin. "Yes," she hummed. I see." Chelsea clapped her hands together and turned to address us. "Well, it's warded alright," she remarked with resolve. "If you blow up that door Ned, we're all goners."

I tilted my head towards Chelsea and gave her a curious look. "How do you know it's warded?"

"Look at the 'I' in both Collin and Dain. It's not an 'I' at all. It's the Ogham symbol for danger. It's a warning to anyone who knows how to read Collin's magic. Give me a second though. I think I have an idea on how to get past this little hex."

Chelsea pressed her finger along the "O", and then

poked at the symbols as if each letter were parts of a keyboard, pushing the "P," then the "E," and finally the "N." The door flashed red, and then the lock from the doorknob clicked. Gethin stood with a fascinated smile, and DuSable bobbed his head in approval. I stared at Chelsea as she clapped her hands in triumph. She turned to us, and seeing our vacant stares, gave an innocent grin.

"What?" she asked sweetly.

"Madame," said DuSable, tugging on the lapel of his beat up jacket, "Let's talk about a career with the Union after this."

Chelsea blushed. After a brief second, her face froze. "Wait, wouldn't I have to die to do that?"

DuSable laughed like a madman. Chelsea looked to me for an explanation, but I could only offer a slight shrug. As she did, Gethin, who appeared to be teeming with anticipation, hurriedly tried the door handle. The large knob twisted without argument, and as soon as it did, Gethin pushed forward, thrusting his body inside. The three of us watched as the fallen angel scrambled into Collin's office like a rabid dog, waving his head back and forth in order to find Elsberry.

"Thomas," he howled desperately, "Thomas can you hear me?"

We followed in after, cautiously hugging the walls. My gut began to tingle, presumably warning me about the dangerous collection of artifacts and enchantments that we were presently in the company of. DuSable tucked his hand inside his raggedy long coat as if reaching for something. Chelsea safely took cover behind me. The office was exactly how I'd remembered it, though there were a few scorch marks along the bookshelves and ceiling from my earlier scuffle with Dain. Gethin locked his eyes on the statue of Ares behind Collin's desk. The Forsaken then ran to a rack of books on a particular stand and grabbed at a large red tome. He hurried to the statue of Ares, which was still in its usual spot, and rubbed at its chest with optimism.

"Please," he pleaded to Chelsea, beckoning her over with a wild thrust of his hand. "Please come read from the book and free my Thomas."

Chelsea looked to me for approval. I took a moment to think it over, but nodded in consent. It was the first time I'd seen Gethin lose his cool. I wasn't exactly sure why he was caressing the sculpture, but I had a hunch. Perhaps Ares wasn't just some tasteless statue that Dane used in order to make his dick feel bigger. Maybe this damn statue was poor Thomas. Maybe this was how Dane kept an eye on him to ensure Gethin continued to cooperate. Maybe this was the only freaking reason that Gethin helped create the warlock's army at all.

If that were the case, then I was horrified by Collin's lack of boundaries. Only Lucifer himself could have come up with anything so devious, and I quickly realized that I was in the house of a villain so revolting that even *The Punisher* would shiver. It was also alarming to think that Collin, who had somehow managed to cheat death, was creating a level of malevolence so large that it might match the heights of Hell someday. I wondered how far he'd be willing to go to attain power. Had we not rescued Gethin, Collin may have someday had an army large enough to rival anyone who challenged him.

Chelsea hurried to Gethin's side, and began flipping through the tome. After a long minute, she finally honed in on a particular page. She traced her finger along the wording, and began to speak in a sort of singsong voice. Her chanting was thick and throaty. I didn't recognize the language, but I also didn't think it wise to cut her off during an intricate dispelling just to quench my curiosity. Chelsea read and read until cracking and splintering sounds, like the sounds before a large tree falls, began to resonate throughout the office. It was coming from the statue. The white marble began to peel off the figurine's surface as if it were eggshell. Piece by piece, the stone shed off of Thomas, until all that was left was a young man dressed only in a loincloth and Romanesque helmet. Elsberry appeared dazed and weak, and upon seeing Gethin, took a single deep gasp of air before falling to the ground. Gethin hurried to his lover, peeling off the legionnaire helm and combing at the long strands of gold hair with his fingers, clearing it from Thomas's face.

"Oh my love," said Gethin, "fret not. You're safe now. I have come to rescue you."

Gethin pet Thomas's cheek with the back of his hand. His eyes swelled with tears and affection for the young mortal. Chelsea and I locked eyes. We reached out our hands to one another and squeezed them together. I wasn't sure what Chelsea was thinking, but for me, it was simple. *Fuck all of it.*

Fuck Lucifer, fuck me being a corruptor again, and fuck Collin. After seeing Gethin's happiness, all I wanted to do was to go home with Chelsea and sit on her couch, drinking tea and talking about nothing. All of this mad dash for eternal power was starting to get old quick, and I wanted out. I could go straight, freeing myself from the clutches of Hell while staying neutral in any spooky affairs -- the Switzerland of supernatural beings.

"Well then," DuSable called out, breaking the silence, "should we get out of here before Dane gets back?"

"That would imply that I had ever left," called out a voice from nowhere. Suddenly, the smell of ozone infused the room as Collin appeared out of thin air, posed in his desk chair with a nearly empty glass of Scotch in his hand. His face was composed. His eyes calculated. He was wearing a custom fit suit, black with a single red carnation pinned to his chest, as if he were going to a funeral. "Very well done," he complimented. "I had assumed that my forces would have at least destroyed one or two of you before you made it up here."

DuSable's jaw dropped with a popping sound from his decayed joints. Gethin, still cradling Thomas in his arms, took a deep breath before spitting out, "You bastard."

"Oh, come now. Did you really think a bloke like myself would have taken the bait and gone to the museum after you've hidden the place from me so well after all these years DuSable? It was too good to be true. Anyone with the slightest smidgen of intelligence would have realized it was a trap."

"So why then would you allow us to attack?" DuSable begged desperately for an answer.

"Well isn't it obvious?" asked Collin rhetorically. "I needed to finally get all of the hidden pieces on the playing board," he gave a tired wave of his hand. "*My* playing board." DuSable trembled with anger. Collin ignored him, staring at Gethin instead. "I'm shocked that Gethin didn't tell you about all of the demon spawn he's helped me make. Together we've created an entire slew of my favorite musicians." Gethin hung his head, either embarrassed that he'd somehow forgotten or ashamed for his part in their creation. "Not only is there an entire regiment of horrors in reserve just below us, but I have another special surprise."

As if on cue, police lights, all sky blue and fire truck red, lit up the dark skies from under Collin's window. A single siren shrieked into the air, announcing the authority's presence. The group paused, uncertain how to react. There was the crack of a loudspeaker followed by the commanding voice of a man barking orders over the megaphone.

"This is the Chicago Police Department." called out the voice. *"Come out with your hands up Nedonius! We know you're up there."*

Dane leaned back in his chair, taking a sip of his drink. The ice clanked in the glass as he savored the gold whiskey. Gethin hurriedly picked up Thomas, lifting him in his arms before withdrawing behind us. Collin watched with a bemused smirk. As he did, DuSable dug at his pocket. Suddenly he plucked out a pair of chicken's feet bound with a rubber band. *Great DuSable, chicken feet, just what we needed.*

I thought about leaping on top of Chelsea in order to shelter her from anything the warlock had planned, but didn't feel as if doing so would actually protect her from Collin. So instead, I arched both hands like coiled cobras and lit them with hellfire.

"Please don't be silly," Collin pleaded without any real color or concern in his voice. "I've been preparing for this moment for some time. I have a hex ready for your little hellfire trick Nedonius." He then turned to Gethin. "I've also cast an enchantment for your whistle my friend, so please save your breath." Collin then turned and studied the chicken talons in DuSable's hand. The warlock pressed his fingers across his lips, pretending to suppress a laugh. "Really DuSable?"

DuSable ignored Dane and turned his dried up face to me. "Think he's bluffing *mon ami*?" he whispered.

I shook my head. "No," I said in a hushed tone. "I think it's safe to say that Collin has us by the balls." I cleared my throat. "Alright Dain, you have us right where you want us. What now?"

"Well first," he said after finishing the contents of his drink, "I want to tell you what I've been planning. I know that it might be a bit cliché, but unlike those villains in the movies, I've already taken every measure in order to guarantee that I win. Of that, I'm certain."

Wow, the ego on this guy.

Chapter Twenty-Two

I assumed that if we tried to run to the stairs or elevator, some primed magic would trigger and we'd be screwed. I also expected that if we tried to fight Collin in his office, some prepared magic would trigger we'd be screwed. If we jumped out the window, we'd look like assholes in front of the entire Chicago Police Department, and then some prearranged magic would trigger, and we'd be screwed. Collin, from my short time knowing the bastard, only acted if he took chance and risk out of the equation. Long story short, we were screwed.

"Well," Collin hummed, "let me first start by saying that many of my followers bet that none of you would make it out of the basement, but I knew better. I must admit, I was very curious how you planned on defeating Mr. Jalacy Hawkins," he spun his computer monitor towards us so that we could see. It was the security camera system's interface. The display was divided into several different smaller split screens, each numbered accordingly. On camera 5, we could see the squid monster still mopping blood from the dungeon's cement floors. "But you managed to do one better, and simply outsmart the poor fool. Bravo." Collin removed a bottle of Scotch from his top drawer and began to refill his empty snifter.

After filling it half way, he returned the bottle to its drawer before casually taking a sip from his glass. I watched as a slight glow lightly colored the flesh along his throat, highlighting the highway of veins in his neck as the alcohol went down. The liquid was more than just Scotch. It must have had some type of magical properties. *Mental note, if you survive this Nedonius, stop being stubborn and start learning magic already.*

"I was hoping, *but* not counting on the lot of you figuring out a way to destroy Jalacy," Collin declared, "as his upkeep was skyrocketing. But oh well. I'll figure something out." Collin glanced at the computer screen before staring directly at me. "On the other hand, I fully intended on Nedonius besting all of my mortals waiting for him on the first floor." I rolled my eyes and sighed. Collin didn't seem to care. "I figured that even if the Negative-One Union didn't come to rescue him, my mortals would be no match for the undying Legionnaire's flames, especially since I didn't arm the fools with anything that could affect him."

"Wait," DuSable interrupted with disgust, his milky eyes still fixed on the computer. "You knew that your mortals would die?"

"Yes," said Collin with resolve as he watched one of the camera views stationed above the dance floor. The screen displayed the dead nightclub personnel. "The humans have been around for far too long, and some of them know too much. I needed them gone so I could refresh them with newer, younger employees," he was plain faced as he observed a bloody security guard drag himself across the glass-covered ground. "It's a necessary precaution that I must take every few decades, as much as it pains me," he sighed. "As for Gethin's creations that you all bested, they were expendable, especially with the dozen or so more I have at my disposal. I had to sacrifice *some* in order to keep any of your suspicions from growing. Everyone knows that one does not merely step into The Citadel without peril."

With that, Collin pressed a button on his keyboard. One of the cameras, which had been fixed on the bar where the Undead Union was picking apart Michael Stonewall Jackson, zoomed out. We watched from every camera angle stationed on the main level as steel awnings dropped down along the windows. Alarmed, the Undead Union hurried towards one another, creating a perimeter circle. Mary raised her book, and though there was no sound, we watched as her zombie animals raced to each of the main doors, ready to strike anything that might come out.

"Don't worry," the computer light bouncing off of his face,

"I'll take care of your friends later."

"You Sir," Gethin annunciated slowly, "are the most vile scoundrel I've ever come across."

"Very rich coming from a devil," said Dain. "Oops," he snickered, covering his mouth, "did I use the 'D' word again?" Collin looked to me with a wicked grin. "My apologies. Where are my manners?"

"You Sir," I said in my best Gethin impersonation, "are an ass-hat."

"Maybe," said Collin as police lights reflected off his face from the window behind him, "but it doesn't keep you from suffering what I have in store for you. You see Nedonius, from the moment you stepped foot into my little nightclub, I knew that this was my ultimate test. Gethin was easy to manipulate, but you were the real deal. You *are* hell- ruthless, unrelenting and above all, clueless." I turned to Chelsea, who was frowning at me. Collin's words struck me deep. I was ashamed by who I was- a pitiless, but bumbling agent of Satan. "I knew that if I could defeat you, I'd send a message to the entire supernatural community that this realm and the next are mine. My reputation would skyrocket," he said thirstily, "Like John Lennon at his marketing height."

DuSable clenched his bony fist, shedding dust from his knuckles. "But what did the Union ever do to you? Why must you make every other creature suffer?"

Collin laughed degradingly. "Again, is that a real question Jean?" DuSable nodded in reply, seemingly curious to Dain's genuine motives. Personally, I could give two shits. "Fear is the pillar of what I desire most- power. Show the weak what happens to those who challenge you, and they'll submit to your will."

"I repeat," called out the policeman's voice over the loudspeaker, interrupting Collin's moment. *"This is the Chicago Police Department. Nedonius, come out with your hands up. We have you surrounded. If you do not comply, we will be forced to come in and use deadly force."*

"Uh oh," said Collin. He opened up his mouth and swallowed a small piece of ice from his Scotch, crunching it like rock candy. "They sound like they mean business. You'd better do something Nedonius. Someone has tipped them off."

"Alight Collin." I held my hands up in surrender. "No need to get any mortals involved in this. You've had your fun. What do you want from us?"

"What do I want from you?" Collin repeated, obviously caught off guard. He took a moment to swallow the ice and Scotch in his mouth. "Oh Nedonius, you still think there are options. There isn't any bargaining. I've already made my decision. I finally get to rid myself of all of my enemies in one fell swoop while sending a message to the rest of the supernatural community in the process." I looked to DuSable who was slowly inching the chicken feet behind his head in a throwing position. "I just wanted to share my plans beforehand. I wanted you to know during your last dying breaths that your first mistake was to ever think you could challenge me." His voice became angry and fierce. "Think of your deaths as a way to preserve lives in the future. You'll be a deterrent for those fools who are bold enough to even think about testing my authority."

"And pray tell," I challenged, "How do you plan on ridding yourself of Gethin and I? We're fucking exalted beings you dumbass."

"Ha," laughed Collin. "I've already told you. I don't need to kill you. Gethin helped me design a ritual that will allow your brothers and sisters do it for me. Just like that annoying little quasit, I'm going to portal you both to heaven." Gethin stared up at Collin fretfully. "That's right Gethin. I don't need you any longer. I've studied your methods and can create spawn on my own. You have no value to me any longer." Gethin took a deep breath, and then spit a large wad of saliva onto Collin, hitting the warlock on his cheek. Collin cocked his head back, wiping the spittle off with his fingers in disgust.

And with that, Collin irritably pressed a button along his drawer, and four of the bookshelves leaning along the wall lifted like mechanical garage doors. I didn't waste any time closing the distance between Chelsea and I, holding my arms out in order to shield her. To our shock, waiting behind the shelves were four beings of abnormally concerning proportions. All of them were sizzling, crackling or steaming from their humanoid bodies. They had bright glows of lightning yellow, toxic waste green, blood red and moonlight blue emanating around them. All four of their exteriors represented one of the traditional elements of earth, fire, wind and water, only with a slight twist. Each elemental was sculpted to look like the hybrid of a different conventional chess piece, but much like all of Collin's demon spawn, with a famous musician's face as well. They were all seriously freaky.

The bishop nearest Gethin appeared to be Michael Lee Aday, better known as Meatloaf, but with a stationary scowling face. He was short, fat and made of clay. The helmetless knight nearby was mostly made of metal plates that strangely were hovering above the ground with nothing more than a short cyclone of air. The knight's gauntlet grasped a sword and shield over his whirlwind body, and his cloudy head, made entirely of swirling air, had the powerful hair, jawline, eyes and nose of Jimi Hendrix. As for the queen, she was made entirely of embers and burning coals, but molded to look as if she was adorned in fine robes, jewelry, and a crown. Though she had the body of a female, the face was that of Freddie Mercury during his mustache phase. *Scaramouche, Scaramouche, will you do the Fandango?*

Finally, there was the king, tall and skinny. His body was constructed of plumbing pipes that said "Property of the Chicago Water Department," and crisscrossed to make a skeleton shaped figure. Peculiarly, his head and hands were made out of some clear and gelatinous material, like colorless JELLO that leaked along the ground. Though I half expected the king's jelly face to be that of Elvis, instead, it appeared to be in the likeness of Collin, only with a massive royal crown topped over his temples. Obviously, Dain's ego knew no bounds.

The elementals quickly hurried over and tried to capture us. Freddie Mercury decided he wanted a piece of me, which was a good thing since I was perhaps the only guy in the room immune to fire. Though the coals didn't burn me, the elemental was still incredibly quick and strong. I tried to push Freddie away, but as the elemental closed in, his thick black and searing-orange hands grabbed at my neck. I desperately tried to break free of his grip, but Mercury easily pulled me in and put me into a headlock. These were not simple creations, rather constructed masterpieces that must have taken plenty of time and effort to build. They were mighty and fast with intricate designs. As I tried to pry the burning orange arm from my neck, I saw that the rest of the party had fared just as poorly as I had.

The air-knight's shield was painted with a cloud in the shape of a guitar. His sword pointed at Chelsea's throat. The sharp end pushed into her skin, creating a dimple under her chin. Meanwhile, clay Meatloaf had not only managed to grab Gethin by the hair with one hand, but was also using his other hand to drag an unconscious Thomas by his leg. The young man's skin squeaked on the glossed floors as he was dragged across the wood. Gethin squeezed onto the creature's hand, wincing in pain, but unable to free himself. Maybe most bizarre of all, the water king had somehow managed to cover DuSable in the very goop that made up its hands and face. The undead leader was now encased in what looked like a mound of clear jelly.

"Good work my children," Collin complimented as he walked to the center of the room with a burlap sack. "Now, bring the humans here. I'll need their sacrifice in order to close the portal back up later." Anger bubbled in me as I watched the elementals bring Chelsea and Thomas behind Collin's desk. Each of them stood behind their prisoner, ready to act at Dain's word. I could tell that Gethin was feeling just as nervous as I was because he was violently thrashing to free himself from Meatloaf. For once, I tried to take a deep breath and remain calm. *I know right?* My usual methods of reckless warfare weren't going to work this time around. I needed to think outside the box.

Collin took out my satchel and cellphone, and placed them next to one of the gaudy diamond earrings I'd seen Gethin wearing before. Collin then began to prepare the ritual. He removed a few items from his sack and placed them on top of the nearby coffee table. There was a piece of chalk wrapped in yarn and a ceremonial dagger with an ivory handle. He grabbed the effects and sauntered over to us. He bent down and drew a circle around Gethin and myself with the chalk, before writing unrecognizable symbols along both rings' outline. DuSable's milky eyes moved back-and-forth, though the rest of him was helplessly frozen in the gelatinous heap.

"Alright," called out the policeman's voice from outside. *"You've left us no choice. We're coming in."* The echo of multiple feet marching in unison clapped loudly as their respective boots made it towards the club. Collin looked up at me with an amused smirk.

"Oh," laughed Collin, "it's going to be a long night

for the boys in blue." I could hear the faint sounds of the main nightclub door being smashed open. The vibration shook the floor beneath us. From the camera views on Collin's computer monitor I could see several armed police officers marching in. A wild zombie monkey leapt onto one of the officer's heads, and a rhino with half of a face charged the gate. After hurling the monkey off of his head, the police officers backed up and shut the broken door behind them before the rhino could smash into its exterior.

"Get back to the cars," cried a commanding voice from the streets below. Seconds later there were the brief sounds of automatic gunfire, followed by shouting and strident footsteps retreating from the front of the building.

"What do you mean wild animals?" said the muffled voice of the spokesman over the megaphone. There was a brief pause and then the boisterous call of the policeman's voice again. *"Alright you sick freak. You think you're really funny huh? We're going to get Animal Control out here pronto, and then we're coming back in to get your ass."*

"Looks like your undead zoo bought you some time," Collin complimented. "I'll let the authorities and your Union work things out with one another before I unleash my demon spawn to finish the survivors." I gave the warlock my best stink-eye. Dane ignored me and grabbed at my hand, poking my finger with the end of his knife. Black blood and a spit of fire rose from the wound, leaking across the blade. Collin studied it for a moment before smearing it on the end of my satchel and cellphone in an odd Gaelic pattern. "What is in this pathetic bag anyhow?" he questioned, pouring the contents from my satchel near my feet. Clearly, Collin didn't know everything, because the items that were stored in the pocket dimension, including the user's manual, didn't pour out. Instead, only knickknacks like the flower T-1000 had gifted me with, Mary's charmed necklace and the crucifix that

Joliet had tried to kill me with, tumbled down onto the floor. *Holy shit, the crucifix!*

"Ha," he laughed as he looked at the items on the ground. "Stupid keepsakes."

It was a long shot, and most likely an end all, but perhaps the crucifix could work. If I could get it around my neck, Archangel Michael would definitely come to deliver final judgment onto me, and in the process, might also stop Chelsea, Thomas and all of the police from being murdered. I looked to Gethin with urgency. He tried to read my expression as Collin walked toward him, but I could tell that I wasn't doing a good job of conveying myself. I waited for Collin to continue writing in chalk along Gethin's feet, and then mouthed the words, "Archangel Michael," while staring hard at the crucifix.

Gethin cringed and whispered, *"No way."*

I scowled and fizzed, *"Yes."*

Collin didn't seem to notice. He reached up and grabbed at Gethin's hand, pricking him in the finger with the knife, and smearing the blood onto the small earing and briefcase. As he did, I stretched my foot ever so gently so that Freddie Mercury wouldn't notice, and stepped on the crucifix. Dragging it toward me, I waited for the religious pendant to be within arm's length before slowly reaching out my hand and picking it up by the cross. Chelsea watched what I was doing, but tried to show her best poker face.

"Now," said Collin, "let the portal be opened." He stationed himself between Gethin and I before holding up the dagger into the air. "Powers of the North, South, East and West, hear me. I use the blood of these fallen angels to not only summon your attention, but to ask you to recognize and permit these two fools to be sent through your borders."

Gray mist, like that of a storm cloud, began to form along the ceiling. Loose papers flew through the air as a brisk wind swirled inside the office.

"I am Collin Dane my lords, warlock, and eldest son of Carman. Gift me with a window that will send these Forsaken back to where they belong."

A tearing sound, similar to the noise that occurred when Michael first appeared on the Riverwalk, emanated throughout the office. Suddenly, a swirl of twisting brilliant blue light circled above Collin. Dane began to laugh as his long frosty hair twirled in the air. As the portal expanded even further, I could hear choirs of angels singing from inside it. Collin heavily panted with anticipation as he looked to his bishop and queen. His eyes were wide like a madman's when he pointed to the portal.

"Throw them inside," he ordered, gesturing to the pair of us.

I could feel the overpowering grip of Freddie Mercury around my neck release, only to quickly be replaced by a powerful throbbing as the fire elemental carelessly grabbed me by my shoulders and legs, lifting me above its head. As I struggled, Gethin desperately tried to grab at the nearby couch as Meatloaf dragged him by his collar towards the portal. It was now a race to see who would get killed first, and I was winning. With no time to lose, I fought to take the crucifix and wrap it around my neck.

Almost instantly, as if it were a bolt of lightning, a blue burst of flame jetted down from the heavens and exploded just outside of Collin's office. A sharp pain jabbed into my gut, piercing and tender. There, floating just outside of Collin's floor-to-ceiling window was Archangel Michael, his dangling penis and all. He held up his sword, now surging with gold flames, and plunged it into the surface of the window. The glass did not shatter, but instead, melted away like iridescent syrup.

"Finally," Michael called out in a boisterous voice, locking eyes with me as I flailed in the suspended grip of

Freddie Mercury. "No more of your tricks Nedonius. You will pay for your insurrection against God."

"Alright..." called out the policeman over the loudspeaker. *"Animal Control is on its way. It won't be long now buddy."* The mortal eyes of the police officers below were unable to make out Michael, though I feared that it might have been better if they could. Michael paid no attention, instead flying into the office with his massive pairs of wings and standing beside Collin's desk. Infuriated, Collin ran between Michael and I, possessively holding out his arms. He threw his piece of chalk to the ground, smashing it into hundreds of fragments.

"Who dares to break up my ritual?" Dane demanded. "What is this, another Fallen?"

Michael kicked his head forward as if someone had hit him. He turned towards Collin, and with a flare of his blue eyes, glowered.

"See me mortals," Michael called out in an imposing tone, "I am no Fallen. Now step aside. Anyone who interferes with the duties the Lord will suffer my wrath."

Collin responded with a cheekily degrading laugh.

Okay now I'm feeling cramped. This room is way too small for both of these guy's egos.

Chapter Twenty-Three

Michael loved his blade more than most men love their dicks. Like most men and their dicks, the angel could hardly ever be found without it in his hand. Any picture of the angel or excerpt from the Bible always described him with his fiery blade at his side. It had been a reward from God after Michael had personally defeated Lucifer during the war for heaven, and was the archangel's only possession. In retrospect, perhaps God should have also gifted Michael with holy swim trunks or divine trousers.

The sword was beauty for sure. The surface of the white steel blade was polished like a mirror, with a deep fuller and edge that reflected the screaming faces of evil before cutting them down. The hilt was gold with a simple but sturdy pommel that shone at its end. The flame that enveloped the blade was a yellow brighter than any sunrise. The weapon surged and flickered according to Michael's mood. At the moment the flame had swollen larger than I'd ever seen it before, crackling like a forest fire as the angel stared down Collin.

Dane seemed unconcerned. Perhaps it was the high he'd been riding after duping the lot of us. He looked to the pair of elementals who were safekeeping Chelsea and DuSable. "Stop this fool," he ordered. "We'll throw him in the portal with the others." The Hendrix-knight pushed Chelsea to the ground with a shove of his shield. She fell hard, but quickly lifted her head up as if to defiantly show that she was unharmed.

The water elemental stepped up first, extending its arm at Michael. A thick stream of clear goo poured out, smothering the archangel in JELLO. The weight of it must have been immense, because Michael fell to his knees before being completely encased. DuSable's eyes frowned, as if empathizing with the archangel. Dane gave a smug laugh before turning his back to Michael. The warlock was just about to address the rest of us, but before he could catch his breath, a bright gold light began to pierce through the murky sludge coating Michael. Before long, the entire room was illuminated in the brilliant glow.

Shockingly, even though Freddie Mercury held me over his head, Michael's holy rays were once again washing my human disguise away. My skinny biceps began to inflate into large and muscular arms. Black wings sprouted from my shoulders and the suit I'd worn during my interview with Armen began to appear, still crisp and unwrinkled. Gethin, who was now mere inches away from being thrown into the gate by Meatloaf, seemed to be affected by the rays as well. His true form was tall and wiry with bronze skin, a shaved head, and sable wings. He had a short black beard growing only out of the end of his chin with several red bands tied along it. He wore a caramel pair of pants and an elegant white collared shirt with rolled up sleeves. Michael's powers had completely cancelled out our mortal disguises.

I looked up to Chelsea. Her gaze was locked on me, a look of horror across her face. I frowned, but it did nothing to change her expression. I had to look like a complete stranger to her now, bizarre and cartoonish, like He-Man if he went through a gothic phase. The pain it caused was too much, and in order to keep from falling into eternal despair, I focused on the other activity going on in the room.

Both the water elemental and the Hendrix-knight hurried to Michael, who was still trapped in a now boiling bubble. They raised their arms, ready to strike the fizzing slime. But another large pulse of light caused the clear goop to explode outward, sending both elementals to the ground. Collin's desk flipped over, nearly landing on Thomas, and the bookshelves and musical memorabilia along the walls crashed onto the floor. The JELLO covering DuSable began to melt away too, freeing the undead leader from his prison. Collin leapt behind a leather sofa, taking cover on the ground as he dug into his coat pocket.

Michael stood up proudly, straightening his back and raising his blade. The elementals returned to their feet, charging the angel with haste. The water-king swung hard at the archangel's head. Without effort, Michael blocked the blow with his flaming sword, sawing the plumping-pipe that once represented itself as an arm in half. Still the elemental lingered, clumsily trying to bash at Michael with its good hand. Michael easily sidestepped the blow, and then whirled his blade, cutting through the elemental's chest and dividing the creature in two. The clear gelatin that made up the water-king's head and hands splattered across the room as its two halves hit the ground.

Michael stepped over the heap just as the Hendrix-knight's broadsword came down towards his arm. Michael quickly flapped his great gold wings, sending the air construct backwards by at least a foot. The air-knight's blade barely missed, instead striking into Collin's upturned desk, where the weapon became lodged. Without hesitation, the air-knight lifted its shield at Michael, attempting to bash him. However, Michael's flaming blade, forged by God himself, thrust through the shield, splitting the metal barrier into pieces. The archangel followed up his attack by plunging the sword into the Hendrix-knight's airy head. Static fizzled throughout the office as the fiery edge of Michael's weapon split through Hendrix-knight's cloudy round bundle of hair. The cyclone of wind that made up the knight's body quickly evaporated into nothing, causing the random pieces of armor that still remained to fall to the ground.

I don't know how long I'd been suspended in the air, but the altitude must have done something to my brain because I found myself rooting for Michael. Perhaps it was because I knew that if Michael were victorious, regardless of the fact that he'd eradicate me like vermin, at least Chelsea would be safe. She'd be free from Dain's plans of sacrificing her and could go back to leading a mostly normal life. So, as Michael moved deeper into the office, and Freddie Mercury wound up its arms in order to throw me into the portal, I couldn't help feeling a deep satisfaction knowing everything was going to be all right.

Then suddenly, as if to rain on my parade, time came to a complete halt. I could still see the room, but everything inside of it stood frozen, as if we were all part of a movie that had been put on pause. I tried to wiggle free from Freddie Mercury's grip, but my body wasn't responding. Everyone else, including the elementals, had the same difficulties. DuSable, who had only recently freed himself from the mounds of clear gelatin, stood mid sprint with his pair of chicken feet in hand, pointed towards Meatloaf as he dragged Gethin to the mouth of the magical gate. Gethin posed with his teeth gritted and his fingers raking at the ground as he played tug of war with the clay bishop. Chelsea, who'd taken cover behind the turned over desk, stared motionlessly at me with wide eyes. Even Michael, who was once marching towards yours truly, his blade extended at his side, was now locked in place.

Though the police's red and blue lights still flashed from the outside, only two things remained in motion within the confines of the demolished office. There was the portal, which still spun wildly like a miniature hurricane in its dazzling blue, and Collin. Dane had abandoned his hiding spot behind the couch, and ambled to the center of the room. His skin shined with the same gold glow I'd seen previously trickling down his neck from the Scotch. It pulsated through his body like a strobe light. His pocket watch dangled from his hand, and swung like a pendulum as he moved to the center of the room. I half expected the miniature warlock to come to me, using his hex magic to levitate both Gethin and myself into the portal. Instead, he walked to Michael.

"Now I know who you are," he said with great understanding. "The Great Archangel Michael," he snorted, rubbing at Michael's strapping bicep. "How very," he paused, "fortuitous." Collin did a few casual laps around Michael, examining him like someone would a Corvette at a car lot, before taking his hands and grabbing onto Michael's oversized index finger. One by one the warlock pried the fingers off of Michael's sword, until finally only the archangel's pinkie held the blade upright. From there, Collin easily removed the blade. He stared at it as a child would with a new toy, spinning the weapon around, and unskillfully swinging it in the air. *Michael must have been screaming bloody murder in his head.*

"The wrath of God, aye?" Collin said with spite as he moved over to DuSable. "Well, let's see how powerful it really is." I watched in horror as Dane swung the blade upward like a baseball bat towards DuSable, cleanly cutting into the revenant's neck. Anger and fury bottled up in me as the undead leader's gray and emaciated head rolled across the floor, his collar cauterized from the flame. A volcano burned in my stomach as hellfire built up, coursing through my veins, though I could do nothing to release it. "Wow," Collin said with false enthusiasm, "I finally have a lightsaber."

"Now Michael," Dane jibed, his Irish accent growing more prominent as his frustration intensified, "I don't know why ya' thought you could show up here without invite, but I'm tellin' ya' now, if you supposed that *you* were going to be the one to put an end to these two wee devils," he poked upwards at Michael's chest, "you're undoubtedly mistaken. For his attack upon me, I shall be the one to taste the gratifying nectar called revenge on Nedonius."

"However," Collin said teasingly, his brow arched as he smiled, "I think I could find use for you Michael." Collin, still pulsating with bright gold, directed his hands to the heap of metal that was once his water elemental. The copper piping lifted into the air, and hovered around the archangel. The metal squealed as it reshaped itself so that it was now tightly coiled around him. "To think," he said flippantly, "if I could harness the power of the Almighty, don't that kind of make me God?"

Collin spun around to face Gethin and I. He waved his hand again, and the pair of us were torn away from the elementals and levitated just inches from the portal. From my angle, I couldn't see Chelsea, but I assumed she'd still be watching as I was sent back to heaven in order to be slain. I couldn't imagine the emotional toll it would have on her. I stared up at the ceiling, wondering what it would be like to just not exist. How it would be to just be nothing.

Maybe it was for the best. I mean, everything I'd ever done had gone to shit. I was a flawed model. The rebellion, being a corruptor…hell, even being a good boyfriend didn't work. In a few seconds, just after I was ripped apart like fresh meat in a piranha tank, Chelsea was going to die. Collin would most likely slit her throat, as he would with Thomas, in order to close the portal. It was all about to come to a head. I'd killed the only person I'd ever loved. *Yay me!*

As I floated forward, and the sounds of angels singing rang in my ears, I readied for my closing scene. At least I could hold onto the memories of camaraderie and love that I'd experienced here on Earth within the last few days. That was slightly comforting. Collin someday would get his, and he'd have no memories to cherish as he moved on, just death. Too bad I wouldn't be there to see it. Then suddenly…

"*Ned,*" said a dopey, yet familiar voice from the megaphone outside. It was Billy. "*Your loyal minions are here.*"

Although he stopped speaking, the loudspeaker's static resonated through the streets as if Billy was still holding down the megaphone's talking button. I could hear the muffled beats of someone pounding on a hard surface.

"*Billy,*" a muffled voice in the loudspeaker's background hollered, "*Open this car door now!*" It was the spokesman from the police department who'd been barking orders from the streets below.

"*Sorry Dad,*" said Billy apologetically, "*I'll explain later. Stevie, give us a visual.*"

Though I could barely see a thing, the sounds of helicopter propellers and tiny engines emerged from just outside Collin's office window. I could hear Collin shuffle. "What is the meaning of this?" he hissed.

"*Hey scumbag,*" shouted Billy from the loudspeaker. "*Death from above!*"

Chapter Twenty-Four

I could hear the *thump, thump, thump,* of paintballs being fired followed by the sounds of Collin grunting in pain. Suddenly, time returned, and Gethin and myself dropped to the floor. I looked up into the portal, which was now just centimeters from my face, and could see the hazy outlines of angels on the other side, shields and spears at the ready. *There is no way I'm letting them put me in there.* I used my own wings to glide myself back to my feet before taking in my surroundings. It was anarchy at its finest.

A pair of helicopter drones armed with paintball guns floated just outside of the windowsill. Dangling from the landing gear of Billy's *Raptor* was his book bag. The satchel seemed to be heavy, hampering the drone's movement. The room's lamps twitched on and off. Collin's computer screen was now sideways on the floor. The screen blinked with the image of a computerized skull that had the title, "You've been Virexed!" flashing above it. Without warning, all of the lights in the nightclub, as well as the streetlights outside, shut off.

The drones flew inside of the office, and upon reaching safe ground, released the bag. Two pint sized hellhounds burst from the small opening, their eyes blazing red. The little guys charged towards us, and leapt onto the clay-bishop and hot coal Freddie Mercury. The elementals were taken off guard, and fell onto their backs. From their prone positions, they tried to strike Simon and Hecubus, but it was like watching sloths trying to swat flies. The demon dogs were far too quick.

Collin had dropped the sword and was grabbing at his eyes, which were now covered in yellow pepper-paint. Snot dribbled down his nose, and his lips fizzed with foam. He extended his hand, which was adorned with a gaudy gold ring, and began blindly firing bolts of lightning from it. The sounds of thunder roared throughout the room. A few rays of electricity crashed into the wall, just near the fireplace, but none of them came close to hitting the team.

As for DuSable, there are perks to being undead. His body wobbled over to his head, and using its free hand, picked up his face by his dreaded hair. The body tucked DuSable's head like a football under his arm. Now mostly in one piece, he hurried to the nearby elementals and used his other hand to throw the chicken feet. The talons crashed onto the back of Freddie Mercury, who was struggling with Simon. The chicken feet bounced off of the construct, and where they'd made contact, a rippling affect surged, flowing through the hot coals. Freddie went still before bursting into a cloud of white feathers. Simon, confused, began to hack tiny quills from out of his little mouth, afterwards joining his brother by leaping onto Meatloaf.

Gethin quickly made it to his feet, and after grabbing his briefcase, flew up to the ceiling, soaring towards Thomas. Once the Forsaken had reached his lover, he opened up his case and dug inside. He removed a large lute, far too big to be carried in a simple carrying case, and strummed the chords. Though I could hardly hear the tune through the madness, it seemed to have some sort of effect on Thomas, whose eyes opened and rapidly blinked. Thomas looked up to Gethin, who was now in his true form, and lovingly brushed his cheek.

The sight reminded me of Chelsea. I'd hoped that she would have found a clear path to the elevator, but to my amazement, she was instead walking towards Collin with an opened tome in her hand. Dain, who was still scratching at his eyes, suddenly and unexpectedly levitated into the air. With a flick of Chelsea's wrist, the warlock violently flew back into the wall behind him. He cringed as his short body smashed into the corner of a bookshelf, falling onto the floor.

Chelsea read from the book in some unrecognizable language. She focused on a baby grand piano that had been tucked into the corner of the office, and with another fluid wave of her hand, lifted the instrument with her new found magic. She began to manipulate the black piano closer to Collin until it was steadily floating above his dazed head. Collin was unaware. He was grabbing at his eyes and back, doubled over in pain.

Chelsea was a great person, but she was now being sucked into evil's most fulfilling temptation. *Wrath*. She'd told me before that Collin had to pay for what he'd done. I had to do something, but I had no idea what. *Who was I to tell her not to do evil?* I was the epitome of evil. Had I been reasoning with rational Chelsea, maybe I'd stand a chance, but when you're thirsty for revenge, a guy like me isn't exactly going to be the best person to inspire wisdom. So, in one of the more stupid moves I've ever made, I decided to go with my gut. Hastily, I flew over to Michael, who was still struggling with his bindings. He glared at me as if I were up to something malicious.

"Mikey," I said, looking at his copper bindings, "You and I have had a merry dance, but it's time for you to claim me. For real this time." Michael looked doubtful. "But first, I need you to help me rescue that girl's soul," I said pleadingly while pointing to Chelsea.

Michael looked puzzled. "You want me to help you save someone's soul?"

"Yes, she's about to do something really bad and I need your help to stop her. I won't let her be trapped in Hell like I was."

Michael hummed curiously. "And how am I to believe that you, Nedonius, Legionnaire of Lucifer, will keep his word this time around?"

I looked Michael dead in the eyes. They were glittering with a beautiful mixture of gold and sapphire. "Michael," I said soberly, "because believe it or not, I love her. Now, are you in?"

Michael looked down, contemplating. Then, with a quick flick of his head, he nodded somberly. "We will save her, and then I shall claim you."

"Agreed." I grabbed at the piping, and together we began to stretch it off of him. As soon as we did, Michael leapt into action. His beautiful wings spread open, smashing into the two helicopter drones and sending them to the ground. Flying gracefully through the confined space, Michael soared between Chelsea and Collin.

"My child," he said empathetically, "I know what you think you must do, but that is evil speaking in the form of reason." Chelsea didn't break concentration with the piano, though her words became whispers. "I have been with you since you were a baby, as I have been with all of God's creatures. In your time, never have you once chose thoughtlessness over purpose. Please, I ask you to reconsider. Put down the piano."

Michael could have easily picked up his sword and hacked the piano into pieces or grabbed Collin and rescued him. But for the archangel, it wasn't right to interfere with the one thing that God gifted all mortals with, free will. He wanted Chelsea to choose. I guess I did too now that I think about it. The veil that hid the supernatural had been lifted from her eyes, and after all she'd been through, it was time to decide her path. All it would take was a flick of her wrist and a quick incantation in order to kill Collin. The question was, did it feel right to her? Was this what she really wanted to do?

Chelsea's eyes were cold and calculated. The briefest pause between her whispered words made me hope she was contemplating the great moral conflict inside her. She looked away from the piano and turned her head not to

Michael, but to me. Her eyes were glossed over and her mouth quivered with uncertainty. I nodded sympathetically and gave her the simplest half smile- a smile that always came naturally to me whenever we were together.

Chelsea locked eyes with me, pursing her lips. She took a deep breath before she turned her attention back to the piano. With a flick of her wrists, Chelsea sent the baby grand past Collin and into the ground. The piano's legs gave out on it, giving a final ring to the keys. Chelsea dropped the book and ran over to me, giving me a strong hug. As she grabbed onto my waist I squeezed her back, and could feel the slightest little trickle run down my cheek.

Michael stared at us before bowing his head as if ashamed. He glanced at his feet, where his sword awaited, and curled his wings gently behind his back. Then he bent down and collected both his blade, and Dain, grabbing the warlock by his collar. I waited for him to come to my side and pry me from Chelsea. Instead, he turned away, crunching through the glass and rubble until he was next to the gate. I kissed Chelsea lightly on her forehead before pushing away in order to follow the archangel.

"Sorry Chelsea," I said apologetically. I took a step back, "but I promised." Chelsea covered her mouth in shock.

"No, no, Ned, don't," she pleaded. "I need you. Please, you can't."

"Chelsea," I said gratefully, fighting to keep up my smile, "I finally get it," I added simply. "Thank you."

To that, I raised my head to Michael. To my surprise, the archangel wasn't giving me the judgmental glare that I'd been accustomed to. Instead he tilted his head, his stare bemused and inquisitive, as if I were doing something foolish like cooking bacon without a shirt.

"What *are* you doing Nedonius?" he asked.

"Uh," I buzzed. *Wasn't it obvious?* "I'm going with

you so that I can be put to final justice."

"And why do you think that I would let you do that?" Michael asked.

I leaned my head like a curious puppy, blinking a few times before opening my mouth again to speak. "Um, because I gave my word."

"Nedonius, you may have been a vile and wretched representative of Lucifer at one time, but you've changed. You've proven to me that you're still part of God's flock. Take care of this young woman." Chelsea wiped her eyes and ran to my side, hugging my oversized arm. "And in that case, take care of Chicago as well," he said firmly. "It's about time that heaven had a few agents on Earth to help sway the masses as well. It might make my job a lot easier."

My jaw dropped. I eyed Michael's sword, thinking that at any minute he'd lift it, shout "Psych!" and bring it down on me. Instead, he gave me a simple wink, and then took a step into the portal. A sizzle of energy sprang from the vortex as he dipped his foot in.

"I'll close the gate from the other side," he said with his usual bravado, "but it's up to you to handle the police. Do not draw attention of our kind as this one did," he raised a sniveling Collin by the collar, "or you will have failed your first task."

Michael gave me one last glance, then dipped his head and squeezed the rest of his body into the portal. Collin looked up, his eyes still watery, and for the first time I saw fear. His arms reached out, briefly beseeching us to save him, before being submerged in the portal's blue overlay. Soon, the brilliant blue swallowed up Michael and Dain, and the gate instantly disappeared, like a television image once you pressed the off button.

Chelsea stared at my tall figure, a smile stretched across her face. I pet her hair with my large hand and grinned. The room went hushed as the action died down.

"So this must be awkward. Do I look weird or what?" As I asked she put her arms back around my waist. "Don't worry, I have a spell that will turn me back into the Ned you're used to."

Chelsea straightened the collar of my interview suit, before reaching her hand up and stroking my cheek. "What's the hurry?" she asked while biting the bottom of her lip, "this look is kind of sexy."

Chapter Twenty-Five

"Are you serious," I argued. "You're telling me that you think that the USS Enterprise could take on the Millennium Falcon?"

"No doubt," spat Billy over the break table. We were in the back room of Chelsea's new bookstore. Well, not so much new bookstore, as rebuilt bookstore- *I still get an earful any time the woman is feeling feisty.* A lot had happened since that night at the Citadel. Stopping Dane created a sort of tidal wave of good fortune, and the crew and I were reaping all of the benefits.

After Michael spared me, the group had to find a way to carry out the archangel's first command, dealing with the police. Chelsea had found Dain's pocket watch on the ground, and hurriedly rummaged through one of his journals in order to figure out how it worked. It took her about ten minutes or so, and the group of us bought time by harassing the officers from above with rude gestures and oinking. Once Chelsea figured out the timepiece, we used it on the police in order to make everything right.

Dain's pocket watch locked *Chicago's finest* in place, giving us plenty of time to free the Undead Union. Once we had Mary's help, we used her Book of the Dead to cast a powerful ancient enchantment. She cleaned the memories of all the responding police officers, replacing their recollections with false ones that suggested the boys in blue merely responded to a false alarm. By the end of it, we'd managed to not only collect Billy and Stevie, who were more than frightened by the mini army of dead escorting them out of a police car, but also send the police back to the station without further incident.

Afterwards, DuSable informed us that since the nightclub was a far superior outpost, the Union would be taking over The Citadel, and would handle the demon spawn still inside. I really wanted to burn the bitch down-but, after some gentle persuading, agreed. DuSable insisted that Chelsea collect all of Collin's rare books and use them to reestablish her bookstore. Later, with the help of Stevie, she auctioned off some of the mundane historical tomes online to museums and private collectors and made a small fortune. Since her bank account was now loaded, she was able to repair *The Prologue* and buy the property that it was located in. With an array of century year old books now at her disposal, Chelsea's bookstore, as well as her new career as a witch, went off without a hitch.

Business booming, Chelsea moved out of her old apartment and into a beautiful old house in Lincoln Park. Might I add that two weeks later I became her first, and hopefully only, live-in boyfriend. *Score.* Not long after, Billy and Stevie needed a place to stay. Since I'd promised to help them, I begged Chelsea much like a child trying to keep a kitten until she allowed the minions to move into the basement. Together, the four of us worked at the store. Stevie and Billy helped with online sales when they weren't at school, and I kind of provided...security as well as moral support.

It was during one of these grueling security shifts that Billy and I engaged in a heated debate about galactic prowess.

"Let me tell you why the Enterprise would win," said Billy, tightening the screws on his latest drone. "The Enterprise not only has an array of weaponry and an entire crew at its disposal, but, it also has the best Captain in the universe."

"Blasphemy," I shouted, now back in my human form due to Mary's book. "Not only will the Falcon do loops around the Enterprise, but it will do so with style, because the best captain in the galaxy is Han Solo, bar none."

Stevie snorted. A dungeon raid was ongoing on the giant monitor in front of him. We'd made the backroom our hangout, enhancing it with the high tech computer we'd inherited from Collin's office, comic book posters, and an industrial size coffee maker. It wasn't that we didn't like to help Chelsea. It was just that we had no idea what anything was whenever customers asked. Chelsea insisted that we only come out when needed, and banished us to the break room. I'd occasionally come out to check on *she who must be obeyed*, but for the most part, we knew our place. Plus, when we weren't arguing about the best captain in the galaxy, we used the converted storage space as our research center in order to do God's will.

I'd been given orders by Michael to help the good guys again, and I didn't want to disappoint him. So together with Chelsea, Billy, Stevie, and of course Simon and Hecubus, we tried to aid those mortals who were burdened by evil. And by burdened by evil, I don't mean that we came in like high school counselors during an intervention. No, I mean that if evil lurked, like Hell spawn or malevolent spookies, we took care of them. We weren't exactly the X-Men, and we were still sort of working the kinks out, but with Chelsea's newfound magical talents, Billy and Stevie's arsenal of experimental drones, and the awesome power of yours truly, we were doing well enough to get by. Plus, whenever the going got tough, we knew that we had friends we could call on.

The Negative-One Union was now thriving. Undead from all over the Midwest had flocked to the union after the defeat of Collin Dain. Apparently, everyone wanted to be in Chicago so long as the warlock was gone. Although they weren't exactly the police, the Negative-One Union did try to keep order in the city's supernatural circle by means of their magical headquarters, a private art museum they dubbed as "Studio des Morts." Don't ask me what they did with Screamin' Jay Hawkins.

Gethin and Thomas occasionally sent postcards. They'd moved to Europe, where with Gethin's knowledge of art, they looked to make a name for themselves. Gethin would occasionally give me a call to check up on things, offering us his opinion on the latest demonic possession or crazed devil doll, but for the most part he kept a low profile. We knew we could call on him anytime we needed, but tried to leave him alone unless absolutely necessary. All of us knew that secretly, he and Thomas wanted no part in the supernatural any longer.

As for Chelsea and I, when she wasn't using me as a human forklift in order to move her incoming shipments, she was as lovely as always. Life with her was simple, but perfect. We'd work all day at the store, and then go home at night and curl up on the couch, talking about nothing like we always did. I'd never been so happy. It didn't hurt that she was a sex goddess, and did things that they didn't know about in hell.

Anyhow, back to the future. After calling a truce with Billy about galactic supremacy, I came out to the storefront to see if I could help Chelsea with anything. She was returning books to their shelves, Simon and Hecubus at her heels, while humming to Danzig. Her hair was up in a bun, showing the delicious curve along her neck. She wore a form fitting Black Sabbath shirt that looked like it was tattooed to her skin, and a pair of jeans that showed off her wonderful rear end. She looked up and gave her classic Chelsea smirk.

"Um, can I help you with anything Sir?" she asked lightheartedly.

"Yes, I'm looking for a book that I can give as a gift for my girlfriend. I need something that says, 'I love you so much that I turned my back on Lucifer.' You know, something that will get me laid."

Chelsea snorted. She rested the stack of books on a nearby shelf, and then walked over to me. "Well, sir we do have some lovely jinx tomes that might do the trick. They're in aisle five next to those smutty erotica books with Fabio on the cover. I warn you though, be careful what you wish for...lover boy."

I grabbed at her and pulled her into my skinny human arms. "So," I said with a fake Antonio Banderas accent, "which Nedonius would you like between the sheets tonight? Tattooed hipster Ned or mysterious black winged Ned?" Chelsea rolled her eyes. I straightened my back, wiping the grin off of my face. "Seriously though, want to get a pizza tonight and watch the original Star Wars movies?"

"Hmm," Chelsea contemplated, "Let's negotiate. We can do pizza and movies, but only if you help me learn how to cast a sleep curse."

"Deal," I kissed her on the forehead. "But you can't use the sleep curse in order to dodge watching the trilogy."

"Ned," she gasped sarcastically, "I'd never."

We chuckled like a bunch of hyenas before collecting the rest of Chelsea's book stack and shelving them. For once, there was no one inside the store; so putting away the tomes wasn't too difficult, even for a Brainiac like me. But shortly after Chelsea showed me where she wanted a 1st edition "Protection Against Lycanthropy" volume, the power in the store went out. A deep rumble belched from the store's foundation. It was the moan of metal, and it didn't take long for us to figure out that it was coming from the pipes. Simon and Hecubus began to growl like wolves and sniff the air. Billy and Stevie came out from the backroom in a panic. Billy held up a drone, while Stevie readied the remote control. I could feel a stabbing in my gut, and knew that we had a spooky on our hands.

"Nedonius," a high pitch voice wailed from the

walls. Billy turned the power on the miniature helicopter. Stevie triggered the propeller button so that the robot took flight. The air cannon armed under the drone's belly had several different ammunition options, including wood bolts, silver tipped darts, and of course, pepper paint. Stevie used the controls to spin the gun around to pepper paint. As he did, Billy grabbed Simon and Hecubus, ready to hurl them at the enemy like dodge balls with teeth. At that same time, Chelsea quickly drew out her new wand and readied it. The wand was whittled like a *Dio de los Muerte* skeleton in a burlesque outfit. She'd traded it during a trip to Mexico in return for some Chupacabra repellant, and had been kicking butt with it ever since. She whispered under her breath, and the skeleton's skull began to glow green. The group used the light to inspect the store.

As for me, though the hair and wings of my true form never went back to their original color, my hellfire abandoned me shortly after Michael had spared my life. *Never fear.* Because the frightening fury of hellfire had quickly been replaced with the awesome power of holyfire, compliments of the good guys. Holyfire, unlike hellfire, worked on nearly every spooky, solid or ethereal, and didn't need me to be pissed off in order to use it. All it took was my continuing to be a good guy, which was easier said than done sometimes. Since the store was under attack-*again*, I decided it was time to initiate my new divine powers in order to defend our headquarters.

I held out my hands, and pure blue flames flickered from my palms. I couldn't see the spooky, but the turning in my stomach told me that it was near. My instincts couldn't say whether or not the creature was evil, but I calculated from its shriek that it was angry.

"Nedonius," the voice called out from the walls again, its pitch similar to nails on a chalkboard.

Suddenly, the sprinklers in the ceiling popped, and water began to spray across the storefront. But instead of pouring all over Chelsea's precious books, the water stopped midair, flowing into several streams. The multiple jets snaked into the air before meeting at a focal point directly in front of us, and merging together. The collection of water slowly started to form into a humanoid shape. As it did, I could make out a narrow old face, beady eyes, and a slender female body. *Oh shit.*

"Nedonius," Catherine O'Leary repeated, fury in her voice. "You promised me that you would help in exacting revenge on that foul reporter once you returned to hell. Now, here you are in this damnable bookstore."

"Uh," I hummed, creating a shield of holyfire between Catherine and the group, "yeah, about that."

"You tell untruths you wicked rapscallion," she howled, flying across the room like a madwoman. "I knew I shouldn't have trusted you."

"Cat," I begged, "come on. You know that circumstances have changed things. Be reasonable. I can't go back to Hell any longer."

O'Leary's eyes flashed with red as bookshelves began to lift above her. "If I can't have revenge on Michael Ahern, then I'll have to exact it on you."

I turned to the group, and with a clownish grin on my face, gave them instruction. "Alright team, set your phasers to stun. We need her." The team charged.

It was one Hell of a day, and that's saying a lot where I come from. It began as cliché as one might expect when living as an angel in Chicago. My girlfriend woke me up to breakfast, my dogs caught a ghost, and work was way too much fun. Things were looking pretty promising. Oh, if only I knew then that by this time tomorrow I'd have to defend Earth from a legion of evil, I might not have acted so giddy.

...Cue credits and epic music.

About Justin Alcala

Justin Alcala is a novelist and nerdologist. He's the author of Consumed, The Devil in the Wide City and Dim Fairytales. His short stories such as It Dances Now and The Offering have been featured in multiple magazines and anthologies. When he's not burning out his retinas in front of a computer, Justin is an adventuresome tabletop gamer. He's also a blogger, folklore enthusiast and time traveler. He's an avid quester of anything righteous, from fighting dragons to acquiring magical breakfast eggs from the impregnable grocery fortress.

Most of Justin's tales and characters take place in The Plenty Dreadful universe, a deranged supernatural version of the modern world. When writing, Justin immerses himself in whatever subject he's working on, from research to overseas travel. Much to the dismay of his family, he often locks himself away in his office-dungeon while playing themed videos and music over, and over, and over again. Justin currently resides with his dark queen, Mallory, their malevolent daughter, Lily, and their hellcat, Misery. Where his mind might be though is anyone's guess.

Social Media

Twitter: https://twitter.com/JustinAlcala

Goodreads:
https://www.goodreads.com/author/show/7862799.Justin_Alcala?from_search=true

Wordpress: http://justinalcalablog.com

Amazon: https://www.amazon.com/Justin-Al-cala/e/B00SN2VJAM%3Fref=dbs_a_mng_rwt_scns_share

Author Website: https://www.justincalcala.com

Facebook: https://www.facebook.com/justin.alcala.33

Acknowledgements

To my wife, Mallory, who supports me in everything I do, my daughter, Lily, who teaches me the importance of being a Dragon-Spiderman, and everyone else that appreciates the weird dude that I am.

www.ingramcontent.com/pod-product-compliance
Lightning Source LLC
Chambersburg PA
CBHW051629260626
47170CB00004B/1099